# The
# *Are You*
# *Being Served?*
## *Stories*

# The
# Are You
# Being Served?
## Stories

*"Camping In"*
and other fiascos

JEREMY LLOYD

**KQED**
BOOKS
SAN FRANCISCO

Stories © 1975 by Jeremy Lloyd and David Croft

Foreword © 1997 by KQED Books & Video

KQED Books & Video, 555 De Haro St.,
San Francisco, CA 94107.

PUBLISHER: James Connolly

EDITORIAL DIRECTOR: Pamela Byers

BOOK DESIGN:
Raul Cabra, Margie Blatchford/Cabra Diseño

All photos © British Broadcasting Corp.

Educational and nonprofit groups wishing to order this
book at attractive quantity discounts may contact
KQED Books & Video, 555 De Haro St.,
San Francisco, CA 94107.

**LIBRARY OF CONGRESS
CATALOGUING-IN-PUBLICATION DATA**

**LLOYD, JEREMY.**
 The Are you being served? : stories : "Camping In" and other
fiascos / Jeremy Lloyd.
  p.   cm.
 ISBN 0-912333-02-2
 1. Department stores--England--Fiction. 2. Humorous Stories.
English.   I. Are you being served? (Television program) II. Title.
PR6053.H36A89  1997
823'.914--dc21                                           97-366
                                                         CIP

**ISBN 0-912333-02-2**

Manufactured in the United States of America

10 9 8 7 6 5 4 3 2 1

Distributed to the trade by
Publishers Group West

# Table of Contents

### ARE YOU BEING SERVED? THEN AND NOW

9

BY ANTHONY BROWN

*In which the series stars reflect on the place of the show in British popular culture, and in their careers*

### THE BIRTH OF ARE YOU BEING SERVED?

21

BY JEREMY LLOYD

*In which the author and series creator looks back from 20 years' vantage to its beginning*

### INTRODUCTION TO
### THE ORIGINAL EDITION

25

*In which the author introduces the dramatis personae and improbably opines that Grace Brothers Department Store represents an island of sanity*

## The Stories

CHAPTER ONE
### CAMPING IN

27

*In which a transit strike strands the Grace Brothers staff at the store overnight and a predictable round of crises ensues*

CHAPTER TWO
### UP CAPTAIN PEACOCK

57

*In which Mr. Peacock discovers that honors can be distressingly short-lived*

# WEDDING BELLS

*In which Young Mr. Grace's apparent interest in Mrs. Slocombe changes her relations with her colleagues*

CHAPTER FOUR

# HIS AND HERS

107

*In which the staff of the Men's and Ladies' Wear Departments are alternately lustful and indignant as business is drained away to a new line of perfumes*

CHAPTER FIVE

# COFFEE BREAK

133

*In which the staff vow to stick up for each others' rights—until "We're behind you all the way" takes on new meaning*

CHAPTER SIX

# THE HAND OF FATE

159

*In which Mr. Humphries reveals a hitherto unsuspected talent for palm reading*

CHAPTER SEVEN

# THE CLOCK

189

*In which Mr. Grainger approaches a significant birthday celebration with some trepidation*

# ABOUT THE AUTHORS

221

GRACE
BROS.

7

# *Are You Being Served?*
# *Then & Now*

THE BBC MAKE THE BEST TELEVISION PROGRAMMES IN THE WORLD. Everyone knows that, and just in case we forget, they remind us often enough. The trouble is, they often find it difficult to spot which of their programmes are the greats.

*Are You Being Served?* began as a one-off play in 1972. For ten years the BBC had been producing seasons of playlets under the Comedy Playhouse banner, and since the first-season episode *The Offer* launched *Steptoe and Son* (the basis for America's *Sanford and Son*) in 1962, the assumption had always been that one or two of each year's ideas would be good for a series. But nobody expected *Are You Being Served?* to be the one.

Certainly, actor Nicholas Smith didn't imagine he was about to begin a twelve-year stint as Grace Brothers' jug-eared manager, Cuthbert Rumbold. "My agent called and said, 'They want you to do a Comedy Playhouse called *Is Anyone Serving You, Sir?* set in a department store.' The money was OK, and the director was David Croft, whom I'd worked with before, so I went along and did it. It seemed to work pretty well, and the audience certainly laughed a lot, but the BBC didn't like it. The show didn't have any social message or political slant, and it wasn't nostalgic. It was very funny, but the BBC weren't too interested in that, so they aired the Comedy Playhouse series without it."

It should have taken a miracle to save *Are You Being Served?* Instead, it took a tragedy. When terrorists kidnapped and murdered the Israeli team competing in the 1972 Munich Olympics, the games were canceled as a mark of respect for the dead. Suddenly, the BBC found themselves with a gap in their schedules, and looked around for anything they could show.

"Because of this ghastly do at the Olympics," Smith recalls, "the BBC were suddenly faced with blank screens, and found they had this awful

Comedy Playhouse piece on the shelf. Even that was better than shutting down, so they showed it, and because the people who'd been at work hadn't heard about those murders they tuned in expecting to see the Olympics. Apparently, 19 million people—almost half the people with TV sets—watched that first episode, and eventually David Croft was able to persuade the BBC, very much against their wills, to make it into a series."

Even once the series was up and running, its success was less than certain. For Mollie Sugden, who played the formidable head of ladies' wear, Mrs. Slocombe, under a variety of multi-coloured wigs, the next few years were a test of faith. "I thought it was going to be a success when I read that first script. I'd been doing a Comedy Playhouse with James Beck and Ronald Fraser, and afterwards David Croft came round to the dressing room and said, 'There's something in the pipeline for you. You'll know when you read the script.' I read it the minute I got it, and thought, This is going to be a success. Unfortunately, the first season was up against *Man About the House*, which inspired America's *Three's Company* and was equally successful, so nobody watched it. The following year it was up against *Coronation Street*, ITV's big soap opera, so it seemed no one would ever watch it.

"Our hopes did droop. We wondered how it could take off if nobody watched it. There was no way they could know it's funny. But once they saw it, it happened very quickly. On one of the first episodes we made they must have shown part of the original show to the studio audience, because Wendy Richard and I were crawling along the floor looking for a diamond and I asked, 'Is that you, Captain Peacock?' as she tapped me on the shoulder. And they laughed. They already knew the characters. But you had to know the people a bit before you could appreciate the humour.

"But then the third series was up against a current affairs series, so people tuned in to us instead and thought 'How wonderful.' And we were finally off."

Suddenly the cast members were household names.

The impact of this differed for each of the cast. For Nicholas Smith, Cuthbert Rumbold was the latest in a long series of television roles—but he almost became the last. "So far as I was concerned, Mr. Rumbold was a character part to be created. It was clear that he was a complete idiot, so I wondered whether to give him an unpleasant whining voice, or a weedy little moustache. But David Croft didn't want me to change my appearance, so I settled for wearing my glasses and taking up my eyebrows, which gave him a permanently worried look."

The image soon entered the public imagination. "The effect in the theatre was terrific, because it meant I would get a lead role, and that's remained the case for the last twenty years. But whereas I'd been making my living entirely from television with hardly any theatre up till that point, directors suddenly starting saying to my agent, 'Well, Nicholas Smith, we know the sort of acting he does, and he'd be wrong for this.' On one occasion someone said, 'Nicholas won't be right for this,' and my agent reminded him that eighteen months ago he'd used me as an old cockney tramp, yet he was saying I couldn't do anything but Mr. Rumbold."

Frank Thornton, Grace Brothers' stiff-necked floorwalker Captain Peacock, explains why television directors prefer actors to stick to a single image. "You can't go in for big character acting with wigs and make-up and funny accents on camera. It's looking right at you, close up, so physically you have to be as close to yourself as you can. You play characters for which you look right. I'm tall, which means I can look down my nose at people, so I tend to play supercilious characters.

"Similarly, we all spoke more or less as we do naturally. Wendy Richard exaggerated her cockney accent a bit, but Mollie Sugden and John Inman are both north country people, so when their accents slipped it was a matter of falling into something they knew instinctively. Mollie's a Yorkshire woman, and Mrs. Slocombe was a Yorkshire woman, though not as well educated as Mollie, so she tried to talk posh but got it wrong. You do well to stay as near as you can to what you are."

Like Smith, Frank Thornton found that the recognition Captain Peacock brought him cost him character roles on television while opening up a new career on the stage. Thornton had worked extensively in the theatre in the past, but had been concentrating on television for the past twelve years except for a Christmas production of *Winnie the Pooh*, which saw the stage debut of future *Doctor Who* companion Sarah Sutton. "*It's a Square World* had established me as a useful character man in light entertainment, comedy and sketch shows for the BBC. In addition I was doing straight plays for ITV, and for ten years I'd hardly worked in the theatre. Then up came the pilot of *Are You Being Served?* in 1972, and they made the first series the next year. You might say the rest is history—69 episodes over the next 12 years.

"For the first time I became established as one character, Captain Peacock, which, alas for my bank balance, meant all the other work faded away. I'd been working in television for 25 or 30 weeks a year up till that time, but all of a sudden people who were prepared to use Frank Thornton until then didn't want Captain Peacock, which meant the only television work I did was two months of *Are You Being Served?* each year.

"In America we'd have done 26 episodes a year, but the dear old BBC only makes 6 or 7 a year, which is artistically very good, because you can stick with the two original writers rather than having a team. The original character of the show remains intact, as the writers are far more important than the actors. But doing it like that isn't so good for the actors' bank balance, so in the other ten months of the year I had to get back to the theatre."

Fortunately, Thornton soon found a particularly challenging arena for his talents: the prestigious Royal Shakespeare Company, which offered him weighty Shakespearean roles that contrasted nicely with the knock-about comedy of *Are You Being Served?* "I've never been the ambitious type who knows what he wants to do and goes out to set it up; I've always sat waiting for the phone to ring. But I let it be known that I was available for theatre, and in 1974 I was asked to join the RSC down at Stratford, where I played Sir Andrew Aguecheek in *Twelfth Night* and Duncan in *Macbeth*.

"Television is the one place where success works you into the unemployment line! Fortunately, I could go back to my theatre reputation as a solid character actor. Some actors say, 'That's it, I'm off' after a series or so if they see identification with a character coming up. You must either do that, or stay right to the end. *Are You Being Served?* was a very successful thing, and I never saw any reason not to come back to it."

*Are You Being Served?* had a far more beneficial impact on the careers of Mollie Sugden and John Inman, who played the flamboyant Mr. Humphries. As Mollie Sugden explains, "I was fairly established because I'd done several series, but none was the startling success that *Are You Being Served?* was and that really did move me up quite considerably. I hadn't done much stage work until then because I had twin boys, but I was able to get a lot of stage spin-offs like pantomimes and summer shows because of *Are You Being Served?* The two months of work on the series each year brought in so much more that I never needed to have a single week out of work.

"At one time the attention from the public did get a bit trying, especially when the boys were small. It's par for the course and something you have to accept, but it's not so easy for ten-year-old boys. Somebody once asked one of my sons what it was like having a famous mother, and he said, 'Well, what's it like not having a famous mother?'"

In addition, Sugden was able to take the lead in other TV series while working on *Are You Being Served?* After John Inman was hired to star in an ITV series, the BBC put her under contract and eventually asked *Are You Being Served?* writers Jeremy Lloyd and David Croft to create the science-fiction comedy *Come Back, Mrs. Noah* as a starring vehicle for her. "I was lucky that all the parts were slightly different, so I didn't become known as Mrs. Slocombe, but as Mollie Sugden. Those parts really didn't rely on Mrs. Slocombe at all, except that they wouldn't have wanted me had they not seen Mrs. Slocombe. Certainly before that nobody would have wanted me for anything other than a supporting role."

John Inman also found that *Are You Being Served?* brought him starring roles on television. "Before then I was working mainly in the theatre, as I do now. Television was just a flash-in-the-pan bonus for me. But because of the huge success of *Are You Being Served?* I did many other television shows, taking the lead in *Take a Letter, Mr. Jones* and *Odd Man Out*. I have to make myself remember the details of those days, otherwise it's just a whirlwind of success. At its peak I was appearing at the Windmill Theatre twice nightly, rehearsing *Are You Being Served?* during the day, and recording it on Sundays. It was a mad time, really."

Still, Inman suffers from the same blinkered attitudes from television directors that Thornton and Smith encountered. "Every single thing I get sent now is a pale version of Mr. Humphries. I'm 61 years old. I can't go mincing around a counter, I'm far too old to do that. If it was something else and it was right, I'd do it, but in television they tend to think of me as Mr. Humphries. For now I'm quite happy to work on the stage. That's what I wanted to do as a little boy. I was seventeen before I had a TV set, so TV acting didn't occur to me. Traditional stage work is what I always wanted to do, on the musical and pantomime side, and I'm very lucky because that's what I've been able to do."

Each of the cast is quick to credit writers Jeremy Lloyd and David Croft with the show's success, with Mollie Sugden noting the way they'd bring a new twist to the situation in the store every time. "It was a bit different each week, and that's why I like television. It was the same character from a different angle, and that kept it fresh. I suppose the characters developed a little; but I looked at that first episode when it was reshown recently, and I was amazed to see it really was very similar to what we all did later. I think that shows what strong characters they were, and how well written the script was. Nothing to do with the actors—you're just lucky to get material like that.

"Some writers are very protective of their work, but Jeremy and David were also very good about accepting people's ideas if you suddenly thought of something. They were good to work with. It was a very happy time."

As Nicholas Smith notes, it was the power struggles among the characters that gave the show its edge. "When you put pips on a man's shoulder, then he has to be obeyed even if he's an idiot. They all knew Rumbold wasn't up to the job, but because he was the manager he could hire and fire them, so they had to knuckle down. It was curious that people always said, 'It's such a friendly show,' but someone only had to step out of line and it would be daggers drawn. Similarly, people said it was such a clean show, without *double entendres* or sexual innuendo, yet there were some lines that at the read-through we thought, 'We can't say that, we'll be arrested.' But if we just said the lines as if we had no idea they could possibly have any other meaning without any hint of a nudge or wink, we'd be all right."

That's something Mollie Sugden discovered when dealing with Mrs. Slocombe's tendency to confuse certain words. "She was totally innocent, really, utterly unaware of what she was saying when she confused 'organisms' with 'orgasms.' Everybody knew except Mrs. Slocombe, and she was totally unaware and stupid. Also very vulnerable, of course. I remember people saying they liked the show because it was good clean fun that they could watch with the family. But to the pure, all things are pure."

For Sugden, trips to the department store were soon enlivened by the confidences of shop workers who'd calmly inform her they had a colleague just like Mr. Humphries ("And John told me they were always telling him they worked with someone just like Mrs. Slocombe"), or tales of floorwalkers like Mr. Peacock ("You'd just think 'Oh, the poor man!' "). But there's one real-life Mrs. Slocombe Sugden never got to meet—even though she was Sugden's inspiration for Grace Brothers' head of ladies' wear. "A friend of mine who was a window dresser in a department store came to me with horrendous tales of this buyer who ruled the roost and would lay down the law about what you could have in the window. A bit of her went into Mrs. Slocombe, along with other people whom I'd seen in shops and rubbed up against. I think that's part of the reason the audience liked it. They knew people like this, and that's why it's still so popular."

That popularity led to a film version and a stage play, as John Inman recalls. "That was wonderful. Hard work, because it was twice nightly for 15 weeks, and the theatre was so full that they let the box office ladies go on holiday three weeks early as the place was sold out. It was only a one-off because I didn't want to do it again. You can't afford to work solely for the love of it—you have to think of the next step—so I wanted to do a big summer show the next year. We wrote a big summer review, *Fancy Free*, around me, and then did it for three years."

Unfortunately, only some of the TV cast were able to do the stage show. "It was curious adjusting to that. It was written so the TV cast did most of the work; but you had to have the characters the audience expected, and even though they were so strong it wasn't the same with look-alikes."

While most of the cast insist stage work is their first love, Mollie Sugden has always preferred the variety television provides with a succession of fresh scripts. She admits the principal challenge of the stage show was to bring continued verve to the same story. "You can't let it show, of course, as it's always got to be as if it's the first time. I'd done a season in Blackpool at the same theatre, the Winter Gardens, and that's an absolute barn—a wonderful rococo barn with chandeliers and everything, but it's still a barn. So two years later David Croft said, 'You've played the Winter Gardens, so make it big, and make it loud.' And it worked, you see.

"There was a lot of visual stuff. I'll always remember when Nicholas, John, Frank and I were on centre stage, as some false teeth started clattering in a pair of men's underpants, and the noise of the laughter was deafening. John just said, 'That's the sound—that's what you want.' And we had time to do all that—we could have conversations while we were waiting for the audience to finish laughing."

Despite the series' high ratings, and its success in raising its cast to starring roles on stage and screen, its own future was never guaranteed, as Nicholas Smith recalls. "David said that every time he asked the BBC whether they were going to do another series, they'd say, 'Well, it's a bit down-market for us, and it doesn't have any message, it's not educational. . . .' 'Yes, but we get an audience of 15 million,' he'd reply, and somehow we'd scrape through."

But the decision was never taken until the last minute, and it was this uncertainty that caused the first of many cast changes the series suffered, in the departure of Larry Martyn's character, the maintenance man Mr. Mash. "Larry Martyn's agent called the BBC to ask when they were going to be doing it again, and was told they weren't sure they would," says Smith. "He'd been offered a theatre tour in a good part around about the time of the year *Are You Being Served?* was usually done, and as the BBC wouldn't commit to anything he accepted the part.

"Larry gave everyone else something to bounce off. When Arthur English took over as the maintenance man, he was marvellous; but he wanted to be loved by the audience, so his character was never as abrasive and rude. He was a great chap, but since his character was more one of the team, it wasn't as good as the aggression Larry brought to the series. It was entirely the BBC's fault that Larry left—they called him three days after they said they wouldn't be doing another series, and treated it as if he was choosing to refuse when he was already booked up."

The series was lucky not to lose Frank Thornton's services the same way, and similar circumstances eventually forced Trevor Bannister to abandon his role as junior salesman Mr. Lucas. "That was a very unfortunate situation," explains Thornton. "In America they'll tie you down to a six-year contract, but the dear old BBC would call up at the last minute asking you to do another six episodes of the show. While I was with the RSC they set up another series of *Are You Being Served?* so I ended up working seven days a week, appearing on stage six nights, coming up each day to rehearse, and recording *Are You Being Served?* on Sunday. Seven weeks of that was quite heavy going; but I was a bit younger then. And I was lucky, as *Are You Being Served?* was recording on Sunday, and it wasn't that far away, so I could come in for rehearsals."

John Inman had done something similar during the first season, but that option wasn't open to Trevor Bannister, Frank Thornton says. "Trevor was doing a tour and might be as far away as Glasgow some weeks, and it was a Friday recording, so he had to do one or the other. It was really a shame because he was a great loss, as were all the original cast."

One change was a matter of particular sorrow for the cast, and would lead to years of changes in the cast. Arthur Brough, who'd played the curmudgeonly Mr. Grainger since the first episode, died in 1977, having been the life and soul of the rehearsal rooms.

John Inman recollects, "We used to fill in for him during rehearsal while he nipped out for a drink. About eleven he'd check that he only had three pages at the end left, and off he'd go. So if we got to his entrance, Trevor and I would start a discussion about the script, and whether one or the other of us should have a line, until he came back through the door." Frank Thornton takes up the story. "When Arthur Brough died, he was a great loss. A lovely man and a great actor. We had one good replacement, James Hayter, a very, very good character actor who fit perfectly into the group, but he was doing the voice-overs for the Mr. Kipling's Cakes adverts, and the BBC didn't want that distinctive fruity voice to become associated with a TV series. So they bought him out, offered him money not to do other work. When you're 75, a little rheumatic, and are living on a mountainside in Spain, to be paid not to work is paradise! So eventually, after a series of attempts to replace him, they just dropped the character and left two men, John Inman and Mike Berry, in the men's wear department."

Berry had joined the cast as Bert Spooner following Trevor Bannister's departure, and John Inman is full of praise for his new junior. "I enjoyed working with Mike. I was upset when Trevor left, as I liked working with him very much; we're still good mates. Now Mike wasn't the greatest actor, though he's got a good career, and he sings and writes his own music; but he was a sensational audience. He laughed at everything I said, so I loved working with him."

With Mr. Grainger's chair left vacant, Mr. Humphries became the senior salesman in men's wear, but his promotion never received formal recognition on the show. "That was my decision. I didn't want to be head of men's wear because they all died. It was a very unhealthy job to have, and they kept replacing them—and not with anyone better! Nobody could be better than Arthur Brough. The one who came close, who was very good and marvellous to work with, was James Hayter. After he left, everybody else was dreadful, I think.

"They made the same decision with Young Mr. Grace, who wasn't replaced. There was an Old Mr. Grace for a while, but that was a failure, so they just put him on the other end of the telephone."

Eventually, the series adapted to the new cast, as Frank Thornton recounts. "It altered the balance of the show. We'd started out as an ensemble piece with everybody getting an equal bite of the cherry; but as we lost good people, the balance veered towards Mrs. Slocombe and Mr. Humphries, because they could fill the gap. That was fair enough, because characters like Captain Peacock were like the feed to the comics, the straight men. Captain Peacock was the central rock which all the others bounced off, and he stayed the same as he was before."

After a twelve-year run, *Are You Being Served?* came to an end in 1985, ironically, says Nicholas Smith, just as the BBC began to see the series' worth. "The last two series we did, there must have been some change at the top, because they suddenly decided it was rather good, and started to spend more money on it. We had bigger sets, nice costumes and excellent guest stars. But after we'd done the final series, the BBC decided to call it a day."

Frank Thornton still believes the BBC were wrong to end it so soon. "The BBC had a series that had a great public behind it. If you've got a property which is worth having, then you shouldn't just junk it and start from scratch on something else—or so it seems to me. But then, I'm just an actor!"

~Anthony Brown, December 1996

*Jeremy Lloyd*

# The Birth of
# Are You Being Served?

THE IDEA FOR WRITING *ARE YOU BEING SERVED?* WAS ONE OF THOSE inspirational hot flashes that writers get when the bank overdraft sky-rockets out of sight.

I'd returned to England after a couple of seasons writing and acting on *Rowan and Martin' s Laugh-In.* I'd been well paid, but had spent almost everything on entertaining friends, and not just in L.A. but in wild trips to Mexico during the occasional break in the show. Even if we didn't have a break, I'd slip down to Acapulco for the weekend and party with George Hamilton, dance under the palms with Merle Oberon, and race Kirk Douglas down the beach beside the bluest sea in the world. Life was one big party, spending money with no thought of tomorrow.

But it had to end sometime, and as my dear ex-wife Joanna Lumley remarked when I revealed at the end of our honeymoon that I only had eight hundred dollars left, "Darling, I have the perfect epitaph for you: 'Made lots, spent more.'" How true!

So there I was back in England, pretty broke and desperate for an idea. All I had left was an old Rolls-Royce Silver Cloud, a deep suntan, a rep-utation as a party animal and a bride who was already wondering how I'd managed to talk her into marrying an impecunious writer.

When I left England to write in America I'd had quite a respectable reputation as a writer, but how quickly people forget! For months I tried to think of a show—I had ideas but they got turned down. Then came the bombshell letter from the Bank Manager. Inspiration was kicked into gear and I wrote the outline of *Are You Being Served?* on the back of the bank's best notepaper.

Now I've often had a good relationship, albeit platonic, with Dame Fortune; and the good old Dame directed my thoughts to one of English

GRACE BROS.

television's most successful writers, David Croft. So I posted my idea to him.

He phoned and congratulated me on the size of my overdraft, and, oh yes, he loved the idea for the show. The rest, as they say, is history.

Looking at one's life as history, it's easy to see how the train of events arrived at their destination. In my case, no planning was required—all I had to do was spend the lot on a good time to end up desperate enough to have an idea, and then to find to my surprise that the show was a hit! A hit is always a surprise; on the other hand, failure is easy to achieve.

And so my life changed once again. During the ten-year run I was able to buy a lovely house with four garages, and my spending managed to keep pace with my frequent change of exotic cars. My bank manager invited me to lunch at the head office, and *Are You Being Served?*, which is enjoyed by all walks of life, opened many doors to places and people who were pleased to tell me they loved the show. I was even invited to lunch by the Queen Mother. I felt almost as flattered when I was given a free jar of pickled onions in Fortnum & Masons—as swanky a store as you can find—just because the top-hatted floorwalker was a fan.

But did I plan all this out of a driving ambition? Of course not. I just did what I enjoy most, writing, and in so doing entertained myself just as much as the viewers.

*Are You Being Served?* has given me a wonderful life. As I write this, I still thank a slightly younger Jeremy Lloyd for his enthusiasm and stamina to survive, with his friend and partner David Croft, the writing of sixty-nine shows which still provide an income to support me should I feel inclined to daydream on my red velvet sofa and gaze into the fire on a cold winter night and see what new shows are on television and wonder what inspired those writers. And look forward to seeing repeats of *Are You Being Served?*, because they still make me laugh, and nostalgia is very inexpensive yet wonderfully rewarding.

~Jeremy Lloyd, December 1996

# *Introduction*

IN THIS RAPIDLY CHANGING AND UNCERTAIN WORLD OF INFLATION, strikes, hijackings, corruption and cinema audiences thirsting for "Erotic Arabian Nights", "Virgins on Venus" or lessons in "How to Seduce a Vampire", it is reassuring to know that sanity still exists, that somewhere the "Empire Spirit" still burns unconverted to North Sea Gas, that there is a world where authority still wears a white collar, a stern expression and, if it can afford it, a carnation.

The world is none other than GRACE BROTHERS DEPARTMENT STORE, with its ancient lifts creaking up to the restaurant on the fourth floor and wobbling down to Hardware in the basement, where to be a moment late back from a coffee break could result in a severe reprimand, where time has stood still for several decades and it feels better that way.

Our story, however, concerns only one floor of Grace Brothers. The first.

Here, between the marble columns and polished countertops, male and female dummies stare at each other across the threadbare carpeted floor with as bored an expression as the salesmen and sales ladies themselves.

To the right, in men's wear, **Mr. Grainger**, the doyen, the elderly states-man of the undergarment and trouser leg, blinks over his glasses and folds his fat little hands over his fat little tummy invariably fearing that his digestion will again cause him embarrassment.

**Mr. Humphries**, blond and nearly beautiful, or so he would like to think, smiling a smile practiced since childhood on his doting mother, ever hoping that the day will bring a romantic adventure the like of which even he could not dream up, waits for male customers with the optimism of the fisherman.

**Mr. Lucas**, a comparative newcomer, ambitious in a lazy sort of way, certainly never missing an opportunity to have a day off, or charm an attractive pair of legs, awaits the chance to have a verbal swipe at Mr. Grainger's counterpart in the ladies' section, opposite.

**Mrs. Slocombe**, who must have been beautiful a long time ago and was definitely brought up proper, has the manner of one who has rubbed shoulders with the aristocracy. She can look down her nose with the best of them, and does so most of the time, while her protégée, young and well-endowed **Miss Brahms**, whose very accent would hurt the ears of any elocution teacher, smiles radiantly and sends Mr. Lucas into a welcome dither.

Down in the basement, **Mr. Mash**, the stolid shop steward, knows every inch of flooring in the department, examining it daily with his broom, as he waits impatiently for the overthrow of the capitalist society.

In the Department Manager's Office, **Mr. Rumbold**, perplexed by the difficulties which life sends his way every minute of the day, nervously anticipates another disaster. And upstairs, out of sight most of the time, **Young Mr. Grace** himself, The Founder—young no longer in years—but never giving a pretty girl a second look, being much too busy with the first one.

Last but not least, the most immaculate and dependable figure of them all, **Captain Peacock**, the floorwalker in charge of both men's and ladies' wear, keeping a watchful eye on the lift doors with such good effect that on many occasions the doors would open and a customer, on meeting Captain Peacock's fierce gaze, would hurriedly press the button to go up to the Tea Lounge where they could sit down and recover from the shock.

~Jeremy Lloyd & David Croft, 1975

Camping In

"All we need now," said Mr. Lucas

"is Lawrence of Arabia."

# Camping In

RECENT HEAVY FOG AND RAIN PUT A DAMPER ON EVERYBODY'S SPIRITS. The only cheerful person was Young Mr. Grace, who sat in his staff discount shorts and Grace Brothers social club shirt, reading the *Tailor and Cutter* while his yacht was anchored in the calm blue waters of the Caribbean. By contrast, the fog seemed to have been an everyday part of London's life for the past week. It even pervaded precincts of the ancient emporium and hung listlessly in a faint haze between the marble pillars, causing Mr. Grainger to don two pairs of long johns to combat the nearly sub-zero temperature, and long wistfully for his summer holiday, which he had been asked to take at the end of September.

"It is chilly, sir, isn't it?" he said to the thin, red-headed customer who stared anxiously at the gloves he was trying on. "And don't worry about the fingers, sir, they will ride up with wear." He turned to Mr. Humphries: "I'm sure these will give every satisfaction. Don't you think so, Mr. Humphries?"

"Oh yes, Mr. Grainger, it's almost impossible to distinguish that plastic imitation leatherette from the real imitation leatherette."

"Yes indeed, and you will find the lining will keep your hands wonderfully warm, won't it, Mr. Humphries?"

"Warm as toast I'd say, Mr. Grainger." Mr. Humphries smiled his bright-as-a-button smile and looked towards Mr. Lucas for confirmation. Mr. Lucas, who had been dozing slightly at the counter, woke up and acknowledged the presence of the customer.

"What? Oh yes, sir, yes, that's because the lining is made of real imitation simulated nylon fur fabric."

"Thank you, Mr. Lucas," said Mr. Grainger heavily. "I think that will be enough from you."

"I wore a pair last season," said Mr. Humphries, conversationally, "and

I got a lot of satisfaction out of them, didn't I, Mr. Grainger?"

"I believe you did, Mr. Humphries."

Mr. Lucas began to enjoy himself, and joined in.

"And the year before that, during the freeze up, when I couldn't fill my hot-water bottle, I wore a pair on my feet, and I got a lot of satisfaction out of those, didn't I, Mr. Humphries?"

"What you say," said Mr. Humphries nodding his head, "has a distinct ring of truth about it, Mr. Lucas, despite the fact that you have only been with us for two months."

"As a matter of fact," said the customer a little put out, "I want them for my wife's brother. I don't like him very much."

"In that case," said Mr. Humphries, "you couldn't have made a better choice." And with speed that deceived the eye, Mr. Grainger removed the gloves, Mr. Humphries rang the till and Mr. Lucas popped them in a bag.

Across the department through the fog, Miss Brahms nudged Mrs. Slocombe and indicated a tall customer standing near the ladies' display counter.

" 'Ere, Mrs. Slocombe, that man's been around our underwear counter for ten minutes."

Mrs. Slocombe raised her jeweled glasses and held them in front of her eyes slightly away from her face to view the situation.

"Oh dear," said Mrs. Slocombe. "Do you think he is," she dropped her voice, "one of those?"

"One of what?"

"A *bon voyeur*," said Mrs. Slocombe. "They're the ones who look and don't touch."

"Ooh," said Miss Brahms, "I have never been out with one of those."

"Leave it to me," said Mrs. Slocombe and, sailing forward, put on her sales smile. "Are you being served, sir?" she asked.

The customer, a fresh-faced, rather nervous young man, looked startled.

"No," said the customer. "Er… do you have a male assistant on this counter?"

"No, sir," said Mrs. Slocombe. "This is ladies' underwear."

"Oh!" said the customer and thought for a moment. "I thought there might be a man to help one."

"There is," said Mrs. Slocombe, "very little demand for that sort of thing at Grace Brothers."

"Ah, I see," said the customer and, glancing round nervously, he leant forward and said, "Well, I want to purchase a bra."

"What size are you?" asked Miss Brahms.

Mrs. Slocombe turned round slowly and gave Miss Brahms a penetrating look.

"That will do, Miss Brahms!"

The young man cleared his throat.

"It's for my fiancée, she's… er… well, she's a young girl."

"Congratulations," said Mrs. Slocombe. "Have you any idea what size she takes?"

The young man looked around furtively, then putting his hand in his raincoat pocket he pulled out an enormous bra and held it up in front of Mrs. Slocombe.

"I managed," he said, "to knock this off while she wasn't looking."

Mrs. Slocombe put her glasses on, took the bra and gazed at it with pursed lips.

"She's a big girl, isn't she?"

"Blimey," said Miss Brahms. "Storm in a 'B' cup."

"That will do, Miss Brahms," said Mrs. Slocombe. "Get out the forties, will you, the Kilimanjaro range."

Miss Brahms opened a drawer containing an assortment of brassieres and as she sorted through them began to hum "Climb Every Mountain."

Meanwhile, the eagle eye of Captain Peacock spotted Mr. Lucas standing at the bottom of the marble staircase looking up at the lift. Clicking his fingers imperiously, Captain Peacock caught his attention and beckoned him over.

"Mr. Lucas."

"Yes, Captain Peacock, did you beckon?"

"Well, as I clicked my fingers and waved my hand, you may assume that I am beckoning and I would appreciate it if you would come over here. I do not wish to raise my voice."

"Of course, Captain Peacock," said Mr. Lucas, and with a mock military step he marched up to Captain Peacock and stood rigidly to attention. Captain Peacock pretended not to notice the insubordination.

"By standing there, Mr. Lucas, near the lifts, you are out of your territory. Your place," and he pointed to emphasize it, "is at the end of the counter to allow Mr. Grainger and Mr. Humphries the first choice of customers."

"It's all very well," said Mr. Lucas, "but I haven't had one all day."

Captain Peacock gazed over Mr. Lucas's shoulder and clicked his fingers imperiously towards Mr. Grainger to attract his attention. Mr. Grainger, who was in the act of putting some cotton wool in his ears to keep out the cold, failed to hear. Mr. Humphries tapped him on the arm and pointed.

"Captain Peacock wants you, Mr. Grainger."

"What?" said Mr. Grainger. "Oh yes, coming, Captain Peacock." Captain Peacock waited patiently while Mr. Grainger made his way over, slowed down by the restricting effect caused by his two pairs of long johns.

"Thank you, Mr. Grainger," he said heavily as Mr. Grainger eventually arrived.

"Anything amiss, Captain Peacock?"

"Yes," said Captain Peacock. "Mr. Lucas is moaning about the fact that he hasn't had a chance to serve any customers today."

"Oh, I wasn't complaining," said Mr. Lucas. "I mean, if I am not allowed to make any commission, I could probably live," he paused for effect, "another three or four days before I starve to death."

"Well," said Mr. Grainger, "I dare say we have been a bit hard on him, you know. I'm sure my colleague and I could hold ourselves back a little."

He turned round and beckoned to Mr. Humphries. "Mr. Humphries, are you free?"

"Yes," said Mr. Humphries, "I am free, Mr. Grainger," and with his quick little steps appeared round the side of the counter and joined them. With a wave of his hand, Mr. Grainger announced that the next customer would be Mr. Lucas's.

Mr. Humphries nodded. "Understood, Mr. Grainger."

"Oh thank you, Mr. Grainger," said Mr. Lucas with mock servility. "And thank you too, Mr. Humphries, and thank you, Captain Peacock. You have probably saved my widowed mother's life."

Mr. Grainger looked at his watch. "Isn't it time for your tea break, Mr. Lucas?"

"Yes, but I can't afford it, so I have had to give it up."

"In that case," said Captain Peacock, "your customer is approaching."

Mr. Lucas turned in time to see a Scotsman in tam-o'shanter and kilt coming down the steps.

"He's all yours," said Mr. Grainger.

"Who's having all the luck," said Mr. Humphries. "Haven't had one of those for weeks."

Waving his sales book to attract the Scotsman, Mr. Lucas approached him.

"Good afternoon, sir, can I help you?"

The Scotsman, like all Scotsmen, took some time to reply while he gazed at Mr. Lucas suspiciously. Eventually he spoke, with an accent so broad that Mr. Lucas had to listen very carefully to understand anything of what he was saying.

"Do you have," said the Scotsman, "any guid, stout, long-lasting, hard-wearing tweed?"

"Let me think," said Mr. Lucas. "Good, stout, long-lasting, hard-wearing tweed." The Scotsman nodded.

"Something in the jacket line, sir?" said Mr. Lucas, trying to get a clue as to the customer's intention.

The Scotsman shook his head. "No, something in the trews line."

"Trews?" said Mr. Lucas, puzzled.

"Trews, man… breeks!"

"Aah," said Mr. Lucas. "Harris tweed briefs."

Captain Peacock gave a long-suffering sigh as he intervened. "Breeks, Mr. Lucas. That's Scottish for trousers."

The Scotsman stared disdainfully at Mr. Lucas. "Dae ye no ken the Gaelic?" he asked.

"Yes," said Mr. Lucas brightly, "he's a tall fellow with glasses."

"That will do," said Captain Peacock. "Just find the gentleman some trousers."

"Yes, sir," said Mr. Lucas, "trousers, sir, certainly, sir. Er, what waist are you, sir?"

"Thirty-six," said the Scotsman, "but forty-three is more comfortable."

"Aah yes, thirty-six," said Mr. Lucas, "and your inside leg, sir?"

"Measure it," said the Scotsman.

Mr. Lucas took a step back anxiously. "I beg your pardon, sir."

"I said measure it."

"Most people normally know their inside leg."

"I have never worn breeks, I have always worn the kilt."

"Would you mind waiting there just a moment?" said Mr. Lucas. "Excuse me, Mr. Grainger, can I borrow your tape? I have to take that gentleman's inside leg."

Mr. Grainger pulled the tape off his neck, but then a thought struck him. "I think," he said, "I'd rather you borrowed Mr. Humphries."

"Mr. Humphries, do us a favour, take my customer's inside leg."

"Don't ask me," said Mr. Humphries, "I've given it up for Lent. Anyway, he's your customer, I'm not allowed to touch him."

"All right then," said Mr. Lucas. "Lend us your tape."

"Don't lose it," said Mr. Humphries, and as Mr. Lucas took it, he put a restraining hand on his arm. "Hang on a minute, it's ever so chilly this morning…," and grabbing the tape he held up the metal end to his mouth and breathed on it a few times.

"We don't want him to jump through the roof, do we?"

"Here we are, sir," said Mr. Lucas, a little unnerved. "Are you ready?"

"I am ready!" said the Scotsman.

"Now," said Mr. Lucas, as he knelt down in front of him, "there's a very important question I must ask you. Do you wear the sporran on the left or the right, sir?"

"Get on with it, man."

Mr. Lucas very gingerly edged the tape up past the Scotsman's knee, and stopped about two inches under the edge of the kilt when a booming voice asked, "And where do you think you are going with that thing, laddie?"

"I am measuring your inside leg, sir."

The Scotsman grabbed the tape irritably. "In Scotland, young laddie, we always take the inside leg from the outside."

And taking the tape he placed it outside his leg and peering closely he announced, "Thirty-two, including the sporran."

With a look of relief, Mr. Lucas leapt up and disappeared towards the trouser rail.

"I'm glad they've given Mr. Lucas a customer at last," said Miss Brahms as she leant on the counter.

"He does walk on a tightrope," said Mrs. Slocombe. "I mean, one more complaint from me about him being cheeky, and he could be out."

"It must be frightening to have so much power," said Miss Brahms.

"It is," said Mrs. Slocombe.

A shadow fell across them.

"Do you think it suits me?" said a voice.

Mrs. Slocombe glanced up to see a rather morose looking middle-aged lady, wearing an enormous hat with cherries hanging all round the edge. Mrs. Slocombe ran her eye over it, making sure it was one of hers before she answered. Noticing the price tag hanging down by the customer's ear, she nodded.

"Oh yes, it does indeed, and the red artificial cherries are very youth making. Don't you agree, Miss Brahms?"

"Oh yes," said Miss Brahms taking her cue. "It takes years off of you, madam."

"Thank you, Miss Brahms. And the blue goes very well with madam's eyes."

The lady thrust her head forward. "I've got brown eyes."

Mrs. Slocombe put her glasses on and peered. "Ah yes, that's what I mean," she said. "It's one of those browns that goes so well with the blue. Gives you the sort of Marlene Dietrich look."

The lady looked even more morose. "She's in her seventies."

"Well," said Mrs. Slocombe defensively, "she wasn't when she was about forty."

"Do you think," said the lady, "that the brim is better up or down?" And grasping the brim with both hands, she turned it down, obscuring the rest of her face.

"Down," said Mrs. Slocombe.

"Where's the mirror?" said the lady.

"Lead the lady," said Mrs. Slocombe.

"Yes," said Miss Brahms. "This way, madam." And taking her by the elbow she led her along the counter to the mirror at the end. The lady forced her head back to peer under the brim to look at the effect.

"I don't think I like it," she said.

"Try something else," said Mrs. Slocombe.

"I tried all the other ones on while you were talking," said the lady. "This was the only one I thought I liked. I think I shall have to look elsewhere."

Mrs. Slocombe gritted her teeth. "I'm sorry," she said, "that we couldn't find anything to go with your face, madam, but do try again."

"Awkward cow," said Miss Brahms as the woman departed.

Mrs. Slocombe and Miss Brahms settled down again.

"Pssht!" came a rude voice from somewhere behind. The unexpected sound made Mrs. Slocombe spin round on her heels. A rather grubby hand protruding from a brown overall waved at her from the end of the line of fitted drawers.

"Over 'ere, " said the unmistakable tones of Mr. Mash.

"Please don't 'pssht' me," said Mrs. Slocombe angrily. "If you have anything to convey to me, Mr. Mash, you can either phone me up from your position in the basement, or speak to me before we open, or convey a message in the course of your official duty of delivering things to my department."

"I shan't tell you then," said Mr. Mash.

"Tell me what?" asked Mrs. Slocombe.

"If you don't want to know about it," said Mr. Mash, "I'll tell everybody else first, then you will be the last to know."

"Know what?" asked Miss Brahms.

"Know what?" insisted Mrs. Slocombe.

"They're out," hissed Mr. Mash, "they come out."

"Who've come out?" Mrs. Slocombe was becoming irritable.

"The transport," said Mr. Mash, "trains, buses, the lot. Look," and producing an early edition of the *Evening News* he pointed at the headlines. 'Transport workers out. Traffic chaos.' "There you are," said Mr. Mash, "it's one up for the workers. That'll teach the nobs a lesson."

"I don't see," said Mrs. Slocombe, putting on her glasses and studying the print, "how it's going to affect them. They've all got their Rolls-Royces. It's us workers what's going to suffer." The phone gave a ring. Taking off her earring, she picked up the receiver.

"Mrs. Slocombe, Ladies' ready-mades." She paused, "I see." Cupping her hand over the mouthpiece she spoke. "It's Mr. Rumbold. He says there is to be a meeting in his office at 5:30, re the transport strike."

"They're in a panic," said Mr. Mash.

"Is it," asked Mrs. Slocombe, "for us heads of departments or staff as well?" Her mouth fell a little. "I see, everybody."

" 'Ere," said Mr. Mash, "does that include me?"

"Does that," said Mrs. Slocombe, "include Mr. Mash from the cellar?" Her eyes closed in relief. "I see. It does not include you," she said as she replaced the receiver.

"Blimey," said Mr. Mash. "Isn't that bloody marvellous? I'm not even everybody, I'm a nobody."

"True," said Mrs. Slocombe.

At exactly 5:30 that evening, Mr. Rumbold sat behind his desk, the fingers of his hands pressed together in front of him in the way he had seen politicians press theirs together when being interviewed on television, and stared at the assembled staff. The evening paper with the news of the disaster lay on his desk.

"Well," said Mr. Rumbold, "you've all seen the news. I'm afraid the situation is very grave." He took a sip of water and continued, his voice getting slightly higher. "I'm proud to say that Grace Brothers are going to rise to the occasion."

"Are we going to man the buses, sir?" asked Mr. Lucas. "Because Mrs. Slocombe will make a marvellous clippy."

"Why?" asked Mr. Humphries, taking his cue.

"Because," said Mr. Lucas. "she has plenty of room on top."

Miss Brahms put her hand to her mouth too late to stifle the laugh.

Mrs. Slocombe turned on her. "There's no need to encourage him, Miss Brahms."

"This is not a laughing matter," said Captain Peacock. "This is very, very serious indeed. The future of the country is probably at stake."

"Now come, come," said Mr. Rumbold. "We must try and keep a sense of humour."

"Oh. Yes, quite right," said Captain Peacock.

"Now," said Mr. Rumbold, "hands up those who have cars." As he spoke he put his hand up.

"Drat," said Mr. Humphries with mock annoyance, "I've let the chauffeur have mine."

Mr. Grainger leant forward and spoke earnestly.

"I used to have an old banger before the war."

"But," said Mr. Lucas, "Mrs. Grainger found out and made him give her up."

"Mr. Lucas!" said Captain Peacock warningly.

"I don't think," said Mrs. Slocombe, "that any of us is fortunate enough to possess a vehicle."

"And although," said Mr. Rumbold, "you can see from my raised hand that I have one, it is unfortunately off the road at the moment being prepared for my continental touring holiday."

"Oh," said Miss Brahms. "Going to the Isle of Wight again?"

Mr. Rumbold ignored her.

"Now, are there any of us within walking distance?"

"Well," said Mr. Humphries nodding, "I could be home by morning if I set off now."

"Dear, dear," said Mr. Rumbold. "It is as I thought. We are stranded here. Well, assuming this would be the situation, I telexed Mr. Grace who, as you know, is holidaying on his yacht in the Caribbean."

"I hope he is having good weather," said Mr. Lucas.

"And," said Mr. Rumbold, "he has kindly telexed back giving his permission for the employees to spend the night in the store."

"He's got a heart of gold," said Mr. Humphries.

"Which he keeps in Fort Knox," said Mr. Lucas. "Mind you, we are very fortunate to be able to spend the night in the store. It's so much better than standing outside the staff entrance and coming in with the milk."

"Just a minute, just a minute," said Mrs. Slocombe. "Where are we going to sleep?"

"On the floor," said Mr. Rumbold.

Mrs. Slocombe gave a short, sarcastic laugh. "I'm not sleeping on the floor," she announced.

"I mean," said Mr. Rumbold, "on the department floor. On whatever bedding or other devices we can improvise."

"I've got an idea," said, Mr. Lucas. "How about Miss Brahms and I bagging the water bed on the fourth floor?"

"Good idea," said Miss Brahms. "As long as you sleep inside it."

"Everybody is staying on their own floor," said Mr. Rumbold. "It has already been agreed."

"Well," said Mrs. Slocombe, "I mean, what are we going to do for privacy? We can't all kip down like Sodom and Gomorrah."

"Or Swan and Edgar," said Mr. Humphries.

"I think," said Captain Peacock, "that Mrs. Slocombe has raised a very valid point. I think we should have some separation between the sexes."

"Perhaps," said Mr. Rumbold, "the ladies could sleep in the fitting rooms."

"I'm not," said Miss Brahms, "sleeping in that pokey hole with no air."

"I'll tell you what," said Mr. Lucas. "You sleep with the rest of us, and I'll get a couple of chastity belts from the novelty department."

Mrs. Slocombe drew herself up to her full height and inflated her bosom menacingly in the direction of Mr. Lucas.

"Because it is after five thirty, Mr. Lucas, it doesn't give you carte blanche to be coarse."

"I'm just trying to do what Mr. Rumbold suggested, best to keep our spirits up."

"Yes, quite right," said Mr. Rumbold. "What we will have to do is improvise. Now let's all think carefully."

There was rather a long silence while everybody furrowed their brows and thought very carefully. Finally, Mr. Rumbold banged his fist on the desk.

"Camping," he said.

"I beg your pardon," said Mr. Humphries.

"Camping," said Mr. Rumbold. "That's it. Were you never in the Scouts, Mr. Humphries?"

"Well," said Mr. Humphries shifting from one foot to the other, "not officially."

"One has to have the equipment, of course," said Mr. Rumbold.

"Oh, I have the equipment," said Mr. Humphries.

"I mean the equipment for camping here, tents, that sort of thing. I shall have to requisition it."

"Just a minute," said Mrs. Slocombe. "If we are going to have tents, I'd like one with a very stout bolt."

Mr. Rumbold stood up and paced the small threadbare area of carpet behind his desk.

"Mrs. Slocombe," he said, "I'm sure I speak for the rest of the men here when I say we will not, as you seem to suppose, behave like mad dogs as soon as the lights are out."

"Hear, hear," said Mr. Grainger.

"We are," continued Mr. Rumbold, "all in this together, and we are going to have to make the best of it, that's all." He picked up the phone and asked to be put through to the camping department.

Due to the emergency, the canteen at Grace Brothers bad been kept open and as a special concession everything was half price. Unfortunately, as there had been a rush at lunchtime of people staying in rather than braving the cold weather, all that was available at half price was an individual pie each, and tea or coffee.

"My pussy's going to go mad," remarked Mrs. Slocombe. "I mean, it just won't know what's happened to me."

"It'll see the fog." said Mr. Humphries, "and guess that you are held up somewhere."

"This pie," observed Mr. Grainger, "is getting under my plate."

"That remark," said Mrs. Slocombe, "will cause me to leave mine on my plate. Anyway, pastry always gives me wind."

"I'll tell you what," said Mr. Lucas, taking Mrs. Slocombe's pie, "I'll have yours and hoist a gale warning."

"You're so coarse," said Miss Brahms. "I'm surprised girls go out with you at all."

"They don't if I can help it," said Mr. Lucas. "I stay indoors with them."

"Your tent is up," shouted Mr. Mash. "Marvellous, isn't it? Here you are all noshing away, and there's me been working myself to death down there just so's you can have a comfy night."

"You are getting overtime," observed Mr. Rumbold.

"True, brother," said Mr. Mash, "otherwise it would have taken far less than the three hours I have just clocked up."

With a ping, the lift arrived on the first floor and disgorged the victims of the transport workers" dispute. Mr. Lucas gazed at the row of tents.

"All we need now," he observed, "is Lawrence of Arabia."

"We should be so lucky," said Mr. Humphries.

"It's a very familiar sight to me," said Captain Peacock. "But it's quite clear that Mr. Mash was never in the army. He's made a very sloppy job of erecting them."

"I don't see," said Mr. Lucas, "why I couldn't have gone up to the toy department and stayed in Peter Pan's house with Wendy and the crocodile."

"They wouldn't need the crocodile if you was there," said Miss Brahms. "Which is mine?"

"I know which one is mine," said Mrs. Slocombe. "I'm having the big one at the end."

"Aren't we going to toss for them?" asked Mr. Lucas.

"As head of the ladies' department," said Mrs. Slocombe, "I think it is only fitting that I should have the best tent." Bending her head slightly she walked into it and disappeared. A moment later her head popped out again.

"Captain Peacock, are you free?"

"Yes, Mrs. Slocombe."

"Could I have a word with you for a moment?"

Mrs. Slocombe pointed to the perspex window in the side of her tent. "There are no curtains."

"I shouldn't worry," said Captain Peacock. "You will be sleeping on the floor. Only a very tall person could see anything and even then he'd have to stand on tiptoe." To demonstrate the point Captain Peacock stood on tiptoe and looked through the perspex window.

"Yes," said Mrs. Slocombe pointedly, "that's what I meant."

"Apart from that," said Captain Peacock hurriedly, "one usually finds that condensation steams up the windows."

"I can assure you," said Mrs. Slocombe, "that lying down here on my air mattress I shall not be getting any steam up. And there's another thing. How am I supposed to do my flap up from the inside?"

"Perhaps," said Captain Peacock, "the best thing would be to get someone to zip you up after you are in."

"Oh, really," said Mrs. Slocombe. "And what if for some reason or other I wanted to leave in a hurry during the night?"

Captain Peacock smiled. "Well, if you think that sort of emergency might occur it might be wiser to leave your flap open."

"It all seems very primitive," said Mrs. Slocombe.

The rattling of wheels attracted their attention. Turning, they observed Mr. Mash with several pairs of winceyette striped pyjamas. He called out coster fashion: "Pyjamas, pyjamas get your lovely ripe pyjamas. Fresh pyjamas straight from the sales discount department."

Stopping the trolley he grasped a pair of very large pyjamas and held them up for Mrs. Slocombe. "There you are, Missis," said Mr. Mash. "Room for you and a friend."

"Oh," said Mrs. Slocombe recoiling, "what awful common things. Still, I suppose they are better than nothing."

"I prefer you in nothing," said Mr. Mash winking, and moved on with the trolley, stopping by Miss Brahms's tent.

"Sleepwear!!" he called out.

"Miss Brahms," said Mrs. Slocombe, "your pyjamas have arrived."

Miss Brahms's head popped out in front of her small beach tent.

" 'Ere," said Mr. Mash, "what size are you?"

"Mind your own business," said Miss Brahms. "Anyway, I never wear nothing in bed. I don't like rough things next to my skin."

"Cor," said Mr. Mash, "aren't you lucky I'm not in there with you then."

Mrs. Slocombe walked over to Miss Brahms's tent and took the pyjamas from Mr. Mash.

"Miss Brahms," she said, "you will wear pyjamas tonight. I mean, supposing there was a fire and you'd got nothing on."

"In that case," said Miss Brahms, "I'd be first to be rescued."

Mrs. Slocombe thrust the pyjamas at Miss Brahms. "Get 'em on."

"I can't wear those," said Miss Brahms. "They're men's—they got a flap at the front."

"Get a safety pin," said Mrs. Slocombe, "and wear them the other way around."

Mr. Mash wheeled his trolley on and stopped at the next tent. Seeing a moving bulge in the side he slapped it.

"Who's in there?" said Mr. Mash.

"I am," winced Mr. Humphries, "and mind where you're putting your hands."

"Do you, or do you not," said Mr. Mash, "require a pair of pyjamas?"

The flap parted and Mr. Humphries appeared and stood up to reveal that he was wearing a full-length black nightshirt with a Chinese dragon motif embroidered on the front.

"No, thanks," said Mr. Humphries. "I made arrangements with a friend of mine, in the gentlemen's boutique."

"Cor blitney," said Mr. Mash, "Anna May Wong rides again."

Mr. Mash stopped at the next tent from which came the noise of gnashing teeth and much grunting.

"Are you in there, Mr. Grainger, sir?" inquired Mr. Mash politely,

The answer was more grunting, then the whole tent rose in the air, collapsed and from its folds emerged Mr. Grainger's head.

"Are you all right?" asked Mr. Humphries.

"No," said Mr. Grainger, "I am trying to remove my trousers."

The struggle continued under the tent. "It's not easy, is it?" he said. "Ah... that's it." And triumphantly he held up a pair of trousers by their braces.

"Nice pair of pyjamas, Mr. Grainger?" said Mr. Mash, holding out a pair of winceyettes.

Mr. Grainger stood up among the remains of his tent to reveal himself in shirttails, long johns, shorts and suspenders. Mrs. Slocombe stared at him, shaking her head in disbelief.

"It's amazing," she said, "what you see when you haven't got a gun."

"I think," said Mr. Grainger, "that it would be more dignified if I changed in the men's cloakroom."

"Mr. Grainger," called Mr. Lucas, "you've left your flap open."

Mr. Grainger paused halfway up the stairs and his right hand shot over his posterior defensively.

"On your tent," explained Mr. Lucas.

"I don't think," said Mr. Grainger, turning round and staring sternly at Mr. Lucas, "that was very funny."

"Here you are, Captain Peacock," said Mr. Mash, handing Captain Peacock a pair of pyjamas from the trolley. "Top-quality passion killers."

Captain Peacock gazed at them disdainfully.

"Haven't you anything else but stripes?"

"Oh," said Mr. Mash. "What do you want, pips?"

Captain Peacock glanced round and leaned forward and spoke confidentially.

"I think," he said, "having regard to my position, I should have something that makes me look a little different from the rest."

"Well," said Mr. Mash, equally confidentially, "leave the trousers off then."

Captain Peacock was not amused.

"Don't you worry," said Mr. Mash. "I'll try and find something for you, Captain."

Taking the last pair of pyjamas, Mr. Mash went up to Mr. Lucas's tent.

"Not much room in here," said Mr. Lucas, crouching inside and gazing around dejectedly. "It would be easier to pinch one of Mrs. Slocombe's bras and use it as a hammock."

"Oi," said Mr. Mash, "here's the last pair for you, sir."

"Thanks," said Mr. Lucas, crawling out of his tent and standing up. "Just a minute, what's this?" Mr. Lucas held up the pyjamas to reveal that one leg was missing.

"Cor," said Mr. Mash. "How did those get in there? They must be the ones from the window display."

"Window display? How many one-legged men go window shopping?"

"Ah." said Mr. Mash. "It was from a bed advert. The 'he' dummy was getting out of one side and the 'she' dummy was getting out of the other, and they made one pair of pyjamas do for two."

"I can't wear these in mixed company," said Mr. Lucas.

"It's all right," said Mr. Mash. "Stick both legs down one leg and hop into bed."

Pulling up his trousers, Captain Peacock got down on his hands and knees and crawled purposefully into a tent. A piercing scream from Miss Brahms caused him to crawl out backwards at great speed. The scream was followed by Miss Brahms's face staring indignantly at Captain Peacock.

"'Ere," she said, "what are you playing at?"

"I'm sorry, Miss Brahms, but I was under the impression that this was where I was sleeping."

"Not on your nelly," said Miss Brahms.

Captain Peacock tried to clear up the situation. "But you are supposed to be sleeping in the big tent with Mrs. Slocombe."

"In that case," said Miss Brahms, "you'd better take it up with her. And you'd better knock first."

"By the way," said Captain Peacock, "your pyjamas should be worn the other way around."

"You do your thing your way," said Miss Brahms, "and I'll do my thing mine."

Rising to his feet Captain Peacock walked to Mrs. Slocombe's tent and knocked as best he could on the canvas. There was a pause. He knocked again and coughed and from within came a prolonged raspberry that died away, leaving an expression of surprise tinged with horror on Captain Peacock's face.

"Er, Mrs. Slocombe," he called nervously, "are you by any chance free?"

The only answer was another prolonged high-pitched raspberry.

"Just a moment, Captain Peacock," came the muffled voice of Mrs. Slocombe.

"I can come back later," said Captain Peacock embarrassed.

A further raspberry that came in short, sharp bursts answered him.

"Or indeed not at all," continued Captain Peacock, moving hurriedly away.

"It's all right," said Mrs. Slocombe, appearing at the doorway of her tent. "I have the stopper in now." And holding up the airbed she indicated the source of the trouble. "Just blowing up my air mattress. It took puff after puff after puff."

Mr. Humphries chose that moment to pop his head out of the tent. "Can I help anybody?"

"It's all right, thank you, Mr. Humphries, I've managed."

"Can you tell me," asked Captain Peacock, "what Miss Brahms is doing in that tent?"

"Knowing you," said Mrs. Slocombe, "I'm surprised you haven't looked."

"He did look," said Miss Brahms popping her head out. "I was getting into my pyjamas, and he told me I was doing it the wrong way round."

"Oh really," said Mrs. Slocombe. "You are a *voyeur*, nothing less than a *voyeur*."

"The point is" said Captain Peacock, "that this big tent is for yourself and Miss Brahms, and that one is supposed to be for me."

Mrs. Slocombe shook her head.

"There's going to be no one in my boudoir when I blow out the candle, Captain Peacock."

"But then that leaves me without any accommodation. Where am I supposed to bivouac?"

"I don't care whack, it's nothing to do with me." She emphasized the parting shot by disappearing and pulling the flap to.

"Left hand down a bit," called out Mr. Mash.

Captain Peacock turned to see Mr. Mash and three men in brown coats approaching with what appeared to be a large wardrobe on a trolley.

"What on earth is that?"

"Glad you asked," said Mr. Mash. "It's a bed, sir. Mr. Rumbold ordered it."

"Oh," said Captain Peacock, "how very thoughtful of him."

But immediately in the wake of the bed appeared the large figure of

Mr. Rumbold in striped pyjamas waving his arms and calling.

"Not there, Mr. Mash, not there! Over there!"

"It won't go through your office door, Mr. Rumbold."

"Shsh," said Mr. Rumbold, taking Mr. Mash to one side he dropped his voice to a confidential tone.

"I can't," said Mr. Rumbold, "sleep out here with the staff."

"What, sir?" said Mr. Mash, in a loud voice. "You can't sleep out here with the staff?"

All flaps opened and head popped out again. With everyone's eyes on him, Mr. Rumbold raised his voice and gave a false laugh.

"Well... of course I can sleep with the staff, Mr. Mash. I meant the female staff. Now, how does this thing work?"

"Well," said Mr. Mash, "this is a collapsible bed and should be screwed up against the wall of a bedroom. That's so when your bird's father knocks at the door you press the button and she goes up the wall instead of him."

"Enough levity," said Mr. Rumbold.

"Ah," said Captain Peacock, "an ingenious device, is it not?"

"Yes," said Mr. Rumbold, "most ingenious."

"Very, very roomy," said Captain Peacock.

"Well," said Mr. Rumbold, "it is sold as a small double."

"In that case," said Captain Peacock, "it might well solve a slight problem."

"What problem?"

"Miss Brahms," said Captain Peacock, "refuses to leave my tent."

"Well, of course you're quite right to tell me, but what you do after hours, in normal circumstances, is entirely your own affair, but you certainly can't go through with this sort of thing under our noses though, so to speak."

Captain Peacock sighed. "I think you may have what might be termed as the wrong end of the stick, sir."

"Have I?" queried Mr. Rumbold.

"Yes, sir. You see, I have already arranged for Mrs. Slocombe to have the larger tent because I was quite sure she would be willing to share. But to my surprise, she wouldn't hear of it."

Mr. Rumbold nodded, trying to take in the situation.

"Do you think she suspects you and Miss Brahms?"

Captain Peacock shook his head, very patiently. "Again you don't follow me, sir. I was trying to get Miss Brahms and Mrs. Slocombe together in the same tent."

"What?" said Mr. Rumbold aghast. "All three of you? This permissive society has really gone to your head, Peacock."

"No, *no*, sir," said Captain Peacock. "You have misunderstood again. I don't want to share with any of the ladies."

"Thank heavens for that," said Mr. Rumbold.

"I want to share with you."

There was a gasp of surprise from the direction of Mr. Humphries's tent.

Some time later, once Captain Peacock had managed to explain to Mr. Rumbold his reasons for wishing to share his sleeping accommodation, everyone sat cross-legged round an electric log fire, the red glow of which lit up their faces as they clutched cups of hot cocoa in their hands.

Led by Mr. Rumbold, they sang "Keep the Home Fires Burning," Mr. Humphries's voice coming over loud and clear on the line…"though the boys are far away they dream of you"….The song echoed round the marble columns declaiming that there was a silver lining through the dark cloud shining, and Mr. Rumbold held up his hands to hush them all so that he could sing the solo.

"Turn the dark clouds inside out," he sang in a whisper and was extremely annoyed when Mr. Humphries joined in for "till the boys come home… ."

"Wonderful, Mr. Rumbold," said Mrs. Slocombe as they all applauded. "Didn't you think so, Captain Peacock?"

"Ah yes," said Captain Peacock, sipping his cocoa reflectively. "It brings back so many memories of the army and the lads; the heat and the sunset; the endless shifting sands."

"How long were you at Bognor Regis?" asked Mr. Lucas.

Captain Peacock smiled his desert smile. "Mr. Lucas, when you were at school, I was with some of the toughest soldiers in the world, chasing Rommel."

"Some people have all the luck," observed Mr. Humphries.

Mr. Rumbold nodded. "Yes, Lucas, many people seem to forget that men like Captain Peacock and myself were instrumental in making this country a place for heroes to live in."

"Not to mention to strike in," added Mr. Humphries.

"What were you in, sir?" inquired Mr. Lucas.

"Me?" said Mr. Rumbold. "The Catering Corps, actually."

"The Naafi," said Mr. Lucas disdainfully.

Captain Peacock held up his hand. "Not the Naafi, Mr. Lucas. The Catering Corps—they were a very important part of the service. Remember the army used to march on its stomach."

"I suppose," said Mr. Lucas, "they couldn't walk upright because of the indigestion."

Mrs. Slocombe shook her head. "Unfortunately, Captain Peacock, the youngsters of today seem to forget what we went through. I always remember those famous words of Sir Noël Coward's... 'They also serve who only stand and wait'..."

Mr. Humphries looked at her amazed. "Were you in the Naafi too, then?"

"Oh. No, no," said Mrs. Slocombe with a deprecating wave of her hand. "Although I was only a slip of a girl, I was in the air-raid precautions. In fact, that's how I met my husband, during a raid." She paused and glanced upwards.

The others followed her gaze, then leaning forward she continued: "With the bombs coming down, it was awful. I will never forget seeing his face lit up by an incendiary, then he threw me down on my front and said 'Look out, here comes a big one!'"

"I suppose there wasn't much time for chatting up in those days," said Mr. Lucas.

Mrs. Slocombe ignored him and continued. "And after it had gone off, we headed for the shelters, and I knew at that moment it was love at first sight."

"First bomb site you came to?" queried Mr. Lucas.

"Ooh, your filthy mind," retorted Mrs. Slocombe.

Hurriedly changing the subject, Mr. Rumbold addressed Mr. Grainger. "And where were you when it all happened?"

"I was with ENSA entertaining the troops," said Mr. Grainger nostalgically.

" 'Ere," said Miss Brahms, "what does ENSA stand for?"

"Every night something awful?" suggested Mr. Humphries.

"That was the joke at the time of course, but they were very good indeed," said Mr. Rumbold. "You did a grand job, you ENSA chaps." He patted Mr. Grainger on the shoulder warmly.

"Thank you, sir," said Mr. Grainger. "I remember I used to do impersonations—Goring, Hitler, Goebbels, von Ribbentrop, Lord Haw-Haw."

"Whose side were you on?" inquired Mr. Lucas.

"Oh, I used to do Mr. Churchill as well," said Mr. Grainger defensively.

"You must realize," said Captain Peacock, "particularly you, Mr. Lucas, who are too young to remember, that ENSA were up in the front line with us chaps and stood just as good a chance of being lolled or captured as anyone else."

"With those impersonations," said Mr. Lucas, "Mr. Grainger could have got the Iron Cross and escaped."

"I think it's fascinating," said Mr. Humphries. "Of course I've read all about it. How about giving us your Lord Haw-Haw, Mr. Grainger? You know, that propaganda one he used to broadcast to England."

Mr. Grainger sipped his cocoa and shook his head. "Well, I don't know, after all these years, it's been a long time, but I'll try."

Placing his cocoa on the floor he took a deep breath. "I last did this in a concert in Tobruk." Clearing his throat and holding his nose, he spoke in a high nasal voice. "Germany calling, Germany calling. You British cannot win the war. The German army is invincible. This is the voice of Lord Haw-Haw speaking to you directly from Berlin."

"Just listen to those words," said Mrs. Slocombe. "Doesn't it send shivers up your spine?"

"It certainly does," said Mr. Lucas. "Just like the Daleks."

Mr. Grainger ignored the last remark and stood up.

"Has anybody got a cigar?" he asked.

"I didn't know you smoked," said Mr. Humphries.

"I don't," said Mr. Grainger. "But I was going to do Churchill. A pencil will do."

"I have one," said Captain Peacock, taking his propelling pencil from the top pocket of his pyjamas.

"Thank you," said Mr. Grainger. "Are you ready?"

"We're ready," said Mr. Rumbold.

Mr. Grainger cleared his throat, puffed out his double chins and held the pencil at a rakish angle between his fingers.

"We shall," he croaked, "fight on the beaches! Give us the tools and we will do the job! Some chicken, some neck!" and then reverting to his normal voice, "After which I used to take my hat off."

"I think you were very brave, Mr. Grainger," said Captain Peacock.

Mr. Lucas nodded. "With that act, he'd have to be."

"Do you know," said Miss Brahms, "I hadn"t even arrived when all that was going on."

"Really?" said Mr. Lucas. "Where were you?"

"Wasn't born," said Miss Brahms, "but it was the war that got my father and mother together. We still got pictures in our scrapbook with him in his black face running up a beach."

"Blimey," said Mr. Lucas. "Was he the first of the illegal immigrants?"

"He was a commando!" said Miss Brahms proudly.

"The toughest," interjected Captain Peacock nodding approvingly.

"Absolutely ruthless," said Mr. Humphries. "If they got hold of you it was the end of you. If you were on the other side, of course."

Miss Brahms moved nearer to the fire.

"He met my mum," she said, "when he broke into her bicycle shed during a training exercise at Ipswich… 'What are you doing?' she asked. 'Looking for Gerry,' he said, so she took him upstairs and showed him around, and they just clicked."

"Isn't that romantic?" said Mrs. Slocombe.

"It certainly is," said Mr. Lucas, "and if it happens again despite my pierced eardrums and my flat feet, I'll be the first in the queue."

"Dressed," Mr. Humphries added, "as a lady with a ticket for Sweden, no doubt."

"How about lending me your handbag?" said Mr. Lucas.

"Now, now," said Captain Peacock, "I think it's getting late."

"Yes indeed," said Mr. Rumbold "I think it's time for lights out. It's been a most enjoyable evening. It's just like the old boy scouts' jamboree."

"Yes," said Mr. Humphries, "and it's only half past ten."

Mr. Lucas stood up. "Shall I switch off the camp fire, sir?"

Mr. Rumbold took the suggestion seriously. "Yes, we don't want to take any risks."

A loud snore came from beyond the glow.

"Oh look," said Mr. Lucas, "Churchill's having a cat nap."

"Poor old Mr. Grainger," said Miss Brahms. "He probably retires long before this normally. Shouldn't somebody wake him up and tell him it's time to go to bed?"

"I'll do it," said Mr. Humphries. And cupping his hands he shouted in Mr. Grainger's ear, "Are you free?" Mr. Grainger woke with a start and staggered to his feet. "Yes, yes, I'm free," and peered round shortsightedly.

"We just wanted to say goodnight to you," said Mr. Lucas.

"Oh," said Mr. Grainger. "Yes… goodnight."

"And so," said Mr. Lucas, as Mr. Grainger bent down and crawled wearily into his tent, "after another exciting adventure in the desert the Red Shadow rejoins his harem." He paused and looked at Miss Brahms. "Shirley, how about a game of Ping-Pong in the sports department?"

"No thank you."

"Well, how about a game of sardines in soft furnishings?"

"Why don't you get in your tent and zip yourself up?" said Miss Brahms pointedly.

"We can always go up to the library," continued Mr. Lucas, "and get you a copy of *The Sensuous Woman*."

Miss Brahms gave him a two finger sign.

"All right." said Mr. Lucas. "Two copies."

Mr. Grainger's head popped out of his tent.

"Has anyone set the alarm for the morning?"

"I don't know," said Mrs. Slocombe, "but I have set a burglar alarm for tonight."

"You might be lucky," said Mr. Lucas, "and get one."

Captain Peacock stared longingly at the double bed. "I think we should retire now, don't you think, sir?"

"What?" said Mr. Rumbold. "Oh yes, yes, if you insist. I'm not too happy about this sharing, though."

"I don't see any alternative," said Captain Peacock, "unless you wish me to sleep on the carpet."

"No, no, no," said Mr. Rumbold. "As long as you don't snore."

"My good lady wife has never complained of me snoring," said Captain Peacock.

"I'll have to ask you to leave if you do," said Mr. Rumbold. "And by the way, I hope you don't mind but I'm keeping my socks on. It's rather cold."

"If you insist, sir," said Captain Peacock

He then looked up as the sound of the "Last Post" echoed across the department. Mr. Lucas, hand cupped round his mouth, was standing to attention and saluting with the other.

"Mr. Lucas," called Captain Peacock, "that's quite enough!"

"I'm trying to make you feel at home, sir," said Mr. Lucas, who then shouted, "Goodnight, Mrs. Slocombe."

Mrs. Slocombe called anxiously from her tent, "Who's that calling goodnight?"

"It's me," said Mr. Lucas, walking over.

"You're not standing on tiptoe, are you?" inquired Mrs. Slocombe.

"No, Mrs. Slocombe."

"I like to be private in here," she said. And as she spoke, Mr. Lucas heard a long, wailing raspberry.

"I quite understand," he said.

"Damn, it's my stopper again."

Mr. Lucas moved across the department and paused by Miss Brahms's tent.

"Are you sleeping in the altogether?"

"Yes," said Miss Brahms, "I am."

He stood silently for a moment, then screamed out, "Fire!"

Miss Brahms appeared at the flap of her tent with a glass of water and threw it over him.

"There," she said, "that should damp it down then," and pulled her flap down and fastened it securely.

"Charming!" said Mr. Lucas, then, wiping his face with his sleeve, he walked over to Mr. Humphries's tent and cooed a "Goodnight."

"I can't come out," said Mr. Humphries. "I have just put cream on my face but, night, night, and sleep well."

Mr. Lucas stopped at Mr. Grainger's tent and stared down at the beaker placed outside which contained his false teeth. Bending down Lucas picked it up and gazed into it reflectively.

"Just think," he murmured, "these are the teeth that chewed on Churchill's cigar."

"Goodnight, Mr. Grainger," he called. Mr. Grainger managed an inaudible reply.

As he passed the double bed, he called out a cheery "Goodnight." Captain Peacock and Mr. Rumbold sat up together.

"Goodnight," said Mr. Rumbold.

"Goodnight, Lucas," said Captain Peacock. He was reading *The Adventures of Captain Dangerfield.*

"I say," said Mr. Rumbold, "you're not going to read, are you, Peacock?"

Captain Peacock closed the book with a bang.

"No, sir."

"Good. Could you switch off the light?"

He indicated the strip light above Captain Peacock's head.

"I'll try," said Captain Peacock, searching round for the switch. "But I can't see any switch. It doesn't appear to be on this side."

"Damn," said Mr. Rumbold, "It must be on mine…. No, it's not. Mr. Lucas! Are you in bed yet?"

A muffled voice came from Mr. Lucas's tent. "I'm on my way there, sir."

"Are you free?" asked Captain Peacock.

"I'm just trying to light my candle," Mr. Lucas crawled into view with a box of matches in one hand and a candle in the other. "What is it, sir?"

"It's our light," said Mr. Rumbold. "Can you find the switch and put it out for us?"

"Certainly, sir."

"These wardrobe wall beds are a new line," said Mr. Rumbold. "I'm afraid I'm not too conversant with them."

"Ah, here we are," said Mr. Lucas finding something that looked like a switch.

"Not that," said Captain Peacock warningly. But it was too late.

As Mr. Lucas pressed a button, the back part of the bed folded down and snapped shut like a giant clam, trapping the unfortunate pair inside. Yells and bangs brought the others from their tents, as Mr. Lucas tried desperately to release them.

"What's happened?" asked Miss Brahms.

"It's locked itself," said Mr. Lucas.

"Where's the key?" said Mrs. Slocombe.

"Help!" shouted Captain Peacock from within. "Do something!"

"I just got off to sleep," said Mr. Humphries, "and I really must protest at this noise."

"Do you realize," said Miss Brahms, "that if we can't find the key they will be stuck in there until the morning?"

There was a long pause.

"I don't think we can find the key," said Mr. Lucas.

"They'll suffocate," said Miss Brahms.

"There's plenty of air going through the crack," said Mr. Lucas. "Can you hear me in there?"

"Yes, yes," said the anxious voice of Mr. Rumbold. "What's going on?"

"We're going to get the key for you," said Mr. Lucas.

"Oh good," said Mr. Rumbold.

"In the morning," added Mr. Lucas, "when Mr. Mash gets here. He's gone home because he lives quite close."

"I can't sleep here all night," protested Mr. Rumbold.

"Don't panic out there," called Captain Peacock.

"We shall remain calm."

"Will we?" said the muffled voice of Mr. Rumbold.

"Yes," said Mr. Lucas. "It's no worse than being trapped at the bottom of the ocean in a submarine."

"Help!" said Captain Peacock.

"Remember your Catering Corps background," shouted Mr. Lucas, "the stiff upper lip."

"I'll tell you what," said Miss Brahms. "We'll all keep you company outside here until Mr. Marsh arrives."

"I'll get the cards," said Mr. Lucas.

"Good idea," said Mr. Humphries.

And so, joined by Mrs. Slocombe everyone sat and played whist on top of the collapsed collapsible bed and, after a while, there was nothing to be heard but the regular snoring of Captain Peacock and the anxious voice of Mr. Rumbold inquiring from time to time if everyone was still there.

"You mustn't worry about us," said Mr. Lucas. "We're all right, Jack—Queen, King and all the aces."

CHAPTER

*Up Captain Peacock*

"Oh no Sir," said Captain Peacock shaking his head.

"Not another honour, sir, that would be too much."

Mr. Rumbold nodded. "Yes, it would indeed."

# Up Captain Peacock

ALTHOUGH THE MINUTE HAND OF THE DEPARTMENT CLOCK BARELY indicated 8:45, the ladies and gentlemen of the first floor were already gathered in front of the lifts. With a clatter of footsteps Mr. Lucas came bounding up the main staircase gesturing over his shoulder.

"He's coming up in the lift now."

"Right," said Mr. Rumbold. "Stand by, everybody. Now as soon as the lift gates open you will all applaud, then I shall present Captain Peacock with his twenty years' service badge."

"I remember," said Mr. Grainger, "when I got it. It was a most emotional moment."

"Blimey," said Mr. Lucas, "twenty years in here. It's almost as much as the train robbers got."

The lift bell pinged, a light flashed and the doors opened. The department broke out into loud applause as Captain Peacock appeared, immaculate as ever with carnation, well-rolled umbrella and bowler hat at a rakish angle.

"Oh," said Captain Peacock. "How very unexpected."

Mr. Rumbold stepped forward and cleared his throat.

"Ahem. Captain Peacock, in acknowledgment of your twenty years...."
As he spoke the lift gates shut obscuring Captain Peacock from view. Mr. Lucas rushed forward and pressed the button, but the lighted numbers showed the lift rising.

"I'm sorry, sir," said Mr. Lucas, "I'm afraid I've lost him."

"What a pity," said Mr. Humphries, "cut off in his moment of glory."

"He's going up to Accounts," said Mrs. Slocombe.

"Do you think we ought to follow him?" asked Mr. Grainger.

"Yes! Quick, into the other lift." Mr. Rumbold led a concerted rush and dashed into the lift.

"Quick! Press the button. Everyone in?"

" 'Ang on a minute," said Miss Brahms.

Even as she spoke the doors closed on her, leaving her outside. Banging on them she screamed through the doors, "He's coming down, he's coming down!"

The lighted numbers indicated the welcoming party's up-ward departure, and a ping indicated the return of Captain Peacock.

The doors opened.

"This comes," said Captain Peacock, "as a complete surprise to me and I am most…' he glanced around perplexed. "Where are they all?"

"They've gone up to Accounts with your medal," said Miss Brahms.

"Oh, how stupid." He stepped back into the lift, and pressed the button.

" 'Ang on," said Miss Brahms. But she was too late—the doors closed. She pounded on them with her fist.

" 'Ere, they're coming back!" she screamed.

A ping and the doors of the search-party lift opened, disgorging its passengers.

"You've just missed him again. He's gone up to look for you."

"Oh, drat," said Mr. Rumbold.

"It's like looking for the Scarlet Pimpernel," observed Mr. Humphries. "We seek him here, we seek him there."

" 'Ang on," said Miss Brahms. "His lift is coming."

"Right," said Mr. Rumbold. "Places, everyone."

"It gives me great pleasure," started Mr. Rumbold as the lift doors opened, and then he stopped. It was Mr. Mash with a half-naked female dummy in his arms.

"Yea, and it gives me great pleasure too!" said Mr. Mash.

"Oh, this is ridiculous," said Mrs. Slocombe. "I'm going back to my counter."

"Yes," said Mr. Humphries, "the moment has rather lost its magic."

"Send him to my office when he comes in," said Mr. Rumbold. As the welcoming party started to disperse, a breathless Captain Peacock puffed down the stairs.

"I say," he croaked, "I'm here, I'm here." Before he had time to remove his hat, Mr. Rumbold, with a "tut" of annoyance, marched back and handed him a small box with the words, "In acknowledgment of your twenty years' service to Grace Brothers, I have much pleasure in presenting you with this long service badge with the letters G.B. in eighteen carat gold."

"Plate," added Mr. Humphries.

"My word," said Mr. Lucas, "that was worth risking a heart attack for, wasn't it, Captain Peacock?"

Captain Peacock leant against the wall breathlessly.

"This comes," he said, "as a complete surprise to me and I am most touched, not to say honoured."

"In addition," added Mr. Rumbold, "and as a special token of your particularly excellent service here the management are taking the unusual step of presenting you with this key."

"What's it for?" said Mr. Humphries. "Your flat?"

"It is the key," said Mr. Rumbold, "to the executive washroom."

Mr. Grainger gave a snort of outrage. "The key to the executive washroom?"

"Well, really," said Captain Peacock, "I didn't expect this. It is indeed an honour."

Mr. Grainger snorted again. "Key to the executive washroom! I have served here for thirty-five years and I have never been once."

"You must be bursting," said Mr. Lucas.

"I have been here longer than most," said Mrs. Slocombe, "and I have to muck in with the others."

Mr. Rumbold held up his hand. "I have one more announcement to make."

"Oh no, sir," said Captain Peacock shaking his head. "Not another honour, sir, that would be too much."

Mr. Rumbold nodded. "Yes, it would indeed. This has nothing to do with you directly, Peacock. I just wanted to remind you about the change in the lunch break. The management feel we are losing a lot of trade by closing between one and two, so in future we will take our lunch break between two and three."

"I don't think," said Mrs. Slocombe, "that my stomach can hang out that long."

"Why not?" said Mr. Lucas. "It has been hanging out for the last ten years."

Mrs. Slocombe took a deep breath. "Mr. Grainger, will you tell your junior that if he doesn"t watch his tongue when talking to a lady, he'll get a bat round the ear 'ole."

A ringing of bells indicating that the store was open interrupted Mr. Grainger's reply.

"Right," said Mr. Rumbold. "The store is now open. To your counters, everyone."

As they moved, Mr. Rumbold indicated to Captain Peacock that he would like a word with him.

"Yes, sir?" said Captain Peacock.

"One more thing," said Mr. Rumbold. "Regarding your application for an increase in salary...."

"Oh yes, sir?" said Captain Peacock expectantly.

"It has not been approved."

"Indeed," said Captain Peacock, taking his hat off. "I'm sorry to hear that."

"I am, however," continued Mr. Rumbold, "here to tell you that the management have seen fit to extend to you the privilege of using the executive dining-room."

A stunned look came into Captain Peacock's eyes.

"The executive dining-room?" A smile slowly spread over his face. "I'm very honoured, sir."

"I thought you would be," said Mr. Rumbold. "Well, see you at lunch, Steven."

"Thank you, Cuthbert," said Captain Peacock.

Mr. Rumbold stopped in his tracks and moved back. "It's still Mr. Rumbold," he said sternly.

"I'm sorry, sir," said Captain Peacock. "Please forgive me. Having the key to the executive washroom must have gone to my head."

"I quite understand," said Mr. Rumbold.

"Haven't you forgotten something?" asked Captain Peacock.

"I don't think there's anything else," said Mr. Rumbold.

"Well, you haven't actually given me the key," said Captain Peacock.

"Oh, I'm sorry." Reaching into his pocket Mr. Rumbold produced a small key on a piece of string.

"The key to the executive washroom," murmured Captain Peacock, holding the key up and swinging it around. "The key to the executive washroom," he murmured, as he went to hang his hat up.

"Look at him," said Mr. Grainger. "He's flaunting it. I've wanted that key all my life."

Mr. Lucas shook his head.

"You're not management, Mr. Grainger."

"You're not even in line for the throne," observed Mr. Humphries.

A small, stout, florid-faced man with a raincoat over his arm stood at the top of the stairs and gazed round.

"Are you being served, sir?" asked Captain Peacock as he reappeared still swinging the key on its piece of string.

"It's hardly likely," observed the customer, "I have just stepped out of the lift."

"In that case," said Captain Peacock, "I will rephrase the question. Can I help you, sir?"

"I am looking for a bow."

"Yes, sir," said Captain Peacock. "Tie, violin or Robin Hood?"

"Oh very funny," said the customer sarcastically.

"I beg your pardon, sir. I'm in rather a frivolous mood today, you see it's my anniversary. I have been at Grace Brothers for twenty years."

"In that case," said the customer, "you will know where I can buy a clip-on bow tie."

Captain Peacock effected a look of disdain.

"A clip-on bow tie?"

"Yes." said the customer, "a clip-on bow tie, you know the sort, they…."

"I know, sir… they clip on. Are you free, Mr. Grainger?"

"Yes, I'm free."

"This gentleman," said Captain Peacock with great disdain, "would like a clip-on bow tie."

Mr. Grainger drew his lips back over his teeth and sucked them noisily. "A clip-on bow tie?"

Captain Peacock nodded. "A clip-on bow tie."

Mr. Grainger shook his head. "I'm sorry, I can't help you, sir, I'm just going to the staff bog," and he stared at Captain Peacock aggressively before departing.

"Thank you, Mr. Grainger," said Captain Peacock. "Are you free for a clip-on bow tie, Mr. Humphries?"

Mr. Humphries shook his head. "I have never been free for a clip-on bow tie, Captain Peacock. Mr. Lucas will attend to the customer. Forward, Mr. Lucas."

Mr. Lucas nodded. "Thank you, Mr. Humphries. Good morning, sir. Did I hear you say you required a clip-on bow tie ?"

The customer took a breath.

"Yes," he said.

"If you will step this way. We have a box of them over here." And pulling one from under the counter Mr. Lucas produced an assortment of ties. Diving his hand in, he produced one. "Here we are, sir, one clip-on bow tie. If you would like to remove yours, sir, and try it on."

As the customer removed his tie, Mr. Lucas demonstrated the spring on the clip.

"We sell a lot of these as mousetraps, sir… now, if you would just like to bend over… bend forward a little." With an expert movement, Mr. Lucas snapped the tie into place.

"How does it look?" inquired the customer.

Mr. Lucas glanced towards Mr. Humphries. "How does it look, Mr. Humphries?"

"Awful," said Mr. Humphries.

"What do you mean?" said the customer.

"It's not your fault, sir," said Mr. Lucas. "It's the tie."

"In that case," said the customer, "why are you trying to sell me an awful tie?"

Mr. Humphries shook his head. "We're not trying to sell it to you, you said you wanted it."

"You see, sir," said Mr. Lucas, "no one is wearing them at the moment."

"Except you," said Mr. Humphries. "May we ask what occasion you require it for, sir?"

The florid-faced customer drew himself up and stood to attention.

"It is," he said, "for an army reunion."

Mr. Lucas and Mr. Humphries looked at each other, shook their heads and clicked their tongues disapprovingly.

"Tut, tut, no, no, no," said Mr. Humphries.

"What do you mean, 'No no, no'?"

"Well," said Mr. Humphries, "sir would not want the rest of the regiment to think he had gone to the dogs, would he?"

"What are you talking about? I've got my own building firm."

Mr. Lucas shook his head: "Nobody would ever guess with a clip-on bow tie like that."

An anxious look came into the customer's eyes.

"Er...what do you suggest then?"

"Well," said Mr. Humphries, "for two pounds you could buy a pretty velvet one on a piece of elastic." He selected one out of the drawer and held it up and twanged the elastic. "Nearly everyone's wearing these, aren't they, Mr. Lucas?"

"Oh yes," said Mr. Lucas. "That is, if they can't afford a proper one."

The customer looked even more anxious.

"What do you mean, 'a proper one'?"

"Hand-made watered silk," said Mr. Humphries, producing one, "but they are five pounds, sir."

"I can afford that," said the customer defensively.

"Sale, Mr. Lucas!"

"I'll make out the bill, Mr. Humphries."

The customer gazed at the length of silk Mr. Humphries handed him in exchange for the money.

"Er... how do you tie it?" he asked uncertainly.

"There's a diagram on the box that goes with it, sir."

"But can't you show me?"

"I'm sorry, sir," said Mr. Humphries, "I always wear one of these." And with a quick movement he removed his clip-on bow tie, snapped it open and shut in front of the customer's nose and smiled graciously.

On the ladies' counter Mrs. Slocombe was recounting to Miss Brahms another of her adventures.

"What happened then?" asked Miss Brahms, eyes agog.

"Well, I said to him quite sternly, mind you, I said, 'If you don't take your hands away, young man, I'm getting off this bar stool and going home.' "

"And did he?" inquired Miss Brahms.

"He did not."

"And did you go home?"

"Eventually," said Mrs. Slocombe, then added: "He's taking me to the pictures tonight to apologize. I hope he behaves himself in the back row."

" 'Ere," said Miss Brahms, "how do you know you're going in the back row?"

"Because I've booked."

Captain Peacock paced up and down in the centre of the floor, with a far-away look in his eyes as he remembered the long, hard struggle he had had to reach his present executive position. His reverie was interrupted by a tap on the shoulder. He spun round on his heels and came face to face with a small, dark-haired man with a large mustache wearing a checked sports jacket and flannels and smoking a pipe.

"Good morning, sir," said Captain Peacock. "Can I help you?"

The man removed his pipe and nodded. "The ladies, please."

"Lingerie or powder room?" inquired Captain Peacock.

The man stared at him for a moment. "I'd hardly be asking for the powder room."

Captain Peacock smiled. "Just a little joke."

The man nodded. "Just."

The smile disappeared from Captain Peacock's face and he waved his arm in an imperious gesture.

"Mrs. Slocombe, forward, if you please."

"I'm not deaf," said Mrs. Slocombe, and aside to Miss Brahms, "That key's gone to his head. He's getting above himself."

Taking her time she walked over to the customer and inquired if she could help.

"I want to buy a dress," said the man casually.

"Follow me," said Mrs. Slocombe; then over her shoulder, "For what age group, sir?"

The man blew a large cloud of smoke in the air.

"Forty," he said.

"Younger middle-age rail, Miss Brahms. And the lady's size?" inquired Mrs. Slocombe.

The man produced a small silver stick from his pocket and pressed down his pipe tobacco.

"It's for me," he announced.

"Hold the rail," said Mrs. Slocombe. "I beg your pardon, sir?"

"It's for a fancy dress party," said the man.

Mrs. Slocombe looked relieved. "Oh, I see."

"The men are going as girls, and the girls are going as men."

"Oh how amusing," said Miss Brahms.

"Yes, most original. Tape measure please, Miss Brahms." And taking the tape Mrs. Slocombe reached up inside the man's jacket, and joined the two ends together round his chest. Miss Brahms produced a pencil and piece of paper.

"Forty-two including the spectacle case, Miss Brahms. And will sir be wearing any padding?"

The man puffed noisily on his pipe, blew a cloud of smoke which obscured Mrs. Slocombe for a moment.

"I thought," he said, "that a couple of big oranges would get a laugh."

"Tangerines would get a bigger one," said Miss Brahms.

"And it must be under ten pounds."

"I see," said Mrs. Slocombe, recovering from her coughing fit. "One of the cotton seconds, Miss Brahms, from the maternity range."

"Any colour will do," said the man. "It's only a sort of joke thing."

"How about this?" said Miss Brahms, handing over a three-quarter-length cotton print dress of various lilac hues.

"Yes," said the man. "Can I try it on?"

Mrs. Slocombe shook her head.

"Not here you can't. You will have to use the men's department. Captain Peacock, are you free?"

Captain Peacock replaced his key in his pocket. "You called, Mrs. Slocombe?"

Mrs. Slocombe held up the dress. "This customer is going to a fancy dress do, and wishes to use the gents' facilities to try it on."

Captain Peacock raised his eyebrows. "I see."

Taking the situation in, he came to a quick decision. "Yes, the gentlemen's department would be more suitable. If you would care to come this way, sir."

"Mr. Grainger, are you free?"

"I'm just going to the staff 'cafe' for my coffee," Mr. Grainger snapped at Captain Peacock, stamping off angrily to show how he felt about his senior having the key to the executive washroom.

Captain Peacock appeared quite unruffled.

"Mr. Humphries, are you free?"

Mr. Humphries looked up from the box he was sorting through.

"I'm busy pricing my ties, Captain Peacock."

"The gentleman wishes to try on a dress."

"I'm free," said Mr. Humphries, running round the counter, and taking the dress, "Ooh, nice material."

"It's for a fancy dress party," explained the man.

"Yes," said Mr. Humphries, "they all say that. This way, sir."

Mr. Humphries walked up to the nearest fitting room and pulled back the curtain to reveal Mr. Lucas attending to a customer who was wearing a checked jacket not unlike that worn by the customer with the dress.

"Engaged," said Mr. Lucas.

"We'll try next door," said Mr. Humphries.

Mr. Lucas tugged at his customer's trousers. "Yes… yes," he said. "Throwing well, sir. Also very snug. Try bending, sir."

The customer bent over and shook his head.

"Just too snug, I'm afraid. I think I need the jacket and trousers one size larger."

"Oh dear," said Mr. Lucas.

"I'm not fussy," said the man. "Any bold check will do."

Outside the next fitting room, Mr. Humphries, having divested his customer of his checked jacket and trousers, was hanging them over a rail.

"I've got it on!" called his customer from inside.

Mr. Humphries took a deep breath, adjusted his tie and entered the fitting room. As be disappeared, Mr. Lucas came out of his and, seeing the checked jacket and trousers hanging there, picked them up and disappeared.

Mr. Humphries found himself staring at his customer in shoes, socks, calf suspenders and the maternity dress just above the knees.

"What do you think?" said the man. "Is it me?"

"Definitely," said Mr. Humphries. "I'm only sorry I haven't been invited as well."

He exited to find that his customer's jacket and trousers had gone.

"Mr. Lucas," he called. "Where's that jacket and trousers I hung out here?"

"Sold to my customer," said Mr. Lucas.

"Oh, no!" gasped Mr. Humphries going pale, and he rushed back to the fitting room to break the awful news.

"What?" shouted the man.

"I haven't sold it," said Mr. Humphries. "Mr. Lucas sold it. But don't worry, sir. We'll get it back but it may take time."

"In that case, " said the man, "you'll have to give me a new suit."

"Yes, sir," said Mr. Humphries. "I'll see what I can find, if you wouldn't mind just waiting in here."

"I can't," said the man.

"Why not?" said Mr. Humphries.

"Because I want to spend a penny."

"Oh dear," said Mr. Humphries, "I expect it's the shock. I'll find an overcoat for you, sir, and you can tuck the skirt up out of sight." Before the man could reply he disappeared.

Captain Peacock stopped in mid stride as he observed the pipe-smoking customer emerge from the direction of the men's fitting rooms with his bare legs and suspenders showing below the brown overcoat and make his way furtively across the department.

"Can I help you, sir, or madam, as the case may be?"

"I'd like the gents'," said the man.

"Just down the stairs through china," said Captain Peacock.

"Good Lord, isn't there anywhere nearer?"

"I'm afraid there isn't."

"Oh…," said the man.

"It's a pity you didn't use the powder room when I suggested it."

Captain Peacock watched the victim of fate slink up the steps to the lift. Just as he got to the top the lift doors opened and three ladies came out.

"Don't forget, the lavatory is straight down the stairs through china and glass, sir," Captain Peacock shouted.

The man started back and ran off followed by the curious stares of the customers. Captain Peacock smiled with satisfaction.

Midday found Mr. Humphries staring at the department clock. He shook his head.

"Another two hours till lunch. I wonder if Mr. Grainger will lend me his chair."

"You do look very peaky," said Mr. Lucas.

"Well, you see, I didn't get any breakfast. A friend of mine was supposed to shop for me, but he let me down. And this morning I thought to myself, I wonder what's in the fridge, and when I got there the cupboard was bare."

"It's not like you, is it?" said Mr. Lucas.

"It isn't," said Mr. Humphries. "You know me, I always like to have something tucked away. Anyway, to cut a long story short, I found an egg and put it in boiling water, but could I find my egg timer?"

Mr. Lucas shook his head.

"You're quite right. So I picked up the telephone and dialed the operator."

"And did he know where the egg timer was?"

"No."

"Surprising," commented Mr. Lucas.

"I'll slap your wrist in a minute," admonished Mr. Humphries. "Anyway, where was I? Oh yes. I said, will you give me an alarm call at three minutes past eight. Why, he said, it's eight o'clock now. I know, I said, I'm boiling an egg. Well, he got quite narky. But he had a very nice voice and by the time we'd made it up the egg was like a golf ball, and I had to run for the bus."

"If you play your cards right, tomorrow morning, you could have your breakfast at the telephone exchange," suggested Mr. Lucas.

Then Mr. Grainger appeared.

"I have never had to wait until two o'clock for my lunch before," he grumbled. "I'd take an indigestion tablet if I had anything to digest."

"You know what the Eskimos do?" asked Mr. Lucas. Mr. Grainger shook his head.

"Well, when they are hungry they chew a piece of blubber."

"I am not an Eskimo, Mr. Lucas, and I don't have any blubber."

Mr. Lucas opened a drawer and pulled a glove out.

"How about chewing on sealskin then?"

"There must be something in the Factory Act," Mr. Grainger went on. "Delaying our canteen lunch is a contravention of human rights."

"Eating our canteen lunch is a contravention of human rights," said Mr. Lucas.

"I think," said Mr. Grainger, with a sinister note in his voice, "that I am going to phone the Factory Inspector. Don't try and stop me."

"We won't," said Mr. Humphries.

"Oh," said Mr. Grainger. "Very well then, I will."

Mrs. Slocombe's and Miss Brahms's internal clocks were also complaining.

"I'm starving," said Miss Brahms.

"So am I," said Mrs. Slocombe, "but I have taken steps to keep going." And lifting a counter dummy she revealed a coffee percolator.

"It will be percolating any minute."

"Just what I need," said Miss Brahms. "Look out, Peacock's coming," and Mrs. Slocombe replaced the dummy just as Captain Peacock came into earshot.

"Looking forward to your lunch, ladies?" he inquired.

"At two o'clock," said Miss Brahms, "the canteen will seem like the Savoy."

Captain Peacock nodded sympathetically.

"I'm sorry I shan't be there to watch you."

"Oh," said Mrs. Slocombe, "on a diet again, Captain Peacock?"

"No, but not only have I the key to the executive washroom, but also the privilege of dining in the executive restaurant. I just thought you'd like to know."

"Ooh," said Mrs. Slocombe. "Lord Muck now, are we?"

"Yes," admitted Captain Peacock, "and I'm looking forward to it. It's so nice to have a choice of wine with one's chicken fricassee."

"Oh," said Mrs. Slocombe in mock surprise. "So that's what they call the rissoles up there?"

"I couldn't half do with one now," said Miss Brahms. "It would be worth the indigestion."

A faraway look came into Captain Peacock's eyes. "When I was in the desert we were trained to go for long periods without food or water."

"Really?" said Mrs. Slocombe. "You learnt it from the camels, I suppose."

"I was just making the point, Mrs. Slocombe, that I am better able to cope with the situation than you are."

"Don't you worry, Captain Peacock. My stomach can hold out just as long as yours can."

A loud rumble from the coffee percolator made it sound as though her stomach was contradicting her statement.

Captain Peacock shook his head. "Rommel could have heard that ten miles away."

"Drat," said Mrs. Slocombe.

Captain Peacock, with his hands behind his back, just like Prince Philip, strolled away smiling.

Mr. Grainger appeared from the direction of the Staff Exit.

"Oh there you are," said Mr. Humphries. "Did you get through to the Factory Inspector?"

Mr. Grainger shook his head.

"No," he confided, "I had a change of heart. After all, Grace Brothers have been very good to me and it's not long before I retire. I wouldn't like to be branded as a trouble maker." And then as an afterthought he added, "There's nothing to stop you doing it."

Before Mr. Humphries could reply, the tall figure of Captain Peacock loomed into view.

"A word in your ear, Ernest."

"Yes, Captain Peacock."

Taking Mr. Grainger to one side, Captain Peacock assumed a warm, friendly tone.

"I'm sorry if my election to the executive washroom upsets you. Of course I should have refused. But that might have been taken as a stand against the management."

"Quite," agreed Mr. Grainger. "I think you are far better off standing with the management."

"I'm glad you see it that way, Ernest."

Mr. Grainger sighed. "It's just that I always hoped that one day I'd have that key. I must say I do envy you."

Captain Peacock extended his hand. "No hard feelings then, Ernest?"

Mr. Grainger took it and shook it warmly. "Of course not, Stephen. I would be most delighted if you'd allow me to buy you lunch in the canteen."

"How very kind," said Captain Peacock, "but I'm afraid I can't, Ernest. You see from now on I have to take my lunch in the executive dining-room. I have also, as it happens, been given that privilege as from today."

Mr. Grainger appeared to swell up.

"The executive dining-room?" he spluttered. "Executive dining-room?" Weakly, he staggered to the counter and leant on it.

"A glass of water for Mr. Grainger," called Mr. Humphries.

Mr. Grainger waved Mr. Humphries away.

"I don't want a glass of water. I want that damn telephone."

At exactly two o'clock, the members of the ladies' and gentlemen's departments took their places in the canteen for lunch, each having collected a plate on the way. The last to arrive was Mr. Lucas. Putting his plate down he took his seat.

"What did you decide on?" asked Mr. Humphries.

"What does it look like?" said Mr. Lucas.

Mr. Humphries stared at the brown lumpy pile of gravy on Mr. Lucas's plate. In the end he shook his head. "I give up," he said.

"It's shepherd's pie," said Mr. Lucas.

Mr. Humphries stared at him admiringly. "You always were one for adventure."

"I think it looks very good," said Mr. Grainger.

"Well," commented Miss Brahms, "when I went past, the flies seemed to be enjoying it."

"Take no notice of them," said Mrs. Slocombe. "Plenty of brown sauce and you won't see their footprints."

"Would you mind knocking it off?" said Mr. Lucas.

Mrs. Slocombe pierced a pilchard with her fork and waved it suspiciously under her nose, then held it out towards Mr. Grainger and asked for his opinion.

"I'd rather not," said Mr. Grainger hastily. "It might put me off my roll-mop herring."

"I'll tell you one thing about that pilchard," volunteered Mr. Lucas. "It's definitely dead." He glanced at Mrs. Slocombe's lettuce. "Which is more than you can say about that green thing crawling about right there."

Mrs. Slocombe took off her glasses and magnified the lettuce on her plate.

"Oooh," she said, "how nasty," and picking up her spoon she struck her lettuce forcefully several times.

Mr. Lucas nodded: "Tough little monkeys, aren't they?"

"They have to be," said Mr. Humphries, "to eat here."

"Got it," said Mrs. Slocombe with a final bang. "Ooh, it's quite put me off."

"Shouldn't be surprised," said Mr. Lucas, "if it hasn't given him a bit of a headache too."

There was a loud slurp as Mr. Grainger raised his soup spoon to his mouth.

"Oh," said Mrs. Slocombe, "isn't it disgusting?"

Miss Brahms nodded in agreement. "He always makes that noise when he drinks soup. If you want something really disgusting, get him to order spaghetti."

"I mean," said Mrs. Slocombe, "aren't the conditions in the staff canteen disgusting? Fancy having to wait an extra hour for this rubbish."

"I don't think it will happen again," said Mr. Grainger.

"Really," said Mrs. Slocombe, "and why not?"

"Mr. Grainger phoned the Factory Inspector and complained," said Mr. Humphries. "I think it was very brave of him."

"Well done, Mr. Grainger," said Mrs. Slocombe approvingly.

"You always were a trouble maker," said Mr. Lucas.

"I was not alone in my complaint," said Mr. Grainger. "Apparently, Captain Peacock had already complained about the extra-late lunch. He said it upset his desert stomach. And," continued Mr. Grainger, "the Inspector not only agreed we shouldn't eat so late, but took one look at this place and went to see Young Mr. Grace."

"Oh, good," said Mrs. Slocombe, "I shall be very interested to hear his report."

"If he has lunch here," said Mr. Humphries, "it will probably be a very loud one."

Mr. Rumbold paused by the table on his way to the executive restaurant. "Enjoying your lunch?" he asked amicably.

"Oh yes, thank you, sir," said Mr. Grainger. "Quite up to its usual standard."

"Good, good," said Mr. Rumbold and turning on his heels he walked a few paces to the door marked "Executive Restaurant" and went in.

"I bet they don't get things crawling about their lettuce in there," commented Miss Brahms. "As long as they're all right they don't care about us."

"So it's always been with the workers," said Mr. Mash appearing with a heaped plate of sausage and chips. " 'Ere, move over, Mrs. Slocombe, make room for another one of the workers." Mr. Mash dragged up a chair, but before he could sit down Mrs. Slocombe stopped him with a gesture.

"What on earth do you think you're doing, Mr. Mash?"

Mr. Mash spoke from his half-sitting position: "I'm bending my knees, aren't I, which causes my bottom to plonk on the seat. It's called sitting down." And having made his intentions clear, he sat on the chair and pulled it up to the table.

"I think," said Mrs. Slocombe, using her best head of department voice, "that I am unanimous when I say that this has always been our table."

Mr. Mash took a large bite of sausage and chewed it aggressively.

"Well," he observed, "as Peacock's moved up in the world, I thought I would take his place. Want to make something of it?"

"Yes," said Mrs. Slocombe, "there's a vacancy over there by the pig bin."

Mr. Mash banged his fist on the table and picked up his plate.

"That's it," he said. "That's done it… that's really charming, isn't it?" He shook his fist to emphasize his point. "One of these days," he said menacingly, "we'll all be equal, and then I'll be in the executive dining-room."

"Up the workers," said Mr. Lucas.

Mr. Mash stormed off.

"Look," said Miss Brahms, "here comes Captain Peacock."

"On his maiden voyage," said Mr. Humphries. They began a slow hand-clap as Captain Peacock walked across the canteen. He pretended not to notice them, and to add insult to injury he took out the key to the executive washroom and swung it nonchalantly in his hand as he passed by the table, then replacing it he opened the door of the executive dining-room and disappeared.

"He didn't even speak to us," said Miss Brahrns.

Mr. Grainger's soup spoon stopped in midair. Shaking his head he announced: "Power corrupts. Absolute power corrupts absolutely," and slurped loudly.

"Straw for Mr. Grainger," called Mr. Humphries.

In the executive dining-room Mr. Rumbold sat at a small table in the corner on which was a half bottle of wine and a glass. He glanced up from the junior crossword puzzle of the *Daily Telegraph* as Captain Peacock approached. Extending a hand, he indicated the empty chair opposite him.

"Welcome to the club, Peacock. Perhaps you would like to sit with me."

"Thank you very much, sir," said Captain Peacock and glanced around approvingly. "Yes, this is very nice indeed."

"We think so," said Mr. Rumbold. "Would you care to join me in a glass of wine?"

"Oh thank you, sir."

"A glass for Captain Peacock," called Mr. Rumbold.

"Yes, sir," said the waitress, and taking one from the next table she plonked it down.

"Allow me," said Mr. Rumbold and picking up the bottle, he half-filled Captain Peacock's glass.

"Most kind, sir," said Captain Peacock.

"That will be 25p," said Mr. Rumbold. "You can pay me later."

Captain Peacock's smile froze slightly on his face, and picking up the menu he gazed at it and began to read aloud.

"*Soup de jour*, in brackets lentil, *le* rollmop herring, *le* pilchard salad and *le* shepherd's pie, *et un apres huit* mint. Oh yes," said Captain Peacock, "a big improvement from next door. What?" He sipped the wine and pulled a wry face.

"An amusing little wine, isn't it?" said Mr. Rumbold.

Captain Peacock had difficulty swallowing. "Hilarious," he commented and putting on his glasses he studied the label and read aloud. "Peruvian Beaujolais, er... type. I must remember that!" Then settling down, "Well, this is a great moment for me, Mr. Rumbold. One struggles, one does one's best, most of the time one fails, occasionally one succeeds and finally after a long hard journey, one arrives." His soliloquy was interrupted by a loud hammering on the partition, and a piece of plaster fell from the ceiling, striking him forcefully on the head. Captain Peacock gazed up in alarm.

"What on earth's that?"

"Good morning everybody," said Young Mr. Grace, waving his walking stick as he came through the private entrance of the executive dining-room. Mr. Rumbold leapt to his feet, followed more slowly by Captain Peacock.

"Please don't get up," said Mr. Grace. "I'm so sorry to spoil your lunch, but I have been having a bit of trouble with the Factory Inspector. Somebody in one of the departments sent for him, and it seems the canteen is too small for the number of people using it."

"Yes, sir," said Mr. Rumbold. "I was aware that it should be a hundred square feet bigger, but what can one do?" He waved his hands apologetically as though he would have personally seen to it if he could have.

"Well," said Mr. Grace. "Where there's a will, there's a way. I'm having it all knocked into one."

Captain Peacock stared at him aghast.

"But sir, what about the executive dining-room?"

"That's the least of your worries," said Mr. Grace. "You're going to have to share the staff bog as well. Bash away, boys!"

To Captain Peacock's horror, a number of men in overalls pulled away the intervening partition, which separated the staff canteen from the executive restaurant, to reveal that he was only four feet from the departmental table and that its members were staring at him with smiles on their faces.

"*Bon appétit*," said Mr. Humphries, raising his mug of tea in salute.

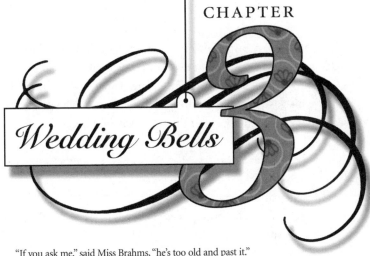

# Wedding Bells

"If you ask me," said Miss Brahms, "he's too old and past it."

Mrs. Slocombe pursed her lips thoughtfully.

"I'm not sure whether that's a pro or a con."

# Wedding Bells

THE MOST IMPORTANT THING IN ANY BIG STORE, AS ANYONE WHO HAS worked in one will know, is the exchange of gossip between the members of its staff on what happened the night before. Though Mr. Humphries likes to save his gossip until the coffee break, he can often be persuaded to part with it earlier, and this morning was no exception.

"Go on," said Mr. Lucas, as he passed a vest from a pile on the counter to Mr. Humphries, who folded it neatly in his vest drawer. "You haven't told me how the fancy dress party went yet."

Mr. Humphries raised his eyes to the ceiling with a pained look on his face. "Oh, I can't speak about it."

"Force yourself," encouraged Mr. Lucas. "I bet yours was the best costume."

Mr. Humphries nodded. "I must admit it was a stroke of genius to go as the Red Shadow, as I had been wondering what to do with that new curtain material I had left over from the guest bedroom."

Mr. Lucas handed him another vest. "I suppose you used a touch of cocoa to stain the old boat race?"

"Nothing so primitive," said Mr. Humphries. "I used that overnight tan, but it wasn't quite dark enough, so you know what I did? I shoved my head in the oven for five minutes regulo two."

Mr. Lucas gave a whistle of admiration. "You must have looked just like Lawrence of Arabia."

Mr. Humphries nodded. "I must say that as I stood in the bathroom and gazed at my clear blue eyes staring back at me out of the mirror, O'Toole did cross my mind."

"I bet you looked the part, Mr. Humphries."

"Oh, I did. I mean, I had even taken the trouble to heat my spare plastic house slippers over the gas, then I pulled the toes out to a point and curled them over, just like the real thing."

"Brilliant," said Mr. Lucas, "and if anyone else had gone as the Red Shadow, you could have said you were Ali Baba and your pots were outside."

Mr. Humphries shook his head sadly. "Alas, I shall never know who went as what."

"What do you mean?"

Mr. Humphries placed the last vest in the drawer and leaned on the counter.

"Well, my minicab broke down and I had to walk. I knew the name of the road, but I'd forgotten the number of the flat. So I had to knock at random."

"I've got the picture," said Mr. Lucas. "There you were in your extended plastic slippers and best curtains, feeling desperate."

"I was," confided Mr. Humphries, "until suddenly two policemen threw their arms round me."

"Ah," said Mr. Lucas. "You'd found the fancy dress party."

"No," said Mr. Humphries, "but you try knocking on doors in Golders Green at midnight dressed as an Arab. I was escorted home in a police car for my own safety."

Mr. Lucas "tut-tutted" sympathetically. "What an anticlimax."

Mr. Humphries gave a slight smile.

"Not entirely. One of them stayed on for a sherry and showed me how his handcuffs worked."

"Mr. Lucas," called out Mr. Grainger.

"Yes, Mr. Grainger."

"Is Mr. Humphries free? I'm afraid I'm in the middle of a bowler hat."

"Are you free?" inquired Mr. Lucas.

With an elbow on the counter, Mr. Humphries gazed round. "Yes, I think I am free."

"Mr. Humphries is free, Mr. Grainger."

"Too late," said Mr. Grainger, "the prospective customer has gone."

"It's all go this morning," observed Mr. Lucas.

Over on the ladies' counter Mrs. Slocombe was just completing a sale and handing a Grace Brothers bag to a tall lady in a feathered hat. She smiled her best early-morning smile.

"Thank you, madam, the bill's inside, and if the garment doesn't give every satisfaction do bring it straight back, because we are only here to be of service." As the lady turned away, Mrs. Slocombe switched her smile off and turned back to Miss Brahms.

"Now, where was I?" she said.

"It was half past nine," said Miss Brahms, "and you had been dressed for an hour and he still hadn't arrived."

"Oh yes," said Mrs. Slocombe. "I was real worried."

"Fancy him standing you up," said Miss Brahms indignantly.

Mrs. Slocombe shook her head. "Men don't stand me up, Miss Brahms. I expect the car broke down. It did last time we had a date and he apologized most humbly when I bumped into him a week later in the supermarket."

"Anyway," said Miss Brahms, "then what happened?"

"Well, to give him a chance," said Mrs. Slocombe, "I waited until 11:35. Then I phoned Mrs. Axby and we went down the Palais together. It was the over 25's night."

"That was lucky," said Miss Brahms. "Did you pick up anyone?"

Mrs. Slocombe waved her arm in a dismissive gesture. "No, no, no, we didn't go for that, Miss Brahms."

"Well," Miss Brahms persisted, "did anyone come over to you and ask for a dance?"

Mrs. Slocombe patted her blue-rinsed hair in the counter mirror. "I don't encourage that sort of thing," she said sternly. "Anyway, I didn't like the look of any of the men there." She paused as she remembered the scene. "So after we had stood by the dance floor for twenty minutes, sussing it out, you know, we went into the bar."

Miss Brahms looked concerned. "You didn't get plastered again, did you?"

"Certainly not," said Mrs. Slocombe indignantly. "We just had a few gin and tonics. Well, one of the tonics must have been a bit off, they are sometimes, you know, because I came over all dizzy, and Mrs. Axby had to put me to bed."

A clatter of wheels indicated the arrival of Mr. Mash with his trolley.

" 'Ere you are, Mrs. Slocombe, twelve pairs of thirty-denier tights. Unlucky for some. And twelve padded bras for the underprivileged." Taking them out of the box on the trolley, he plonked them on the counter. Delving into the box again he produced an assortment of ladies' briefs. "And to continue, 'ere's the *pièce de résistance*, twenty-four pairs of novelty briefs, known to such common persons as myself as naughty knickers."

"I beg your pardon," said Mrs. Slocombe, placing her glasses firmly on the end of her nose.

" 'Ere, look at this," said Mr. Mash, holding up a pair. "See, there's writing on them."

"So there is," said Mrs. Slocombe. "What does it say, Miss Brahms?"

Miss Brahms picked up the knickers and looked at the writing.

"IF YOU CAN READ THIS," announced Miss Brahms, "YOU'RE TOO CLOSE."

Mrs. Slocombe pursed her lips. "It's disgusting."

"Yes," said Miss Brahms, "but true."

"What about these then?" said Mr. Mash, waving another pair. Then holding them between two hands he stretched them out to show that they had a pair of black hands embroidered on the seat.

"What are they called?" said Miss Brahms. "An evening out with Johnnie Mathis."

"That's a good one," said Mr. Mash, delving into his box and pulling out another pair. "Then there's these. They come in four models: HELLO CHEERY, I LOVE ELVIS, YOUR FLIES ARE UNDONE and NO PARKING."

Mrs. Slocombe gazed disdainfully at the offending objects. "Oh Miss Brahms, did you ever see anything like it?"

Miss Brahms nodded. "My boyfriend bought me a pair, but I wouldn't wear them."

"I hardly dare ask," said Mrs. Slocombe, "but what did they say?"

"In case of emergency, pull down."

Mr. Mash gave a coarse laugh. "That'd be worth a five-pound fine."

Mrs. Slocombe waved her hand in a dismissive gesture. "That'll be enough, Mr. Mash," and then, calling out in her best voice, "Captain Peacock, whether you are free or not I want you over here."

Captain Peacock strolled over, hands behind his back, and gazed at the pairs of assorted knickers on the counter. "Are you having trouble, Mrs. Slocombe?"

"I certainly am, Captain Peacock."

Captain Peacock glanced at his watch. "I'm afraid I can only spare you a moment. I have to see Mr. Rumbold in his office." Mrs. Slocombe picked up the knickers and dropped them back in the pile on the counter.

"I positively refuse to display these." Then picking out a pair she held them up for Captain Peacock's inspection and pointed to the "no parking" sign on them. Captain Peacock raised his eyebrows in surprise.

"You're not being asked to wear them, are you, Mrs. Slocombe?"

"Certainly not," said Mrs. Slocombe indignantly. "I wouldn't put them on for a thousand pounds."

"How much to take them off?" inquired Mr. Mash.

Captain Peacock stretched out his arm and pointed a commanding finger. "Mr. Mash, get back to your basement."

Mr. Mash thrust his face under Captain Peacock's nose. "I see. So the worker's not allowed to have a sense of humour, eh? Well, we have our laughs. You should see what's written about you on the walls of our khazi." And having delivered what he considered a crushing blow, he wheeled his trolley off as noisily as he could.

"Horrid man," said Mrs. Slocombe. "Now look, Captain Peacock, I refuse to have anything to do with these vulgar garments."

"They're not all that bad," said Miss Brahms.

Captain Peacock nodded in agreement. "Progress must march on, Mrs. Slocombe."

Mrs. Slocombe waved the offending knickers to emphasize her point. "Not wearing these it doesn't."

Captain Peacock adopted a more soothing tone of voice. "Mrs. Slocombe," he explained, "I must remind you that you are all paid by Grace Brothers to sell the goods purchased by the Buying Department."

"And if I don't," said Mrs. Slocombe.

There was a slight pause while Captain Peacock stared stonily at her. "No one is irreplaceable."

Having issued his threat he turned on his heel and disappeared in the direction of Mr. Rumbold's office.

"Oh," said Miss Brahms. "You're not going to stand for that, are you?"

Mrs. Slocombe gritted her teeth. "I very nearly said something very cutting and rude, I can tell you."

"I'll bet," said Miss Brahms. "What are you going to do now?"

Mrs. Slocombe gathered up the assortment of underwear and stuffed it angrily into a drawer. "I'm seriously thinking of handing my resignation in."

Miss Brahms took a step back and said in a loud voice: "Your resignation?"

Mrs. Slocombe held her hand up in alarm.

"Shhh! Not so loud," she said.

Over in the men's department a short gentleman with a mop of grey hair fought his way gamely into a Fairisle sweater, with the help of Mr. Lucas and Mr. Humphries despite the fact it was quite obviously some sizes too small. Giving it a final tug, Mr. Lucas managed to bring it down till it was only six or seven inches above the customer's waistband.

"There we are, sir," said Mr. Humphries. "It's definitely you, sir. Don't you think so, Mr. Lucas?"

"Definitely the customer," agreed Mr. Lucas.

The customer didn't seem too sure. "It seems rather tight to me," he said breathlessly, as he tried to move his arms up and down.

Mr. Humphries nodded. "They are being worn tight this year, sir."

"Particularly this one," said Mr. Lucas.

"I wanted it for golfing, you see."

"It will keep your arms very stiff," said Mr. Lucas.

"Just try a swing or two," said Mr. Humphries, "to get the feel of it."

Producing a walking stick from his display stand he handed it to the customer, who gripped it, swung and struck an imaginary ball across the department.

Mr. Humphries clapped his hands admiringly. "That's a beautiful movement you've got there, sir."

"Unless I am mistaken," said Mr. Lucas, "that was a hole in one."

"Well," admitted the customer proudly, "I do have a very small handicap."

Mr. Humphries raised his eyebrows. "Have you?"

"With luck," said Mr. Lucas, "we've probably got a tight pair of trousers to go with it."

The customer handed the stick back to Mr. Humphries and pulled at the sweater under his arm.

"It's gripping me very tightly just here."

"It would, sir," nodded Mr. Humphries. "There's a lot of tension with Shetland wool."

"It's the nervous sheep," added Mr. Lucas. "They live near a shooting range."

Mr. Humphries handed the customer the walking stick again. "We know it's all right for driving, sir, but how is it for putting?"

The customer took the stick and bent over an invisible ball, then with a deft movement putted it. He shook his head. "It's pulling."

"Maybe it's the way you are holding the club, sir," suggested Mr. Lucas. "Try locking the thumbs together and keeping your eye on the ball a bit longer." The customer tried another imaginary putt. Mr. Lucas and Mr. Humphries both nodded with approval.

"Much better," said Mr. Lucas. "If Jack Nicklaus had seen that he'd have gone straight home to bed."

"There's no doubt," said Mr. Humphries, "that that sweater has improved your game enormously, sir."

"But," complained the customer, "the sleeves are only just below my elbows."

"It's a good sign," said Mr. Humphries. "You see, it will definitely stretch after the first wash."

The customer looked puzzled. "I thought wool always shrank?"

Mr. Lucas shook his head. "That's a popular misconception, sir. When you think about it, it can't be true otherwise every time it rained the sheep would get smaller."

The customer shook his grey head emphatically. "No, I definitely need the next size."

Mr. Lucas took Mr. Humphries by the elbow and led him out of earshot.

"We don't have a forty-four," he hissed. "We've only got forty-sixes."

"In that case," said Mr. Humphries, "that is the next size." With speed that almost deceived the eye, Mr. Lucas bent over the counter and produced an enormous Fairisle sweater and held it out in front of the customer.

"How about that, sir?"

The customer shook his head doubtfully. "It seems rather long."

"Ah," said Mr. Humphries, "they are being worn long this year, sir."

"And," said Mr. Lucas, "it will be very good for your handicap."

The customer stared uncertainly at the sweater and shook his head.

Mr. Humphries smiled encouragingly. "Of course, it will shrink after the first wash."

"But," stammered the customer, "I thought you said wool didn't shrink?"

Mr. Humphries introduced a patient note into his voice. "That's pure wool, sir, this is half wool and half extruded man-made fibres. The extruded bit shrinks in hot water."

"And," added Mr. Lucas, "the man-made bit shrinks in cold water."

"In fact," observed Mr. Humphries, "there's very little point in your trying it on until you have washed it."

The customer suddenly looked very tired. "Very well," he murmured, "I'll take it."

"Sale, Mr. Lucas!"

As Mr. Lucas rang the till Mr. Humphries produced a carrier bag and placed the sweater in it, but noticed the customer was having trouble taking off the size forty-two.

"Can I help you, sir?"

The customer nodded gratefully.

So Mr. Humphries and Mr. Lucas stood on either side of him and, gripping the bottom of the sweater, began to pull it up, but halfway they ran into difficulties as it stuck over the customer's head.

"Are you all right in there, sir?" inquired Mr. Lucas. There was a note of panic in the mumbled reply.

"If you wouldn't mind bending forward, sir, I'll pull while Mr. Humphries holds your rear. All right, Mr. Humphries?"

"It'll be a pleasure, Mr. Lucas."

As Mr. Humphries grasped the waistband of the customer's trousers to prevent him going forward, Mr. Lucas tugged at the sweater.

"It's just like pulling a Christmas cracker," observed Mr. Lucas.

"Yes," gasped Mr. Humphries, "I wonder who's going to get the novelty?"

Then with a final effort Mr. Lucas heaved and pulled off the sweater as the customer screamed, his hands flying to his head. He was suddenly bald.

"It's gone!" he cried.

"I beg your pardon?" said Mr. Lucas. "What's gone?"

"My toupee!" gasped the customer. "You've lost it!"

"Oh, our Ada!" said Mr. Humphries, his hands flying up with mock horror and falling on his knees to search the floor, while Mr. Lucas shook the sweater.

Seeing what was apparently an unattended customer Mr. Grainger waddled over. "Are you being looked after, sir?"

The customer pointed. "They are looking for my very expensive, undetectable hairpiece," he said grimly.

"And," added Mr. Lucas shaking the sweater and peering down the armhole, "we're having a bit of trouble detecting it. Just a minute, I think I can see it."

Sticking his hand up the arm, he brought out the hairpiece triumphantly.

"Well done," said Mr. Humphries. "Shall we comb it now, sir, or when it's back on?"

Angrily the customer snatched the untidy mop of hair and slapped it back on his head.

"Oh," said Mr. Humphries admiringly, "it takes years off you." Fuming, the man paid his bill and turned to go. As he did so Mr. Lucas nudged Mr. Humphries.

"Look, the sweater price tag's stuck on the back of his hair. Shall we tell him?"

Mr. Humphries shook his head. "He'll see the size, realize it's too big and insist on having his money back. Let's just hope he doesn't notice it before he gets out of the store."

"What if somebody mentions it?" inquired Mr. Lucas.

"I hardly think," observed Mr. Humphries, "anybody would say, 'Excuse me, sir, you've still got the price tag on your wig.' Especially when it looks so awful. If they say anything they'll point out that he's wearing it the wrong way round."

"I'm glad I'm not bald," observed Mr. Lucas.

"So am I," said Mr. Humphries, "although it won't be long if I get another customer like that."

In the ladies' department, Mrs. Slocombe was looking very pleased with herself as she applied a dab of red nail varnish to stop a run in her tights.

"I think I certainly made my point to Captain Peacock about not displaying those awful knickers."

But a worried expression crossed Miss Brahms's face as she observed Captain Peacock striding over with Mr. Rumbold.

"Look out, I think he's reported you to Mr. Rumbold."

Mrs. Slocombe hurriedly put her nail varnish out of sight.

"Oh, he wouldn't sneak, would he, Miss Brahms?"

"Mr. Rumbold's looking very ugly."

"Look at the start he's got," observed Mrs. Slocombe as they arrived at the counter.

"Attention a moment, if you please," said Captain Peacock loftily. "Mr. Rumbold would like to have a word with you."

Mr. Rumbold cleared his throat, took off his glasses and mopped his brow with his spotted handkerchief.

"I must tell you," he said, "that something very important has come to my ears."

Mrs. Slocombe gazed at Mr. Rumbold's large ears and decided that it was better not to comment.

"I'm afraid," said Captain Peacock, "that I had to tell Mr. Rumbold about your insubordinate attitude."

Mrs. Slocombe drew herself up to her full height, and adopted her most refined tone of voice.

"There are," she said, "some knickers I will display and some I won't. The ones I won't are staying in my drawers."

Mr. Rumbold nodded. "I see."

"And," added Mrs. Slocombe, "Miss Brahms backs me up about this, don't you? Miss Brahms…where are you?"

"I'm here," called Miss Brahms, peering through the curtains of the ladies' fitting room. And added, "Mrs. Slocombe feels so strongly about it that she's prepared to resign."

Mrs. Slocombe appeared to have a sudden choking fit. Mr. Rumbold stared at her sternly through his thick-rimmed spectacles.

"Is that right, Mrs. Slocombe?"

"Er…," said Mrs. Slocombe, recovering. "Well, er…that is what I said, I mean, what I said was that I will have to give it my very serious consideration."

"Very well," snapped Mr. Rumbold, who turned on his heel and started to depart.

"Mind you, I haven't had time to consider it yet and I do think a person with my excellent sales record should be allowed some discretion as to what stuff I push." Mrs. Slocombe hurried after Mr. Rumbold. "Don't you agree, Mr. Grainger?" she called as she passed the men's counter.

Mr. Grainger gazed at her unsympathetically. "If you ask my opinion, Mrs. Slocombe, you've been nothing but trouble ever since you put foot on this floor."

"Oh," said Mrs. Slocombe, "you two-faced old crab."

"I take it," interjected Captain Peacock, "that you don't support Mrs. Slocombe, Mr. Grainger?"

Mr. Grainger agreed. "If she wants to resign, let her go. We could do with her floor area to expand my trousers."

Mr. Humphries nodded vigorously. "Yes, our trousers have been rather restricted since the ladies arrived, haven't they, Mr. Lucas?"

"Bursting at the seams," agreed Mr. Lucas.

Mr. Grainger pointed to the centre of the floor which contained the ladies' display dummy.

"That stand," he announced, "has been the focal point of my trousers for the last twenty-five years until the ladies arrived. Correct, Mr. Humphries?"

"Correct, Mr. Grainger. In those days it was known as 'bargain bags.' "

Mr. Lucas stared at Mrs. Slocombe pointedly. "And now they're here, it still is."

Mrs. Slocombe looked outraged. "Captain Peacock, do I have to stand and listen to this?"

It was quite obvious Captain Peacock was enjoying the situation. He nodded. "One must say in Mr. Grainger's defence that his sales have dropped since the ladies took over half the floor."

"Perhaps," said Mrs. Slocombe, bitterly, "because he's a bit past it." Mr. Grainger swelled up like a bullfrog. "Past it?" he spluttered. "Past it?"

Mr. Lucas rushed forward with a chair and called over his shoulder, "Glass of water for Mr. Grainger."

"Some water coming up," said Mr. Lucas.

Sitting down heavily, Mr. Grainger addressed his next remark to Captain Peacock's left knee.

"Tell that woman I am severing my connections."

Mr. Lucas stopped in his tracks. "In that case I'd better cancel the glass of water."

"I don't know why everybody's getting at me," said Mrs. Slocombe. "It wasn't my idea to move into Mr. Grainger's trousers."

"I think," observed Mr. Lucas, "he'd rather have had sports equipment there."

Captain Peacock indicated Mr. Rumbold, who was hovering on the edge of the floor. "It wasn't Mr. Rumbold's idea to have ladies on the floor."

Mr. Rumbold frowned as he tried to remember. "Wasn't it?" he inquired.

"No, sir. It was Young Mr. Grace's idea," Captain Peacock reminded him.

"Aah, yes," said Mr. Rumbold. "Well, I hadn't realized Mrs. Slocombe's underwear was causing so much friction."

"Neither did I," admitted Mrs. Slocombe. "But I could very easily get a top job somewhere else. Harrods have been making overtures."

"Where did they want you?" asked Mr. Lucas. "In the piano department?"

Mrs. Slocombe pretended she hadn't heard.

"I also have very good contacts at Marshall and Snellgrove, and," she added, "the Beauty Department of Swan and Edgar's have made a very interesting offer."

"What was it?" inquired Alr. Lucas. "A free face-lift?"

Mrs. Slocombe's self-control snapped.

"That's it, I'm going!" She turned and marched brusquely towards the steps. Mr. Grainger rose from his chair and hurried after her.

"Mr. Grainger," called Captain Peacock, "don't stop her."

Mr. Grainger turned. "I won't; I was going to ring for the lift."

Miss Brahms, who had been listening intently from behind the counter, picked up Mrs. Slocombe's hat and coat and ran across the department.

"Don't go without these, Mrs. Slocombe."

Mrs. Slocombe pressed the lift bell and turned.

"I'm not going out," she snapped. "I'm going up to see Young Mr. Grace and to put my points before him personally." As she turned back to face the lift the doors opened and the aged Young Mr. Grace staggered out leaning heavily on his stick.

"Aah, good morning to you, Mrs. Slocombe."

Mrs. Slocombe's stern expression disappeared and she took a pace back. "Oh good morning, Mr. Grace."

Mr. Grace waved his stick vaguely towards the members of the department and a chorus of "Good morning, Mr. Grace" echoed from the assembled sales staff.

Captain Peacock stepped forward. "May I say, Mr. Grace, how it does our hearts good to see you looking so flamboyant."

"Thank you," wavered Mr. Grace. "You're probably referring to the flower in my buttonhole."

Captain Peacock's eyes fastened on the anemone that hung limply from the buttonhole in Mr. Grace's tweed jacket. "A touch of spring, sir?"

"I found it in the lift," confided Mr. Grace. "It's a shame to waste it."

"If you have a moment, sir," interrupted Mrs. Slocombe, "I have something I'd like to show you." And running down the marble steps she headed towards the counter.

"What is it?" called Mr. Grace.

"Her knickers," retorted Miss Brahms.

"In that case," said Mr. Grace, "I'll hang on."

Mr. Rumbold cast an anxious eye towards Captain Peacock and hurriedly whispered in his ear, "We don't want a scene here, better keep him talking."

Captain Peacock nodded and, extending his arm, helped Mr. Grace down the steps.

"May I suggest, sir, to go with your flower, one of our range of Foulard squares to go in your top pocket." He snapped his fingers imperiously. Mr. Lucas opened a drawer and produced a silk square and handed it to Mr. Humphries who handed it to Mr. Grainger who handed it to Mr. Rumbold who handed it to Captain Peacock who tucked it into Mr. Grace's top pocket.

"An excellent match I think, sir."

"It's very kind of you, Peacock." said Mr. Grace. "There aren't many floorwalkers who would spend that much on a Foulard for their employers. I shall remember that." Before Captain Peacock could recover, Mr. Lucas pressed the till and called out, "Sale!"

Mrs. Slocombe reappeared from her counter as Captain Peacock hurriedly removed the silk square from Mr. Grace's top pocket.

"Er, I wasn't actually purchasing it for you, sir, it was just to see if you thought it went with your 'ensemble.'" A look of disappointment crossed Mr. Grace's face.

"Credit note for Captain Peacock," called Mr. Lucas, and before Captain Peacock could reply, Mrs. Slocombe appeared holding a pair of bright-coloured briefs.

"What do you think about that?" she asked.

"As a matter of fact," said Mr. Grace, peering at them shortsightedly, "I think I prefer it," and taking them from her he popped them in his top pocket and nodded approvingly. "Thank you, Mrs. Slocombe. Now I have an announcement to make."

"Quiet for Mr. Grace," boomed Mr. Rumbold.

"It may surprise you all to know that I have been a widower now for forty years," said Mr. Grace.

"And," exclaimed Mr. Lucas *sotto voce* for Mr. Humphries's ears alone, "it don't seem a day too much."

"Mr. Lucas," called out Captain Peacock sharply.

"I'm no longer a young man," quavered Mr. Grace.

"I'm sure you have years yet," said Mr. Rumbold encouragingly.

"Certainly hours," murmured Mr. Lucas.

"And," continued Mr. Grace, "there is a certain someone here in Grace Brothers that I have had my eye on for some time." Captain Peacock handed the Foulard square back to Mr. Lucas.

"Any lady," he announced, "who has attracted your attention must have great qualities, sir."

Mr. Rumbold edged forward.

"She will indeed be a lucky lady, sir."

"She'll have lots of lolly too," observed Miss Brahms.

Mr. Humphries nodded. "And not long to wait for it."

"To sum it up," whispered Mr. Lucas, "the maximum of one thing and the minimum of the other."

Mr. Grainger smiled ingratiatingly. "May we be permitted to know the lady's name, sir?"

Mr. Grace tapped the side of his nose with his forefinger. "I'm keeping that secret until I have told her my intentions." Mr. Lucas winked.

"That shouldn't take long."

"But," added Mr. Grace, "I shall reveal everything to you all shortly."

"We will look forward to that, Mr. Grace," said Mr. Humphries.

Mr. Grace turned to Mrs. Slocombe.

"Give me your arm; I would like a private word with you." Leaning heavily on Mrs. Slocombe's arm he took a few paces and then stopped. "How long have I known you now, Mrs. Slocombe?"

Mrs. Slocombe visibly simpered. "Since I was a junior here, Mr. Grace."

"Yes," murmured Mr. Grace, "a very, very long time. Well, I can't discuss it here, so would you have tea with me in the Board room at, say, four o'clock?" He paused and then added significantly, "I want to talk to you about a ring."

Mrs. Slocombe's hand flew to her heart. "A ring?"

Mr. Grace nodded, then waved his walking stick. "Carry on, everybody, you've all done very well."

Mrs. Slocombe helped him towards the lift and pressed the bell.

"Ring?" gasped Mr. Rumbold.

"Ring?" mouthed Captain Peacock.

Mr. Lucas addressed Mr. Humphries from the corner of his mouth. "If he marries Mrs. Slocombe, she'd be in charge of the whole store."

Mr. Humphries nodded. "After the contretemps this morning, Mr. Grainger could lose his trousers altogether."

"Not to mention our jobs," said Mr. Lucas. "She'll be the power behind the throne."

Mr. Humphries looked aghast. "I never like to think of people having power there," he observed.

As Mrs. Slocombe marched purposefully down the steps towards the counter, Miss Brahms was hot on her heels.

"Er," she gasped, "we all heard that. Does that mean that you and him are going to…"

Mrs. Slocombe held up her hand imperiously.

"We don't wish to make any comments at this stage," she announced. "Just get me a chair, Miss Brahms."

Miss Brahms ran into the fitting room and reappeared with the gold wickerwork chair which she placed by the counter.

"Here you are, Mrs. Slocombe."

Mrs. Slocombe slowly sat down, crossed her legs and leaned her elbow nonchalantly on the counter. Captain Peacock and Mr. Rumbold walked slowly towards her, followed by the others. Captain Peacock cleared his throat.

"Er…Mrs. Slocombe, I'm sorry about our little misunderstanding, but I was only doing my job. As a matter of fact, when I mentioned it to Mr. Rumbold I did say my sympathies lay with you."

Mr. Rumbold shook his head. "No, no no, it was you who said we had better put her in her place."

Captain Peacock gave a short laugh. "No, what I actually said was, there should be a better place to put her in."

Mrs. Slocombe gazed at him stonily.

Mr. Grainger extended his hand. "No hard feelings, Mrs. Slocombe. I have been a little on edge lately because Mr. Humphries kept saying men are so much better on the floor than ladies. Though I disagreed with him, of course." Mrs. Slocombe ignored the outstretched hand.

Mr. Lucas leant forward. "On the other hand, I was saying how much I enjoyed having ladies on the floor, particularly Mrs. Slocombe, whom we all love and respect."

"Never in my life," said Miss Brahms, "have I seen such crawling since I went to the insect house at the Zoo. What's more…"

"That'll do, Miss Brahms," cut in Mrs. Slocombe.

"I mean," said Miss Brahms, "just because you're going to marry the head of the firm, they've gone all smarmy. Let me get you a sweetie, Mrs. Slocombe."

"You're very kind, Miss Brahms. I think not, though. I still have to consider my figure, and of course I haven't actually said yes. After all, a girl has to think carefully about all the pros and cons."

"If you ask me," said Miss Brahms, "he's too old and past it."

Mrs. Slocombe pursed her lips thoughtfully. "I'm not sure whether that's a pro or a con. Anyway, he's not that old, he's only about seventy."

"He certainly doesn't look seventy," said Mr. Humphries.

"No," added Mr. Lucas, "he looks about eighty-five."

Mrs. Slocombe produced her handbag from a drawer, opened it, selected a bottle of Eau de Cologne, unscrewed it and shook it down her cleavage.

"Age," she commented, "has nothing to do with it."

A faraway look came in Miss Brahms's eyes. "I wonder where he will take you for your honeymoon?"

"Well," said Mrs. Slocombe, "as he's got a yacht, it could be anywhere. Although I wouldn't say no to Capri."

"Oh, don't go there," said Mr. Humphries. "He might run off with Gracie Fields. She's more his age."

"I've read," said Mr. Lucas, "that they have had a lot of earthquakes in Japan."

"I don't quite see," said Mrs. Slocombe loftily, "what that has got to do with it."

"Well," added Mr. Lucas, "all you have to do is find a nice hotel, book into the bridal suite, lie down and wait for an earth tremor."

Miss Brahms glanced up at the department clock.

"Well, you've got till four to make up your mind. Do you think he's going to pop the question?"

Mrs. Slocombe looked thoughtful.

"And," added Captain Peacock anxiously, "if he does, Mrs. Slocombe, what will the answer be?"

"It's not easy," admitted Mrs. Slocombe, "but of course I shall have to make up my mind one way or the other."

"If you have any trouble," suggested Mr. Humphries, "why don't you do a 'loves me, loves me not' with the tea bags?"

Mrs. Slocombe picked up the counter mirror and gazed at her reflection, then clicked her fingers.

"Miss Brahms, do you mind holding this up so I can see my hair?" Mrs. Slocombe gazed some more with apparent dismay. "Oh dear, it is a sight. I wonder if I can get an appointment at the continental beauty parlour with Madam Beryl? Of course," she looked meaningly at Mr. Rumbold, "that would mean an extra-long lunch break."

Mr. Rumbold opened his mouth to reply, but Captain Peacock interrupted him. "I'm sure that will be in order, Mrs. Slocombe."

A look of annoyance crossed Mr. Rumbold's face. "Those decisions, Captain Peacock, are entirely mine." And then with an ingratiating smile said, "That will be in order."

"Don't worry about lunch," said Mr. Humphries. "I'll send you down a bit of fairy cake."

"That's a good idea," said Mr. Lucas. "You don't want your tum to rumble just as you say, 'Oh, Mr. Grace, this is so sudden.'"

Mrs. Slocombe stood up and gazed at the racks of dresses behind her. "Oh dear," she said anxiously, "what am I going to wear? I do want to look my best."

Mr. Grainger leaned across the counter. "The full facilities of my department, Mrs. Slocombe, are at your disposal."

"How kind," said Miss Brahms, "but she's hardly likely to get proposed to in a three-piece suit."

"I was referring," said Mr. Grainger, "to the superior quality of our fitting rooms and their two-way mirrors."

Mrs. Slocombe turned in surprise.

"Mr. Grainger means you can see the back and front at the same time," explained Mr. Lucas.

Mr. Humphries nodded. "Comes in quite handy sometimes."

"I'm sure," suggested Captain Peacock, "that Mr. Rumbold would welcome your choosing any garment from the stock in the ladies' department."

With a note of exasperation in his voice, Mr. Rumbold said that he was just about to say that.

"How kind," said Mrs. Slocombe. "I shall of course have to choose something appropriate for the occasion."

Leaning over the counter, Mr. Lucas produced a pair of novelty briefs, and held them out and pointed to the writing on them.

"How about 'Opportunity Knocks'?" he suggested.

The department clock indicated it was half past three. Captain Peacock walked up and down nervously, hands behind his back, glanced at the clock and then strolled over to Mr. Grainger, shaking his head.

"Half past three. Mrs. Slocombe still not back from lunch."

Mr. Grainger nodded. "Such a dear person, I'm very fond of her you know, Stephen."

"Oh so am I," said Captain Peacock. "By the way, Ernest, does Young Mr. Grace have any living relations?"

Mr. Grainger shook his head. "Only Old Mr. Grace and he doesn't get about much any more."

"In that case." sighed Captain Peacock, "she stands to cop the lot."

"Yes," said Mr. Grainger. "As I said, such a dear person."

A mechanical ping indicated the arrival of the lift and the doors opened. Mrs. Slocombe stepped out with a massive halo of curls lacquered into place and strolled forward with her head back as though her balance was in jeopardy.

"How nice your hair looks, Mrs. Slocombe," called Mr. Grainger.

Captain Peacock nodded in agreement. "Very *à la mode*."

"It's lacquered solid," confided Mrs. Slocombe. "On the way up I bumped into the commissionaire and broke the peak off his hat."

"Lovely," said Miss Brahms as Mrs. Slocombe moved regally across the floor. "It must have cost a fortune."

"Four pounds fifty," confided Mrs. Slocombe, "but an investment."

Miss Brahms pulled back the curtain of the fitting room. "I've got the clothes that you picked out to try on."

"I'll remember your efficiency," said Mrs. Slocombe. "While I change I shall have to leave you in charge."

With that Mrs. Slocombe disappeared into the fitting room, then came out again with two dresses over her arm.

"The light's better out here," she said.

She held one out and looked at it disdainfully. "Ooh, what a common colour this is when you see it under the fluorescent. Put it back, Miss Brahms."

Dropping it on the floor, Mrs. Slocombe examined the second dress.

"Oh yes, that's very nice, I think brown is so dignified."

"Yes," said Miss Brahms, "and it doesn't show the gravy."

"May I suggest," said Mr. Grainger, "that our fitting room, which has fluorescent lighting, would be a far superior place for you to try on your ensemble."

"Why not?" said Mrs. Slocombe.

"Follow me, madam," said Mr. Grainger.

Mrs. Slocombe followed Mr. Grainger across the floor.

"Mr. Grainger," she said, "your kindness to me will not go unnoticed," then she paused at the gentlemen's counter. "Mr. Humphries, your tie is crooked."

Mr. Humphries's hands leapt anxiously to his tie and straightened it. Mrs. Slocombe waved an arm in a gesture which took in the whole department. "It's so mucky, it all needs decorating. I shall have to decide what colour, of course." Mr. Grainger with an ingratiating smile pulled back the curtain of the fitting room and bowed as he ushered Mrs. Slocombe in, but she recoiled in horror. In the cubicle a customer was in the act of stepping out of his trousers.

Mrs. Slocombe gave a piercing scream and fell back into Mr. Grainger's arms. Mr. Humphries and Captain Peacock rushed to her assistance. Mrs. Slocombe gasped and pointed to the curtain. "There's a naked man in there, in his underpants."

Mr. Humphries patted her hand consolingly. "You've seen nothing yet, Mrs. Slocombe. Just wait until the honeymoon!"

"I think," said Mrs. Slocombe, gathering up her dress, "that I shall use my own facilities, thank you."

"Of course," added Mr. Humphries, "to be fair, Young Mr. Grace will have to get used to it too. Tell me, Captain Peacock, you're a man of the world. From your wide experience of these matters, do you think they will make a go of it?"

Captain Peacock pursed his lips. "Putting it bluntly, Mr. Humphries, neither of them are in a position to be choosy."

Mr. Humphries shook his head. "I can't think what has come over the old boy."

"He wants somebody to be ready to take over, rather like Eva Peron when the Junta collapsed," suggested Captain Peacock.

"I should be surprised," said Mr. Humphries, "if his hasn't collapsed already."

"Between you and me," said Captain Peacock, "I think she could be a bit of a Tartar."

Half an hour later, Mrs. Slocombe reappeared from her fitting room in full bridal regalia, a white veil carefully covering her new hairstyle. The gentlemen's department gasped in surprise.

"Well, Captain Peacock?" said Mrs. Slocombe, posing demurely as she waited for an opinion.

THE *ARE YOU BEING SERVED?* STORIES

"A little formal for afternoon tea don't you think, Mrs. Slocombe?"

Mrs. Slocombe shook her head. "I'm not going to wear it this afternoon. I just couldn't resist trying it on, it makes me feel all young and innocent."

A look of surprise crossed Captain Peacock's face.

"A remarkable garment indeed," he observed.

"It's a quarter to four," said Miss Brahms. "You had better try the afternoon dress on."

Mrs. Slocombe turned back towards the dressing room and warbled in a wavering voice, "Oh be still, my fluttering heart."

Miss Brahms drew the curtains behind her murmuring, "It was probably the wind from the fairy cake."

At five minutes to four Mrs. Slocombe reappeared in the brown dress. She poured another generous helping of the Cologne down her bosom, snapped on her best earrings with a businesslike gesture and with cries of "Good luck" ringing in her ears, entered the lift and disappeared upwards, to her fate.

"Well," observed Mr. Lucas, "it looks as if she's made up her mind."

"Yes," said Mr. Humphries, "in two minutes she'll be up in Mr. Grace's office."

"I wouldn't mind," said Captain Peacock, "being a fly on the wall."

"I'll tell you exactly what you'd see," said Mr. Lucas. "Tea for two, a silly old muffin and a tired old bit of crumpet."

In the Board room Mr. Grace sat in his high-backed chair, eyes closed. A loud knock on the door interrupted his reverie.

"Yes, yes." called Mr. Grace. "Come in, come in."

The young bosomy girl holding a tray of engagement rings entered.

"Here are the rings you wanted to have a look at, Mr. Grace."

"Thank you, Miss Robinson. Where's the tea?"

"It's just coming, Mr. Grace."

A tentative knock at the door indicated the arrival of Mrs. Slocombe.

"Come in," said Mr. Grace.

"I hope," said Mrs. Slocombe, "that I am not late."

"No," said Mr. Grace, "you're early, the tea hasn't come yet. Never mind, come and sit down. I think you know Miss Robinson of jewelry."

Mrs. Slocombe started to nod, then remembered her lacquered hair and stopped just in time. "Yes, yes, her superior and I are old acquaintances."

The sound of a foot kicking the door interrupted them.

"That'll be the tea," said Mr. Grace. "Come in."

The grinning face of Mr. Mash appeared holding a large tray on which was a pot of tea, two cups and an assortment of buns on a plate.

"One pot of Rosie Lee," called Mr. Mash, "and the usual muffin and crumpet." With that he banged it down on the table. "Blimey," he said, "those rings are nice," then aside to Mrs. Slocombe he whispered, "choose a big one, darling, and pick the honeymoon suite on the ground floor, one flight of those stairs and he won't be able to raise his walking stick until after breakfast."

"Get out," hissed Mrs. Slocombe.

"Are you going to be mother?" said Mr. Grace. Mrs. Slocombe almost jumped out of her seat, then recovered.

"We can't be sure," she murmured with lowered eyes. "One must wait and see."

"I mean," said Mr. Grace, "are you going to pour out the tea?"

Mrs. Slocombe looked relieved. "The tea, oh yes, of course."

"Now I expect," said Mr. Grace, "you are wondering why I have asked you up here."

Mrs. Slocombe gave a secretive smile. "A girl does have an inkling, you know."

"What?" said Mr. Grace, leaning forward and cupping his hand to his ear.

"An inkling," shouted Mrs. Slocombe.

"What's that?" said Mr. Grace.

"It's what," said Mrs. Slocombe, pouring with an unsteady hand, "a girl has when something special is in the air."

"Aah," nodded Mr. Grace, "you mean like hay fever."

"Do you take sugar?" inquired Mrs. Slocombe.

"I'm sweet enough," said Mr. Grace.

Mrs. Slocombe threw back her head and laughed. "That's a good one," she said, and to her consternation found that one of her lacquered curls had caught the carved woodwork of her high-backed chair. With a surreptitious effort she managed to release it.

"I expect," said Mr. Grace, "that you think I'm a bit of an old fool getting married at my time of life. After all, I am seventy."

"One or two?" said Mrs. Slocombe, holding up the sugar bowl.

"If I say I am seventy," snapped Mr. Grace, "I am seventy."

"I mean, how many sugars?" inquired Mrs. Slocombe.

"I've already told you," said Mr. Grace, "that I don't take sugar."

"I'm sorry," said Mrs. Slocombe, "it's just nerves. In fact, I thought you were only in your late sixties. And anyway, you are only as old as you feel, and I can see you are very young in spirit. All you need is someone to take you out of yourself. I mean, you hardly ever take a holiday, do you?"

"That's true," agreed Mr. Grace.

Mrs. Slocombe buttered a scone. "It's very difficult being alone for a man of your position, isn't it? I mean, supposing you take your yacht to the Caribbino. You'll have those young girls climbing all over you and all because you're rich."

An interested look crossed Mr. Grace's face. "Will I?" he inquired.

Mrs. Slocombe nodded. "And they are all after you for one thing, you know." She pulled a face to show how she disapproved of that "one thing."

"Are they?" said Mr. Grace, brightening up.

"Yes," said Mrs. Slocombe, blowing her tea. "But if you're married to a wife who is devoted to you, she will protect you from all that. You've always got someone at your side sharing your little problems, helping you through life's weary travels."

The perky look started to disappear from Mr. Grace's face.

"Cherishing," continued Mrs. Slocombe, "each other when you are sick, and all that sort of thing." Taking a large bite of scone she edged her chair a little nearer. Mr. Grace sipped his tea thoughtfully, finally he nodded and put his hand on her knee. She gazed at it anxiously as he continued, "I'm very grateful to you, Mrs. Slocombe, you have helped me to make up my mind. In fact, I brought you up here to choose a ring."

The scone stuck in Mrs. Slocombe's throat, and she had to take a large gulp of tea to get it down. Stabbing her finger into the box she announced breathlessly "that big one there" and picking it up forced it on to her engagement finger. She held out her hand and gazed at it admiringly. Mr. Grace appeared not to notice.

"It's for our Miss Robinson of the jewelry department, whom I have had my eye on for some time, almost three weeks," he added.

Mrs. Slocombe froze. "Miss Robinson?"

Mr. Grace nodded. "Yes, but now I've spoken to you, and you've put me right off the idea of marriage."

"Oh no," said Mrs. Slocombe hurriedly, "that was the last thing I wanted to do."

With an effort Mr. Grace hauled himself to his feet. "Anyway, thank you very much, Mrs. Slocombe. You must come and help me again."

Mrs. Slocombe looked at the ring on her finger, and blinked her eyes rapidly. She tried to smile but failed. "It"ll be a pleasure," she whispered sadly as she removed it.

Mr. Grace opened the door. "When you get to my time of life, you need the advice of an older woman. I'm most grateful."

Mrs. Slocombe rose from her chair. "Any time, Mr. Grace, do feel free."

"Take a muffin with you in case you feel like it after," said Mr. Grace.

"You're too kind," murmured Mrs. Slocombe, pausing as she gave back the ring,

"Well," said Mr. Grace, "is there anything else?"

Mrs. Slocombe shook her head. "I don't suppose there is."

Heavy-footed she headed for the door.

"Oh, Mrs. Slocombe," called Mr. Grace after her, Mrs. Slocombe stopped and her face brightened.

She turned eagerly. "Yes, Mr. Grace?"

"Tell stationery to send me a copy of *Yachting Monthly*. You did say all those girls were in the Caribbean?"

"Yes," said Mrs. Slocombe, "I did."

Mrs. Slocombe stepped from the lift to be greeted by a round of applause.

"Doesn't she look radiant?" said Mr. Humphries.

"Perhaps they've already done it," said Mr. Lucas. "He probably had a vicar upstairs in his office."

"A friend of mine did that," said Mr. Humphries, "and he had a small section of the choir hiding behind the curtain. It was a very moving story in court."

Captain Peacock held up his hands. "Quiet, everybody. Now Mrs. Slocombe, tell us everything that happened."

Mrs. Slocombe glanced round at the assembled faces. "Well," she said, "before I do, I would like to clear up one or two matters. Mr. Grainger?"

"Yes, Mrs. Slocombe," Mr. Grainger hurried forward, hands clasped together.

"I take it," said Mrs. Slocombe, "that you no longer object to the presence of the ladies' department on this floor?"

"On the contrary," said Mr. Grainger, "the ladies' department will always be most welcome."

"And," continued Mrs. Slocombe, "I take it, Captain Peacock, that you will not in future insist upon the ladies' department displaying articles they consider to be in bad taste."

Captain Peacock shook his head. "The goods on display will be left entirely to whosoever is in charge."

"Well," said Mrs. Slocombe, "I'm glad that's all cleared up."

"And may one ask," said Captain Peacock, "when the happy day will be?"

"Today," said Mrs. Slocombe.

"Today!" said Captain Peacock.

"Yes," said Mrs. Slocombe. "I turned him down."

CHAPTER

# His and Hers

"A glass of water for Mr. Grainger," called Mr. Humphries
and then, glancing at the frozen figure,
"and a tranquilizer for Mr. Lucas."

# His and Hers

ON ENTERING THE FIRST-FLOOR DEPARTMENT OF GRACE BROTHERS, YOU might notice Mr. Grainger's trouser-stand, which has occupied a prominent position for the past twenty-five years. As with all landmarks, they are taken for granted and not necessarily missed when removed. Mr. Humphries didn't notice the trouser stand's absence when he stepped out of the lift one bright sunny morning, nor did Mr. Lucas. In fact, all Mr. Lucas did notice was that Mr. Humphries was wearing a deerstalker hat.

"Good morning, Mr. Humphries."

"Good morning, Mr. Lucas."

"I like your hat. Were you hunting last night?"

Mr. Humphries tripped lightly down the steps, "You keep a civil tongue in your head, sauce box. I bought it to save me from being mugged. People aren't so keen to creep up behind you if they think you're looking over your shoulder. It's like having eyes in the back of your head." And with that Mr. Humphries stopped in his tracks. "Look." Mr. Lucas followed his gaze.

"I can't see anything."

"Exactly," said Mr. Humphries. "The centre display has gone."

Mr. Lucas clapped his hand to his face with mock dismay.

"The Phantom Trouser Stealer has struck again."

Mr. Humphries stared at the round, unfaded piece of carpet.

"Whatever will Mr. Grainger say?"

"Perhaps he knows about it," suggested Mr. Lucas.

"If he doesn't he'll have a heart attack."

At that moment Miss Brahms came out of the lift in a brief miniskirt and ran hurriedly down the stairs clutching her handbag. Mr. Lucas gazed at her rear view appreciatively as she bent over the counter and entered her name and time of arrival in the book.

"Good morning, Shirley, there's a ladder in your tights."

"Trust you to notice," snapped Miss Brahms.

Mr. Lucas bent his knee slightly and inclined his head to one side. "Does it go all the way up?"

"There's one person who's never going to find out, and that's you, Mr. Lucas." She glanced at the book with surprise. "Hello, Captain Peacock hasn't signed in."

Mr. Humphries produced his gold propelling pencil. "It won't seem the same signing the book without him looking at his watch and making caustic comments."

Mr. Lucas produced a black comb from his pocket. "Never mind, Mr. Humphries, you sign in and I'll make caustic comments." Clicking his heels he put the comb under his nose to create the impression of a moustache and did a fair impression of Captain Peacock's voice as Mr. Humphries signed. "Tut, tut, tut, Mr. Humphries, 8:46. One minute late for battle again." With a mock gasp of dismay Mr. Humphries fell on one knee, and clasping his hands in a supplicatory attitude gazed at Mr. Lucas imploringly.

"Please, Captain Peacock, spare me. Don't tell the evil Mr. Rumbold or I shall lose my position at Grace Brothers, which I have held as man and boy these thirty summers, not to mention a lot more winters. Please Captain Peacock, please Captain Peacock, I'll do anything, anything."

Miss Brahms fell against the counter giggling helplessly.

Mr. Lucas turned sternly to her. "Miss Brahms, please control yourself. Such displays of human emotion are not welcomed at Grace Brothers."

"I'm sorry, Captain Peacock."

"I also note by my watch that you are two minutes late. That is not good enough. You know what happens when you are late at Grace Brothers."

"No, not that again," gasped Miss Brahms in mock horror, shrinking away. At that moment Mr. Humphries spotted Captain Peacock walking slowly down the steps taking in the scene.

"Peacock!" he warned.

Mr. Lucas turned on him. "Captain Peacock to you, dog! And be quiet while I deal with Miss Brahms."

Unaware that Captain Peacock was now standing with narrowed eyes only a few feet away, he put his arm round Miss Brahms's waist and bent her back. "Come here, my beauty," he growled, "and I'll show you how Grace Brothers deals with deserters." With a quick move he bent forward and gave her a smacking kiss on the lips. Miss Brahms screamed.

Captain Peacock stepped forward and tapped Mr. Lucas on the shoulder. "Mr. Lucas," he murmured.

Miss Brahms screamed again as Mr. Lucas released his grip on her. She fell backwards on the floor, her legs flying.

"Captain Peacock," gasped Mr. Lucas.

Captain Peacock glanced down at Miss Brahms. "Get up, Miss Brahms. And I might mention that you have a ladder that goes the full length of your tights."

"Well," observed Mr. Lucas. "That's one person that has found out."

"Mr. Lucas, I will not have this larking about in my absence."

"I'm very sorry, Captain Peacock. Please forgive me."

"It's disgraceful," continued Captain Peacock, "and very discourteous to me."

Mr. Lucas hung his head.

"I'm truly sorry, Captain Peacock. Mind you," he continued earnestly, "if we weren't all aware of what a real good sport you are, sir, we wouldn't take such terrible liberties."

"Don't let it happen again, Mr. Lucas." He turned to Mr. Humphries. "I'm surprised at you allowing it, Mr. Humphries."

Mr. Humphries smiled an ingratiating smile. "My hand isn't as firm as yours, Captain Peacock."

Captain Peacock produced his pen and signed the book. "Don't let it happen again."

As he glanced at his watch to enter his time of arrival, Mrs. Slocombe made her way down the steps.

"Good morning, Captain Peacock," she called. "You're rather later than customary, are you not?"

"Yes, I had to get my wife off."

"Off what?" inquired Mrs. Slocombe.

"Off on the train, Mrs. Slocombe. She'll staying with her sister in Bognor Regis for a few days."

Mrs. Slocombe raised her eyebrows and gazed at him archly.

"Oh, a grass widower, eh." She gave a tinkling laugh. "We girls had better watch our steps."

"And our ladders," added Miss Brahms.

"May I borrow your propelling pencil, Captain Peacock?"

"Certainly, Mrs. Slocombe. Be careful, I have very little lead left."

"It happens to us all eventually," said Mr. Humphries.

Mr. Lucas nodded.

As Mrs. Slocombe crossed the department, Captain Peacock helped her off with her coat.

"It had occurred to me," he said, "that if you had nothing on one evening I might suggest a little dinner *à deux*."

Mrs. Slocombe stopped in midstride as she noticed the circle of unfaded carpet. "Surely there's something missing, Captain Peacock."

Captain Peacock misunderstood her meaning. "Er…candles, perhaps," he suggested, "or anything else that takes your fancy."

"No trousers," said Mrs. Slocombe. "That's it, no trousers."

Captain Peacock looked alarmed. "My wife is only away for two days, Mrs. Slocombe. I was only suggesting a dinner."

Mrs. Slocombe pointed. "Mr. Grainger's trousers have gone and so has the display stand."

Mr. Humphries piped up from behind his counter. "I noticed that when I first came in, didn't I, Mr. Lucas?"

Mr. Lucas nodded in agreement. "You did, Mr. Humphries. It's gone, you said. What? I said. Mr. Grainger's display stand, you said. So it has, I said. Mr. Grainger will have a fit, you said...." Just at that moment Mr. Grainger appeared from the lift, paused on top of the steps and gave a gasp of horror.

"...and you were right," added Mr. Humphries.

Mr. Grainger's jowls worked overtime as he hurried down.

"Where," he growled, "is the centre display?"

"I forgot to tell you," said Captain Peacock. "An executive's decision was taken yesterday, and Mr. Rumbold ordered its removal. During the night the maintenance men have carried out that order."

"Removal," spluttered Mr. Grainger.

"A glass of water for Mr. Grainger," called Mr. Humphries.

"A glass of water coming up," replied Mr. Lucas.

Mr. Grainger took off his homburg and banged it angrily on the counter. "I shall want to see Mr. Rumbold about this to give him a piece of my mind."

"Morning, everybody," said Mr. Rumbold as he strolled into view from the direction of his office. Mr. Grainger's angry look disappeared as though by magic.

"Good morning, sir, I was just inquiring about the centre display stand. It appears to be missing."

Mr. Rumbold nodded as he crossed the middle of the floor. "Aah yes, Mr. Grainger, I meant to have a word with you about that. In fact, I have an announcement to make."

Raising his voice, Captain Peacock addressed the department. "Gather round, everybody, Mr. Rumbold has an announcement to make."

Taking his cue, Mr. Humphries raised his voice. "Mr. Lucas, gather round, Mr. Rumbold is going to do some announcing."

Captain Peacock took his place on Mr. Rumbold's right and waited for Mrs. Slocombe, Miss Brahms, Mr. Humphries and Mr. Lucas to gather.

"Hurry up, Mr. Grainger," called Captain Peacock. Mr. Grainger pretended not to hear and took some time hanging his coat up, then walked slowly over with his eyes gazing in the direction of the missing stand.

"We're all ready," said Captain Peacock.

"Very well," said Mr. Rumbold and cleared his throat. "Grace Brothers has entered into a special promotion agreement with a perfumery company to promote their product by having a special display on this floor, er, to promote them."

"Does that mean," said Mr. Grainger, "that we're going to sell scent?"

Mr. Rumbold looked uncomfortable. "Er yes, you could put it like that."

"Well if it's scent," said Mr. Humphries, "why can't you take some of the counter space in the ladies' department?"

Mr. Grainger's jowls nodded in agreement. "Precisely. Mrs. Slocombe's displaying far too much underwear."

Mrs. Slocombe stepped forward angrily. "Are you suggesting, Mr. Grainger, that I remove my underwear and put perfume there instead?"

Mr. Grainger stuck his face out aggressively. "Are you suggesting, Mrs. Slocombe, that I remove my trousers and put perfume there instead?"

Mr. Rumbold held up his hand pleadingly.

"I must explain that this was a Board room decision and that the perfume in question is going to be on sale to both sexes under the brand name of His and Hers."

Mrs. Slocombe shook her head. "I'm not selling hers, and I positively refuse to sell his."

"I should be allowed to finish," said Mr. Rumbold. "What I am trying to explain, Mrs. Slocombe, is that it is to be promoted by a member of the perfume company's own sales staff." A look of interest came into Mr. Lucas's eye. "A him or a her?"

"Possibly half and half," said Mr. Humphries hopefully.

"Ices, get your lovely ices," called Mr. Mash.

Everybody turned and observed Mr. Mash pushing a large stand on wheels towards the centre of the floor.

"Ah," said Mr. Rumbold, "here"s the new stand now."

"Where shall I stick it?—as the stamp collector said to Mae West."

"That will do, Mr. Mash," said Captain Peacock. "Everybody lend a hand with the stand."

Mr. Mash gave a lecherous laugh. "That's what Mae West said to the stamp collector."

Mr. Grainger shook his head. "I shall give no help whatsoever. "Mutiny on the counter," said Mr. Lucas.

"Come, come," said Captain Peacock. "Mr. Grainger, that's not like you."

Mr. Grainger stood his ground. "Even in the French Revolution, the victims were not required to chop off their own heads. The members of my staff will not cooperate with the outfitting of this stand."

"I'm behind you, Mr. Grainger," said Mr. Humphries loyally.

"And," added Mr. Lucas, "I'm behind Mr. Humphries unless Captain Peacock tells me not to be, in which case I'm behind Mr. Rumbold."

Mrs. Slocombe stepped forward. "Since Mr. Grainger is behaving like a bear with a sore head, Captain Peacock, perhaps I can give you a hand."

"No, no, Mrs. Slocombe, I wouldn't dream of letting a lady do this sort of work."

"Oh, what a gent! Miss Brahms, give him a hand."

As Miss Brahms went forward and tugged and pulled at the stand which Mr. Mash was trying to guide into position in the middle of the floor, Captain Peacock drew Mrs. Slocombe to one side and lowered his voice.

"How would tonight suit you?"

"Suit me for what?"

"For our little dinner date," said Captain Peacock.

Mrs. Slocombe gave a coquettish laugh. "I'm surprised at you, Captain Peacock, and you, a happily married man."

Captain Peacock shook his head sadly. "Ah, would that were true."

"Oh no," said Mrs. Slocombe, "not another one."

"After fourteen years, you don't know what it's like."

Mrs. Slocombe gazed at him sympathetically. "I didn't know what it was like after seven."

"Think about it," whispered Captain Peacock, "and let me know your decision later." Then in a loud voice he called, "Positions, everyone. The store is open, and please leave the floor, Mr. Mash."

"Yes sit, mustn't let the customers see human rubbish, must we? Cinderella had better go back to the kitchen." Hunching one shoulder and tugging at an imaginary forelock he made the most of his exit. As he did, a ping indicated the arrival of the lift and from it stepped a tall girl with blond hair and dark glasses, wearing a smart trouser suit which did not conceal the fact that she had an amazing figure. Mr. Lucas nudged Mr. Humphries.

"Blimey!" he said. "Get a load of that. What a cracker."

"Men," said Mr. Humphries. "You're all the same."

Captain Peacock's mouth dropped open as the girl progressed down the steps and over to Mrs. Slocombe's counter.

"Here," hissed Miss Brahms, "we got a customer."

"Drat," said Mrs. Slocombe, "I haven't quite finished my face." With her lipstick poised she turned. "Are you being served, madam?"

The girl spoke in a low, husky, musical voice.

"I'm the consultant for His and Hers."

Mrs. Slocombe's half smile froze. "Oh yes."

"Can I see the floorwalker?" breathed the girl.

Mrs. Slocombe gazed at her dark glasses. "I doubt it with those on." Then, in a loud voice, "Are you free, Captain Peacock? This is the sales girl from the scent people."

Captain Peacock quickly adjusted his tie, ran a hand over his hair and strode forward, a charming smile on his face.

"Good morning, Miss, welcome to Grace Brothers. And you are...?"

The girl turned and smiled, revealing a perfect set of teeth. "French," she murmured.

"Ah," said Captain Peacock. "*Pardonnez moi. Boniour, je suis parler français un peu. Je suis dans position supérior...*"

The girl interrupted him. "My name is Miss French."

"Oh," said Captain Peacock. "My mistake."

The girl took off her dark glasses to reveal a pair of beautiful green eyes, which Peacock seemed to think were staring bewitchingly into his.

"I think you're the person I want to talk to," she murmured.

Captain Peacock swallowed nervously, and adjusted his tie.

"Absolutely, if there's anything I can do," and taking Miss French by the elbow he led her away from the counter.

Mrs. Slocombe and Miss Brahms looked at each other. Mrs. Slocombe raised her eyebrows and raising her glasses followed his progress with narrowed eyes.

At the other of the department Mr. Grainger peered shortsightedly through his spectacles at the sight of Captain Peacock, head bent attentively as Miss French held him in conversation. He turned to Mr. Humphries. "Who is that engaging Captain Peacock in conversation?"

"The girl from His and Hers, Mr. Grainger."

Mr. Grainger's jaw set in a firm line. "Indeed. I think it's best if we ignored her."

Mr. Humphries glanced at Mr. Lucas, whose eyes were popping out as he leant over the counter staring in the direction of Miss French.

"Mr. Lucas is trying," he observed, "but he is not doing very well at the moment."

Mr. Lucas dived a hand inside his jacket pocket and took out his wallet and gazed through it.

"Just my luck." he muttered, "for someone like that to sail in on a Thursday when I've got one measly quid. Where can I take a bird for a quid?"

"Well," suggested Mr. Humphries, "you could buy six pennyworth of worms and take her along the canal with a rod and a bent pin."

"Does she look like the sort of girl you can take along a canal?"

"Or," said Mr. Humphries, "how about an evening of your witty backchat over sausage and chips at the local transport cafe? According to you, once they've heard your chat, it's all over bar the shouting."

"It usually is," said Mr. Lucas, "but that's a bit of class over there."

"Look at the way she's smiling at Peacock," said Mr. Humphries. "He doesn't waste any time. Maybe he's hoping she's the sort that goes for the father figure."

"The grandfather figure," said Mr. Lucas sarcastically.

Miss French walked behind the display stand and began opening boxes. She took out bottles of scent and some cards which advertised "His and Hers" and started to arrange them.

Captain Peacock leant on the stand.

"Well, Miss French, I'm sure you'll be very happy here. If there is anything at all that you need don't hesitate to get in touch with me."

"Where do I find you?" breathed Miss French.

Captain Peacock took two paces away from the stand. "About here, actually."

During the next half hour members of both departments watched with interest as Captain Peacock made a number of sorties to Miss French's display stand offering help and advice as to how she should arrange her company's products.

Miss Brahms turned to Mrs. Slocombe. "Do you think he fancies her, he's hopping about there a lot?"

Mrs. Slocombe shook her head, and gave a light laugh. "Oh no, no, not a young thing like that. Men of Captain Peacock's age prefer a more mature woman. Someone they can talk to."

Miss Brahms nodded. "At his age I suppose that's all that's left."

"I'm his age," observed Mrs. Slocombe.

"What do you talk about?" inquired Miss Brahms.

Mr. Lucas, who had not taken his eyes off Miss French since her arrival, breathed a sigh of relief as Captain Peacock turned away from the display stand and walked towards Mrs. Slocombe's counter.

"Keep your eye out for Mr. Grainger," he whispered to Mr. Humphries. "Peacock's leaving the field of battle, it's my turn."

"Before you try your luck in no man's land I should wait for Captain Peacock to leave the department," advised Mr. Humphries.

Mr. Lucas took a couple of paces away from the end of the counter, then his nerve failed him and he walked back again.

At Mrs. Slocombe's counter Captain Peacock gave a discreet cough to attract her attention. Mrs. Slocombe, in the act of changing a bra on a dummy, paused, safety pin between her teeth.

"Captain Peacock?"

"A word with you, Mrs. Slocombe, after you've changed your bra."

Mrs. Slocombe turned the dummy so that the back of it was to Captain Peacock while she completed her task.

"Yes, Captain Peacock."

"About tonight, Mrs. Slocombe."

"Yes, I've been thinking about it and I thought to myself, why not? After all, what have I to lose?"

"What indeed," agreed Captain Peacock, "and I have been thinking about it, too, but on second thought I think it would be unwise to start something we can't finish."

Mrs. Slocombe pushed the dummy aside and leant forward over the counter. "What are you suggesting?"

Captain Peacock chose his words carefully.

"I mean, two attractive people, on their own together, the spark that ignites the tinder, the all-consuming fire."

Mrs. Slocombe looked puzzled.

"I thought it was just dinner."

"It was," said Captain Peacock, "but perhaps lunch in the canteen would be better."

Mrs. Slocombe's lips closed in a thin line. "Are you cancelling?"

Captain Peacock looked embarrassed. "In a manner of speaking, yes."

"Well," said Mrs. Slocombe. "Fancy leading a girl on."

Captain Peacock hurriedly turned on his heel and headed in the direction of the new display stand.

Putting on his best bedroom department smile, he approached Miss French, who was unaware of him as she unscrewed a bottle of scent, tested it on the back of her hand and sniffed it. Captain Peacock coughed to draw attention to himself.

"It's very quiet here at the moment."

Miss French flashed her teeth in a big smile. "Yes, isn't it," she breathed sexily.

Captain Peacock tugged at the knot of his tie. "This may seem rather premature, and I hope you don't mind me asking?"

Miss French turned her bewitching eyes on him expectantly. "Yes, go on."

Captain Peacock clenched his hands behind his back. "Well, let me put it another way. Do you have a particular boyfriend?"

Miss French took a deep breath before she replied, causing Captain Peacock to clutch his hands even more nervously.

"All my boyfriends are particular," she breathed.

Captain Peacock nodded. "Yes, yes of course, but what I was trying to say was, are you by any chance free for a drink when we close the store?"

Miss French's bewitching expression disappeared and a rather hard look took its place. Captain Peacock suddenly looked anxious.

"Well, it's very sweet of you, Captain Pocock."

"Peacock," he corrected.

"But," continued Miss French, "my boyfriend's picking me up at 5:30."

Captain Peacock held up a hand. "Say no more, I was just worried that you might be at a loose end. Er... excuse me." Turning on his heel he called, "Mrs. Slocombe, are you free?"

Mrs. Slocombe gave him a beady look. "Yes, at the moment, Captain Peacock."

Switching on his bedroom smile again, Captain Peacock strolled over and leant nonchalantly at the counter.

"I've been thinking, Mrs. Slocombe, about what I said to you and I have had second thoughts about tonight."

"I haven't," said Mrs. Slocombe, "and with regard to what you said about the fire, I think it's just as well if you didn't get your matches out. Excuse me."

"Excuse me," breathed Miss French from directly behind Captain Peacock, who turned with a sudden start.

"Er yes, what is it?" he inquired.

"Where's your changing room?"

Mrs. Slocombe stepped round the counter. "May I inquire for what purpose you wish to know for?"

"I want to change," said Miss French, indicating the small holdall she was carrying. Mrs. Slocombe looked, then smiled icily.

"I'm sorry," she said, "but our rooms are not for staff."

Miss French gave her a sarcastic smile. "Thanks for your help, Mrs. Slackhome."

"Slocombe," said Mrs. Slocombe crossly, "and," she added, again with an icy smile, "it was a pleasure."

Miss French turned on her heel and marched across towards the gentlemen's counter. Mr. Humphries nudged Mr. Lucas.

"Your turn's coming, she's heading this way."

Mr. Lucas squared his shoulders. "I'll try the direct approach. It never fails with these toffee-nosed birds, you know. All you've got to do is grab 'em and they go mad."

"I've yet to see that," said Mr. Humphries. "Who knows, I might learn something from the Casanova of the cuff links counter."

"I'm not going to do it in front of you, Mr. Humphries."

"Excuse me," said Miss French, "can you help me?"

Mr. Lucas suddenly appeared to be chewing a piece of imaginary gum.

"I'm glad," he drawled, "that you came over. I've got something very important to say to you," and beckoning he led her round behind the rather large display stand. There was a short pause followed by a loud slap, then Mr. Lucas emerged holding his face.

"What happened?" inquired Mr. Humphries.

"I grabbed her," said Mr. Lucas, "and she went mad." Miss French reappeared, straightening her hair.

She approached Mr. Humphries, who took a step nervously backwards.

"I wonder if you can help me," breathed Miss French.

Mr. Humphries smiled. "Tell me, do I need a bodyguard?"

"All I need," said Miss French, "is a changing room."

Mr. Grainger who had been observing the exchange from his end of the counter, waddled over.

"Are you having any difficulties, Mr. Humphries?"

"Not yet, Mr. Grainger. The young lady has just asked if she can use our changing room."

Mr. Grainger gazed at Miss French with a sour expression on his face.

"May I inquire for what purpose, Miss?"

"Would you believe," said Miss French, "to change?"

Mr. Grainger narrowed his eyes. "I don't like the tone of your voice, and I'm afraid our changing rooms aren't to be used by female staff."

"All right," said Miss French defiantly, "have it your own way." Unzipping her trousers she started to pull them down. Mr. Grainger clapped a hand to his forehead and staggered backwards as she stepped out of her trousers to reveal three quarter-length stockings, topped by frilly red garters and above a delectable expanse of bare thigh a minute miniskirt. Mr. Grainger seemed to go through some sort of seizure and clutched wildly at the counter for support. Mr. Lucas, on the other hand, didn't move a muscle due to temporary paralysis. Only his bulging eyes gave away the deep emotion he was feeling inside.

"A glass of water for Mr. Grainger," called Mr. Humphries and then glancing at the frozen figure, "and a tranquillizer for Mr. Lucas."

Seemingly unaware of the chaos she had caused, Miss French strolled nonchalantly back to her display stand, her trousers over her arm. Captain Peacock, who had observed this transformation over the shoulder of a customer, appeared to have a dizzy spell and blinked his eyes rapidly to make sure he wasn't having a bout of desert mirage. Bending down, Miss French disappeared for a moment behind her stand and then reappeared holding a cardboard box from which she extracted a number of ties which she proceeded to arrange in a row at one side of her counter. Bending down again she reappeared with a type-printed card which she propped up alongside the ties. She then produced a box of ladies' stockings and arranged them in a similar manner on the other side of the counter with another card which she propped up next to them.

Mr. Grainger paused halfway through his second glass of water and stared disbelievingly at the row of ties on the centre stand. Mr. Humphries relinquished his grip on Mr. Lucas's wrist where he'd been checking his pulse, afraid his immediate superior might have a serious spasm.

"I have been observing that young lady," said Mr. Grainger, "and I am wondering what is on the cards."

Mr. Lucas shook his head. "Very little at your time of life, I should think."

"On the display cards," corrected Mr. Humphries.

"Oh sorry," said Mr. Lucas, and shutting one eye peered intensely. "It reads, 'With every bottle of His perfume we are giving away a free tie.'"

"Free tie," gasped Mr. Grainger. "Take over, Mr. Humphries, I am going to have a word with Captain Peacock."

At the ladies' counter Mrs. Slocombe held her spectacles a foot away from her face and stared with disbelief at Miss French's display stand.

"It says what?" asked Miss Brahms.

"It says they are giving away a free pair of stockings with every bottle of Hers. I'll have to put a stop to that!"

Miss Brahms nodded in agreement. "It's not very good for our sales, is it?"

"I'm going to complain to Captain Peacock."

"Ooh and what's that she's got on her counter?" Mrs. Slocombe peered through her glasses again.

"It looks like some sort of tape recorder. What on earth…"

And at that moment Mr. Mash popped into view with a plug on the end of a lead. He winked at Miss French lecherously. "Well, darling, let's hope we don't get a short circuit when we plug it in, as Mae West said when she picked up the midget."

Miss French stared stonily at him. Mr. Mash stuck the plug into the back of the recorder and pressed the button.

"I expect," said Mr. Mash, "it will take a few minutes to warm up, as Mae West said to the Eskimo." He clutched his side and laughed loudly at his own joke.

Captain Peacock's shadow fell across the counter cutting his laugh short.

"Mr. Mash, if you are finished, I am sure you are urgently needed elsewhere."

"You're quite right, Captain Peacock. There's a bunged-up khazi in the basement."

"I wonder," said Miss French, "if Mae West ever said that?" Captain Peacock placed his hands behind his back and started his department patrol as Mrs. Slocombe and Mr. Grainger converged on him.

"I think," said Mrs. Slocombe, "that it's disgusting. I mean, it is undermining my underwear."

"And my accessories," chipped in Mr. Grainger.

Captain Peacock stopped in his tracks. Mrs. Slocombe wagged a finger. "You've got to do something, Captain Peacock. You can't let it ride."

"For once, Mrs. Slocombe, I agree with you." said Mr. Grainger. "The girl's sales technique smacks of market trading. She's actually giving ties away."

"And stockings," said Mrs. Slocombe.

Captain Peacock nodded. "Yes, I quite see both your points of view and I shall have to deal with this in my own way."

"Well go on then," said Mrs. Slocombe.

"I'm just thinking about how to handle it."

"That's easy," said Mrs. Slocombe. "Just tell her to push off."

"I will make the decisions," announced Captain Peacock firmly. Adjusting his tie he approached Miss French and gave a polite cough.

"Is everything to your satisfaction, Miss French?"

Miss French looked at her perfume atomizer and gave a quick burst to make sure it was working. "It's all fine," she breathed.

"I must say," continued Captain Peacock, "you caused quite a stir in the trouser department."

Miss French picked up the hem of her skirt. "Yes, this outfit usually gets the men going. It's the gymslip look that does it. That and the stocking tops." She half lifted her leg and snapped her garter. Controlling himself with difficulty, Captain Peacock spoke in an unnaturally deep voice.

"I suppose that if you are that type it does have a certain effect. The stockings seem to have upset the head of the ladies' department."

"Well," said Miss French, glancing towards the stony-faced Mrs. Slocombe, "I suppose that sort of job does attract a rather odd sort of person."

"No, no, no," said Captain Peacock hurriedly. "It's the free sample that's upsetting them." Then he lowered his voice conspiratorially. "I'm having to go through the motions of complaining on their behalf, you understand. Of course, anything you care to display is all right with me."

"Of course," said Miss French, "I understand perfectly."

Captain Peacock reverted to his normal voice. "Well, I think I have made the department's attitude quite clear and there's no more to say." And with a quick wink he turned his back on her and started to walk slowly off.

Miss French then pressed the button on the tape recorder, and her prerecorded voice came bleating out of the loudspeaker. "Hello, you man you, stop just where you are."

Captain Peacock stopped in his tracks as though shot. The voice continued. "Cover your body with me. It was made for you." Captain Peacock raised his eyebrows, totally unaware that Miss French was demonstrating the perfume by squirting it in the air. He started to turn, but the voice stopped him again. "You're sophisticated and dangerous." Captain Peacock gave a slight nod. "You're slightly aloof, yet you have a hint of pulsating virility." Captain Peacock swallowed. "And when you're wearing His, the man-sized perfume…" Turning, Captain Peacock observed Miss French busy picking up bottles and squirting perfume into the atmosphere.

"Very, very nice," he murmured, "I must compliment you on a very arresting sales technique, Miss French."

Miss French shrugged her shoulders. "Well, it's corny, I know, but it works. You wait till you hear what they've cooked up for the girls." She pressed another button on the tape recorder, and as she did so Mr. Humphries walked across the department to adjust the shirt which had come out of the trousers on a dummy. As he bent to tuck it in a very sexy man's voice came from the loudspeaker behind him. "Stay just where you are and don't move a muscle." Mr. Humphries froze on the spot, ears straining anxiously. "If you're looking for a real he-man," continued the sexy voice, "you'll find just what you have been waiting for." Mr. Humphries held on to the dummy for support. "Let me," continued the voice, "caress you and wrap myself round you. You're probably wondering who I am...." Mr. Humphries nodded. Hers, the perfume to attract the perfect Him." Something snapped in Mr. Humphries when he realized the day he had been waiting for hadn't actually arrived. He tottered weakly back to his counter and Mr. Lucas handed him a glass of water, which he drank gratefully.

"Never mind," said Mr. Lucas. At which moment a loud burst of music echoed around the department and from the loudspeaker a bright mid-Atlantic voice announced: "Yes sir, if you are wearing His," Miss French gave a squirt of His perfume, "and you, madam, if you're wearing Hers," Miss French gave a squirt of Hers perfume, "you can be sure of instant results. And remember, this week you get an amazing free gift. For him a tie," Miss French picked up a tie and held it under her chin to demonstrate it, "in these gay, irresistible 'his' colours, and for the lady a fantastic pair of garter grip stockings–they never let you down." Miss French stepped from behind her counter, struck a pose and snapped her garter suggestively. "Keep your chappy happy with something snappy! Get this amazing free gift now with every purchase of His and Hers!!" The customers who had been wandering around the department slowly drifted towards Miss French and gazed at her curiously.

"Today's special price, ladies and gentlemen," said Miss French in a loud voice, "is 85p for a bottle of perfume plus a free tie or a pair of stockings." At the word free, the greedy customers converged on her.

Mr. Grainger marched angrily over to Mrs. Slocombe. "Did you ever see the likes of it in all your born days?"

"I don't think," said Mrs. Slocombe, "that we should take it lying down!"

"Certainly not," and Mr. Grainger beckoned Mr. Humphries and Mr. Lucas over to his side and nodded towards the crowd around the centre stand which seemed to be growing in numbers every moment.

"I expect you've all seen how this lady operates."

"We have indeed," said Mr. Humphries.

"I've even felt it," said Mr. Lucas, feeling his sore cheek.

"She's clearly taking the customers" attention away from our department, and if you will back me up I shall take it to a higher authority."

"I'll back you up," said Mr. Humphries.

Miss Brahms joined in. "It's no good going to Peacock. He'll have his eyes glued on her garters until closing time."

"And," added Mr. Humphries, "it's no good going to Rumbold 'cos he'll back Peacock."

"Men, weak as water," muttered Mrs. Slocombe.

"In that case," said Miss Brahms, "we're lumbered, aren't we?"

Mr. Grainger cast his eyes up towards the fluorescent lighting.

"Will no one rid me of this meddlesome priest?"

"I beg your pardon?" said Mr. Lucas.

"Mr. Grainger," said Mr. Humphries knowledgeably, "is quoting the words of Henry II when he wanted to bump off Becket."

"Becket who?" inquired Miss Brahms.

Mrs. Slocombe turned to her. "Mr. Grainger played Becket in Grace Brothers' production of *Murder in the Cathedral.*"

Mr. Lucas shook his head sadly. "I'm sorry I missed that. I saw Richard Burton playing it in the film, but I'm sure there was no similarity at all."

"As a matter of fact," said Mrs. Slocombe, "Mr. Grainger was very good, in spite of his gammy leg."

Mr. Lucas tried not to smile.

"Becket with a gammy leg?"

"Yes," said Mr. Humphries, "he fell off the Cathedral steps and Mr. Rumbold and the rest of the lads had to murder him in the front row of the stalls. It was very moving."

"Yes," said Mr. Grainger, "it got a very good round of applause."

"Can we get back to our problem," said Miss Brahms impatiently. "What do you suggest we do? Stab her in the staff canteen?"

"I know," said Mr. Lucas, "I've had a brainwave. If I could have fifteen minutes extra in the lunch break, I might be able to carry out a bit of sabotage."

"I didn't hear that," said Mr. Grainger.

"I might," said Mr. Lucas loudly, "be able to carry out a bit of sabotage."

"Yes, yes," said Mr. Grainger, "I mean, I heard it, but I didn't hear it, none of us heard it. Although of course we all heard it."

"I think you put that very clearly," said Mr. Humphries. "To make it even clearer, Mr. Lucas: What Mr. Grainger means is whatever you do, be it on your own head."

"Thanks for your support," said Mr. Lucas.

For the rest of the morning Miss French's stand seemed to be the only one that held any interest for the customers on the first floor. A morose Mr. Grainger watched the scene from his counter and an equally depressed Mrs. Slocombe watched from hers. Captain Peacock found that by standing near the bottom of the steps he could observe Miss French's gartered legs from the rear in a most satisfactory manner. After lunch the scene was the same, customers half a dozen deep crowded round the stand and Miss French gaily went through her sales patter. Mr. Grainger moved anxiously over to Mr. Humphries.

"I thought Mr. Lucas was going to do something! She's still here!"

"Everything's ready," said Mr. Lucas's voice from somewhere nearby. Mr. Grainger glanced round but was unable to see him until a hiss made him look down and he saw Mr. Lucas crouching behind the counter. Mr. Lucas was holding a half bust on which was a bowler hat. He removed the hat to reveal a microphone.

"What are you doing with that?" said Mr. Grainger.

"I've bugged her speaker," said Mr. Lucas. "As soon as she starts the next demonstration, I'll join in!!" and standing up he placed the dummy on the counter.

"I know nothing about it," said Mr. Grainger.

"Neither do I," said Mr. Humphries, "but we're behind you."

At her display stand Miss French pressed the button of her tape recorder.

"Hello, you man you," breathed her voice. A bald male customer on his way to Mr. Grainger's counter stopped in his tracks. "Cover your body with me," murmured Miss French's voice. The man turned and simpered at her. Miss French gave a squirt of perfume in his direction. "You're sophisticated and dangerous," continued the voice. "You're slightly aloof…"

"And—" boomed Mr. Lucas's voice suddenly, "you're as bald as a coot with only one tooth." Miss French stopped in mid squirt and gazed at the tape recorder with horror as the man, deeply vexed, marched angrily off towards the lift. At that moment the sexy male voice murmured. "Madam, just stay where you are and don't move a muscle." A lady in a large, feathered hat stopped and smiled. "She's got a tin bra and starch in her bustle," shouted Mr. Lucas's voice.

"What's going on here?" snapped Captain Peacock.

"Somebody," said Miss French grimly, "has interfered with my equipment." The customers around her were roaring with laughter.

"If you want," breathed the tape recorder's sexy male voice, "a real he-man, you'll find I'm a killer."

"With a face like yours, you'll get Guy the Gorilla," boomed Mr. Lucas.

With that Captain Peacock jabbed his finger at the tape recorder buttons. The tape started to spin round at an ever increasing speed till it snaked out all over the floor.

Mr. Grainger stared horrified. "Just assure me, Mr. Humphries," he murmured, "that we don't know anything about this."

"About what?" said Mr. Humphries with his eyes closed.

A short while later members of both departments found themselves standing in a row in front of Mr. Rumbold, who sat behind his desk with the tips of his fingers pressed together and gazed sternly through his large spectacles. All tried to speak at once.

"Please, please, please," said Mr. Rumbold. "Let's just marshal our facts, and find out precisely why the young lady left. Now first of all, whose finger was on the button that ruined the tape?"

Captain Peacock stepped forward. "It was my finger, sir, but…"

Mr. Rumbold held up his hand. "No, no, no, just the facts. Now how did the other voice come on to it?"

"I was talking through my hat, sir," said Mr. Lucas brightly.

"Perhaps," said Mr. Rumbold, "you could be more explicit, Mr. Lucas."

"I feel I must say," said Mr. Humphries, "that Mr. Lucas's hat was wired for sound."

"I see," said Mr. Rumbold not seeing. "Why?"

Mr. Lucas took a deep breath. "Well, because Mr. Grainger said, "Would somebody rid me of this meddlesome priest.""

Rumbold took out a spotted handkerchief and mopped his brow.

"Did you say that, Mr. Grainger?"

Mr. Grainger shook his head. "Not exactly sir, Henry II did."

"Henry II?" queried Mr. Rumbold. "How old was this hat?"

"It's a new one," said Mr. Lucas.

Mrs. Slocombe elbowed her way forward.

"Perhaps I could explain. Mr. Grainger didn't exactly say it in the play, somebody else said it. You see, he was Becket and got stabbed in the orchestra stalls."

"Which is why he got such a round of applause," said Mr. Humphries.

Mr. Rumbold mopped his brow even more fiercely. "I may be a bit dense, but what has a play about Becket got to do with that girl leaving?"

"Well," said Mr. Lucas, "Mr. Grainger reminded us that Henry II wanted to get rid of Becket and I took the hint because they all wanted to get rid of the girl."

Captain Peacock held up his hand. "I would like to say at this point that I had no hand in the girl's departure."

"I should think not," said Mrs. Slocombe, "the way his eyes were glued to her garters. It was disgusting. And if I may add, it quite ruined sales."

"Hear, hear," said Mr. Grainger.

Mr. Rumbold polished his glasses busily, and placed them back on the end of his nose and looked sternly at the assembled company.

"Well, the pity is that the His and Hers perfume company is a subsidiary of our firm Grace Brothers." He paused significantly. A murmur of surprise went through the ranks.

Mr. Grainger smiled. "Mind you, it was a very attractive smell. I did mention that, didn't I, Mr. Humphries?"

"Now you come to mention it, I think you did. I thought it was most appealing personally. You found it appealing, didn't you, Mr. Lucas?"

"Definitely appealing, Mr. Humphries. Wasn't it appealing, Captain Peacock?"

"Most appealing," said Captain Peacock, "particularly the stockings which I thought were very attractive."

"And," continued Mr. Rumbold sternly, "Young Mr. Grace, the major shareholder, has alerted me to the fact that he will be popping in to see how the campaign is going."

"How unfortunate," said Mr. Humphries, "that the campaign has already gone."

"Exactly," said Mr. Rumbold. "What are we going to do about it?"

"Something fairly immediate," suggested Captain Peacock.

"But what?" asked Mrs. Slocombe.

And there was a pause as they all concentrated very hard on the problem.

The lift bearing Young Mr. Grace stopped at the first floor, and he emerged leaning heavily on his stick, walked slowly to the edge of the steps and stopped in surprise.

Gathered around the His and Hers stand were the members of the ladies' and gentlemen's department of Grace Brothers. Mrs. Slocombe and Miss Brahms were sporting short miniskirts with stockings and brightly coloured garters, on one side of the stand, and on the other Mr. Humphries, Mr. Lucas and Mr. Grainger were sporting His ties while behind the stand Mr. Lucas spoke into a microphone.

"Yes, sir, if you're wearing His, and yes, Madam, if you're wearing Hers, you can be sure of results. Remember that this week only you get an amazing free gift. A tie, yes, a tie in these gay irresistible His colours."

Mr. Grainger and Mr. Humphries waved their ties at the small group of amazed customers that stared back at them.

"And," continued Mr. Lucas, "for the ladies a fantastic pair of garter grip stockings, that never let you down. Keep your chappy happy with something snappy."

Miss Brahms and Mrs. Slocombe snapped their garters with ingratiating grins at the customers and Mr. Lucas continued his patter while Mr. Grace turned around and staggered back weakly into the lift.

"Which floor, sir?"

"Ground," said Mr. Grace. "I think I'm going home early tonight."

CHAPTER

5

Coffee Break

"We are being sacrosanct at Mr. Mash's convenience,"

announced Miss Brahms.

## Coffee Break

MISS BRAHMS PUT THE TAPE MEASURE ROUND MRS. SLOCOMBE'S WAIST.

"Are you ready?"

Mrs. Slocombe exhaled and drew in her stomach. "Now," she hissed through clenched teeth.

"It's…" Miss Brahms peered closely at the tape. "It's 167," she announced.

"Oh," said Mrs. Slocombe aghast, "doesn't it sound a lot in metric."

"Well, whatever it is," said Miss Brahms. "You've just gone up four whatever they are."

"Centrepedes," Mrs. Slocombe said knowledgeably. "We'll have to use them now we are in the Common Market."

"Whatever you call them," continued Miss Brahms, "you're still putting it on."

Mrs. Slocombe sighed. "It's all the Government's fault."

"How do you make that out, Mrs. Slocombe?"

"Well, when they had a sugar shortage, I stocked up so much that if I don't keep eating it, I'll never get rid of it. So of course, I'm eating sugar all the time."

"If you go on with that," said Miss Brahms, "you'll be too fat to get into your store cupboard. Really, Mrs. Slocombe, I do envy you, I wish I could put weight on. I can't understand it, I have a big meal every night."

"I don't know how you can afford it."

"Well, I can't," said Miss Brahms, "I just have to keep going out with men I don't like, just to keep body and soul together."

Mrs. Slocombe pulled a face. "Oh, I couldn't do that, not if I didn't like them."

"Oh, it's easy," chirped Miss Brahms. "You see, I wear my low-cut dress, they have a good look and I have a good nosh."

"These days they expect something afterwards," said Mrs. Slocombe, then as an afterthought added, "Don't they?"

"Oh, yes," said Miss Brahms, "but they don't get it."

Mrs. Slocombe looked puzzled. "Then why do they keep taking you out?"

"Well, it's like a fruit machine," explained Miss Brahms. "Once they've made the investment they keep hoping to hit the jackpot."

A determined look came across Mrs. Slocombe's face and she gave a short laugh.

"They'd have to pull the handle a long time before they got my cherries up," she announced.

Over on the men's counter Mr. Lucas was relating to Mr. Humphries his adventures of the night before.

"Anyway," he confided, "the meat cost me seven pounds. I borrowed a car to take her home so as to be sure of a quick cuddle and what happened…?"

"What happened?" asked Mr. Humphries.

"Half a mile from the house she had her front-door keys out and was fiddling with the passenger-door handle."

"You mean she was keen to make a night of it?" inquired Mr. Humphries.

"No, she was keen to make a run for it. Anyway, I've borrowed the car to take her out again tonight."

"Really," said Mr. Humphries. "What makes you think you'll do any better tonight?"

Mr. Lucas put his hand in his pocket and produced a car-door handle. "I've unscrewed the handle."

Mr. Humphries sighed. "Oh, for the return of the romantic age when one's heart used to pound at the sight of an ankle slipping into a hansom cab. That's all gone now. It's clunk, click, strip off quick." He glanced up as Captain Peacock approached the counter.

"I'm sorry to interrupt this *tête à tête*, but may I inquire the whereabouts of Mr. Grainger?"

"You may indeed," said Mr. Humphries.

"Well, where is he?" asked Captain Peacock impatiently.

"Well," said Mr. Lucas, "I don't like to tell tales out of school, but he's not back from his tea break yet, Captain Peacock."

Captain Peacock nodded and glanced at his watch. "I see," he said. And then a sinister note crept into his voice. "Tell Mr. Grainger I wish to have a word with him as soon as he returns."

"We'll do that," said Mr. Lucas, and at that moment Mr. Grainger appeared round the corner. "Oh, Mr. Grainger," called Mr. Lucas, "are you free?" Mr. Grainger glanced round and made sure there wasn't a customer standing anywhere near, and gave a ponderous nod.

"Yes, I think I'm free at this particular moment in time."

"Oh, good," said Mr. Lucas, "because Captain Peacock just asked me where you were and I, being unable to lie, said you were still having tea, and he said he would like to have a word with you when you returned."

"Thank you, Mr. Lucas. Mr. Humphries?"

"Yes, Mr. Grainger."

"I'd like you to take over from me; I'm just going to have a word with Captain Peacock. It appears he wishes to see me."

Mr. Humphries nodded. "Certainly, Mr. Grainger."

Mr. Lucas nudged him. "Shall I take over from you, Mr. Humphries?"

Mr. Humphries lowered his voice. "Get stuffed, Mr. Lucas."

"Better still, get round the end of the counter with me and we'll hear what excuse Grainger is going to give for being late back from tea."

Mr. Grainger approached Captain Peacock with a benign smile on his face. "You wanted a word with me, Stephen?"

Captain Peacock gazed at him sternly. "Yes, Mr. Grainger," he glanced at his watch pointedly. "It's ten past eleven, you had twenty minutes for your coffee break, your entitlement is fifteen. How do you account for this?"

Mr. Grainger smiled even more benignly.

"I spent a few minutes in the men's room on my way back."

"That," said Captain Peacock, "is not part of your coffee break."

"It's the result of it," Mr. Grainger remarked, his smile disappearing slightly.

Captain Peacock raised his eyebrows. "For five whole minutes?"

"There was a queue," said Mr. Grainger defensively.

Captain Peacock shook his head. "I don't think that Mr. Rumbold will regard that as an adequate excuse."

"You're not going to report me, Stephen, surely?" Mr. Grainger stared at him disbelievingly.

Captain Peacock stared back unsmilingly. "Yes I am, Mr. Grainger."

Mr. Grainger's jaw clamped shut.

"Very well, Captain Peacock," he snapped.

"I'm sorry, Mr. Grainger, but it's part of my job."

"You mean being a sneak."

Captain Peacock put his hand reassuringly on Mr. Grainger's shoulder. "It's not easy for me, you know. On the one hand we have our friendship, and on the other I have my job to do. I have to wear two hats."

Mr. Grainger shrugged the hand off. "You should find no difficulty in that. You're two-faced," and turning on his heel he marched over to Mr. Humphries. "Did you hear that, Mr. Humphries?"

"I did, Mr. Grainger. Now come round this side of the counter and sit down. Mr. Lucas, a glass of water but don't drink it all at once, Mr. Grainger, or you'll need another five minutes off."

For the rest of the morning Mr. Grainger glowered and Captain Peacock pretended not to notice.

After glancing frequently at his watch, Captain Peacock went over to Mrs. Slocombe's counter. "Before you go to lunch, Mrs. Slocombe, I should like to have a word with the floor personnel by the centre stand."

"Is it important?" queried Miss Brahms. "Because I'm dying for my lunch."

Captain Peacock turned round and stared at her. "Miss Brahms, everything I have to say is important," and with that he marched purposefully over to the men's counter, trying to ignore Miss Brahms's hissed "pompous nit." Avoiding Mr. Grainger's baleful glare, Captain Peacock addressed the men's counter. "I'd like a word with the gentlemen's floor personnel before you all go to lunch."

Mr. Grainger spoke through clenched teeth. "I hope it won't take long, Captain Peacock, otherwise Mr. Herbert of Hardware will have pinched my seat."

"Some people," observed Mr. Humphries, "have all the luck."

"I don't suppose you need me," said Mr. Lucas.

"Yes," said Captain Peacock, "juniors as well."

With anxious glances at the department clock indicating that their lunchtime had arrived, the members of both departments gathered in the middle of the floor. Captain Peacock put his hand in his inside pocket and produced a letter ,and from his other pocket a pair of spectacles, which he placed on the end of his nose.

"This won't take a moment" he announced, then coughed and started to read. "From D.M./C.R. to F.W.L. and G.D./S.P. re Tea."

"Excuse me, Captain Peacock," said Mrs. Slocombe, "but what language are you speaking?"

Captain Peacock peered at her over the top of his spectacles. "It simply means, Mrs. Slocombe, from the D.M./C.R.—that's Departmental Manager Cuthbert Rumbold—to the F.W.L. and G.D./S.P.—Floor Walker Ladies' and Gentlemen's Department stroke Stephen Peacock— regarding Tea."

"What does 'T' stand for?" asked Mrs. Slocombe.

"It doesn't stand for anything," said Captain Peacock patiently. "You drink it. T-e-a, tea. They use these initials to save time."

"It doesn't seem to be working very well," said Mr. Lucas.

"It would be," said Captain Peacock, "if people didn't keep asking questions."

"That's simply because people don't know what you are rabbiting on about," said Mrs. Slocombe.

"May I be allowed to continue," said Captain Peacock.

"Yes," said Miss Brahms, "P.C.O."

Captain Peacock looked at her with surprise. "I beg your pardon."

"Please carry on," said Miss Brahms.

"Where was I?" said Captain Peacock.

Mr. Humphries put his hand up. "You'd just got to the part where you were stroking Cuthbert Rumbold."

Captain Peacock took a deep breath. "I see you are…."

Mrs. Slocombe interrupted. "You're not starting those initials again, are you?"

Captain Peacock gave a sigh of exasperation. "Please, Mrs. Slocombe. I see you are concerned about excessively long tea breaks being enjoyed by members of your department under your supervision." He paused. "I must emphasize that the said breaks are limited to fifteen minutes and to ensure no one takes advantage of this arrangement, personnel will be required in future to enter their departure and arrival in a book to be known as the E.L. and T.B. Book—that is the Elevenses Lunches and Tea Break Book."

"It's exhausting just listening to it," said Mrs. Slocombe. Captain Peacock pretended he hadn't heard.

"And," he continued, "visits to the toilet will also be recorded, to which end I have provided a separate book."

"Known," said Mr. Lucas brightly, "as the W. C. Book."

"This," muttered Mr. Grainger, "is outrageous."

"I agree absolutely," said Mrs. Slocombe. "Do you mean we have to clock out and clock in when we go for a cup of coffee?"

Captain Peacock nodded. "That is precisely the idea, Mrs. Slocombe."

"Do you mean," said Miss Brahms, "that every time I want to powder my nose I have got to stick it in a book?"

"That is correct, Miss Brahms."

"Well," persisted Miss Brahms, "what if it's urgent and my biro runs out?"

"If such an eventuality arises," said Captain Peacock, "you will have to get somebody else to do it for you."

Mr. Humphries shook his head. "It's not the same as doing it yourself, you know."

"I mean," said Captain Peacock, "you will have to get somebody else to sign the book."

"I regard this," interrupted Mr. Grainger, "as an intolerable invasion of privacy."

"Yes," said Miss Brahms. "It's just like 1984. Big brother is watching you."

Mrs. Slocombe looked aghast. "They won't be watching us as well, will they?"

Captain Peacock replaced the letter in his pocket. "It only remains for me to say that this comes into effect immediately, and I hope you will all be back to sign the book properly at 2 p.m."

"Here, 'ang on a minute," said Mr. Lucas, "we've spent five minutes listening to you. Don't we get five minutes longer?" Captain Peacock stared at him for a moment before replying.

"I wish," he observed, "that you would think before asking a question like that, Mr. Lucas. The customers will be coming in at two and they will require to be dealt with."

"But what about our five minutes?" said Miss Brahms.

Captain Peacock gazed sternly at her. "Miss Brahms, if you add up all the odd minutes you've taken on top of your normal break, I think the five minutes are more than due to Grace Brothers."

Mr. Lucas looked at his watch. "Six minutes," he announced.

"I suggest," said Mr. Grainger, "that we discuss the whole matter at lunch and bring it up in front of Mr. Rumbold."

In the canteen the clamour and clatter lessened as Mrs. Slocombe, Miss Brahms and the others took their places at the table near the exit, which was always reserved for their department. Mr. Lucas, whose turn it was to take the order, appeared with a large tray on which were a number of plates.

"Who's for 'Cock a Leakey'?"

Mr. Humphries held up his hand.

"Need I ask?" Mr. Lucas placed the plate in front of Mr. Humphries and then removed another plate and put it in front of Miss Brahms.

"Yours is the dumplings, Shirley. It's like taking coals to Newcastle. Whose is the grapefruit cocktail?"

"Mine," said Mrs. Slocombe, "and where's my cherry?"

"I ate it," said Mr. Lucas. "You're supposed to be on a diet."

"I will thank you," said Mrs. Slocombe, "to let me make my own sacrifices." Putting the tray on the table, Mr. Lucas picked up a plate and banged it down in front of Mr. Grainger.

"One open sandwich for you, sir."

Mr. Grainger stared at it with distaste. "I did not ask for an open sandwich."

"I'm sorry," said Mr. Lucas, "but someone nudged my arm and the top fell off. I'll look for it if you like. I think it fell buttered side up."

Mr. Grainger shook his head. "Please don't bother, Mr. Lucas."

Removing the final plate containing salad, he placed it in front of himself and put the tray under his chair. Miss Brahms bent over and looked at his salad, then sniffed it.

"You're brave," she said, "risking a seafood salad."

Mr. Humphries looked at it knowingly and then turned to Mr. Lucas. "Ooh, shellfish, they"re supposed to make you virile. I suppose you chose that because you're having an evening out."

"I don't think," said Mr. Lucas, "that two mussels and a shrivelled-up shrimp will make all that much diff erence to my performance tonight."

Mrs. Slocombe bent forward. "Why, Mr. Lucas, what are you doing?"

"He's got a date tonight," said Mr. Humphries, "with a lady escapologist. He's taken the handle off the passenger door so he can bend her to his will."

Miss Brahms sniffed. "That's why I always carry a tin opener."

"Doesn't that take a long time?" inquired Mrs. Slocombe.

"No," said Miss Brahms, "I just jab 'em in the 'ands with it."

"That's right," said Mr. Lucas, "Mr. Grainger's still got the scars."

Mr. Grainger carefully pulled the crust off his sandwich. "Could we tear ourselves away from sex for a moment and discuss this clocking-in business?"

Mr. Humphries turned to him. "I quite agree with you, Mr. Grainger. It was so humiliating the way you were told off in front of us. Just like a naughty schoolboy."

"I nearly went up to Captain Peacock to say something really sharp and witty to cut him down to size," said Mr. Lucas, tugging with difficulty at the legs on his shrimp.

"Why didn't you?" inquired Mr. Humphries.

Mr. Lucas shook his head. "I couldn't think of anything."

"Well the point is," said Mrs. Slocombe, "what are we going to do about it?"

Mr. Humphries blew silently on his soup. "Well," he observed, "I don't think you and Mr. Grainger should put up with it."

"Let's put it like this," said Mr. Lucas. "If you and Mr. Grainger refuse to sign this book, the company will have to do something about it."

"Yes," said Miss Brahms. "Sack 'em."

Mr. Grainger swallowed the remainder of his sandwich and waved his hand, indicating that he was about to speak. "I think Mrs. Slocombe is right. We should all refuse to sign."

"I agree," said Mr. Lucas. "But I think you two should refuse first."

"I know," said Mrs. Slocombe, "we must all not sign it together."

"Exactly," said Mr. Grainger. "United we stand, divided we fall."

"I wish I'd thought of that," said Mr. Humphries.

At two o'clock Captain Peacock stood in the middle of the floor gazing at his watch. At one minute past two he was still gazing at it and striding over to the men's counter he opened the new black book, took out his pen and held it poised. A ping indicated the arrival of the lift and from it stepped the members of both departments. Mr. Grainger looked anxiously at Captain Peacock and paused.

"Go on," said Mrs. Slocombe. And reluctantly Mr. Grainger led the party down the steps.

"Mr. Grainger," called Captain Peacock.

"Er yes, Captain Peacock," said Mr. Grainger.

"Would you come over here a moment?"

"Go on," said Mrs. Slocombe, "we're all behind you. Off you go."

Mr. Grainger slowly approached Captain Peacock, who made great play of glancing at his watch and then at the book and writing deliberately and mouthing the words he intoned. "Mr. Grainger returned from lunch at 14:03. Now would you just sign against this entry, please."

Mr. Grainger looked behind him for support. Mrs. Slocombe shook her head, indicating that he shouldn't sign. Mr. Grainger took a deep breath. "I'm sorry, Captain Peacock, but I refuse to sign your book."

Captain Peacock glanced at his watch again. "I will ask you one more time, Mr. Grainger. You have returned from lunch at 14:04. Will you now sign, please."

Mr. Grainger stood his ground. "Again, I shall refuse, Captain Peacock."

Captain Peacock started to write in the book speaking as he did so. "Mr. Grainger refused point blank to sign book." He paused, then added "twice" and with that he snapped the book shut and tucked it under his arm.

"Mr. Grainger, I shall now report your action to Mr. Rumbold." Turning, he started to walk towards Mr. Rumbold's office.

"Captain Peacock," called Mr. Grainger, "the others have refused to sign as well." Captain Peacock turned and Mr. Grainger rather pathetically pointed to the group standing by the bottom of the steps.

"On the contrary," said Captain Peacock shaking his head, "I have only asked you, Mr. Grainger, and you have refused, and you will be reported."

Mr. Grainger's legs seemed to give way and he staggered towards the counter.

"A glass of brandy for Mr. Grainger," called Mr. Lucas.

Mr. Humphries rushed up and took him by the elbow. "Mr. Grainger, you were marvellous, the way you stood up to him."

"Yes," added Mr. Lucas, "we'll always remember you for that, sir."

"But," said Mr. Grainger weakly, "we were all supposed to be standing up to him."

Mrs. Slocombe looked at him admiringly. "I hope I am as brave as that when it comes to my turn."

"But," said Mr. Grainger, "it *was* your turn, Mrs. Slocombe, it was all our turns. You should all sign something to say you are not signing it."

"Don't you worry," said Mr. Humphries. "We're all behind you."

"Of course we are," said Mrs. Slocombe. "We're all in this together."

"But," said Mr. Lucas, "you're in it a bit deeper."

The men's department telephone started to ring. Mr. Humphries walked quickly behind the counter and took it off the hook.

"Men's wear," he announced. Then, glancing over at Mr. Grainger, "Yes, he's here." He paused for a moment and listened. "I see." Hanging up the phone he announced that Mr. Grainger was required in Mr. Rumbold's office at once.

"Good luck," said Miss Brahms.

"And remember," said Mrs. Slocombe, "that we're all behind you."

A rather pathetic expression crossed Mr. Grainger's face. "Can't we all go in together, you know, united we stand, divided we fall?"

"I'm afraid," said Mr. Lucas, "they only sent for the ringleader."

"But," spluttered Mr. Grainger, "I'm not the ringleader. I just happened to be first out of the lift."

The telephone rang again and once again Mr. Humphries ran quickly behind the counter to answer it. "Men's wear....No, sir, he's still here....Yes, sir." Hanging up the phone he turned. "Mr. Rumbold's furious. You're keeping him waiting."

Mr. Lucas took Mr. Grainger by the elbow and steered him in the direction of Mr. Rumbold's office. "Better hurry, Mr. Grainger, you don't want to get the reputation of always being late."

Mr. Grainger paused on his way and turned towards them.

"You will all back me up, won't you?"

"If you don't look sharp," said Mrs. Slocombe, "you won't be here for us to back up."

As the phone started to ring again, Mr. Grainger broke into a run towards Mr. Rumbold's office.

"I think Mr. Grainger went too far in defying Captain Peacock like he did," said Mrs. Slocombe.

"Yes," said Miss Brahms, "but we all agreed we weren't going to sign."

"That's true, and we wouldn't have signed the first time we were asked, as a protest, but we would have signed the second time."

"You're right," said Mr. Humphries, "he went too far, but of course I was still behind him."

"Oh yes," said Mr. Lucas, "we're all behind him, but," he added, "not too close."

Mr. Rumbold sat at his desk. Next to him sat his secretary, notebook and pencil poised. Mr. Rumbold looked at her severely. "Miss Ainsworth, is your book ready?"

Miss Ainsworth nodded.

"Good. I shall want a verbatim report of everything that's said at this meeting."

There was a timid knock at the door.

"Come in," shouted Mr. Rumbold sternly.

The anxious face of Mr. Grainger appeared round the side of the door and then the anxious look broke into an ingratiating smile.

"I believe," he murmured, "you wanted a word with me, Mr. Rumbold."

"I have been waiting five minutes to have a word with you," snapped Mr. Rumbold.

"I came as quickly as I could," Mr. Grainger assured him. "I was in the middle of an inside leg when you called." Mr. Rumbold pointed to the black book on the desk. "Do you recognize this book?"

Mr. Grainger approached it as though it were some poisonous insect, and peered at it. "Yes, I think I do."

Mr. Rumbold glanced at his secretary. "Take everything down, Miss Ainsworth."

Miss Ainsworth glanced down at her shorthand notes. "I've taken everything down." Then she started to read: "Knock, knock…come in…I believe you wanted a word with me, Mr. Rumbold…I have been waiting five minutes to have a word with you…I came as quickly as I could. I was in the middle of an inside leg…do you recognize this book?…yes, I think I do…take everything down, Miss Ainsworth…I've taken everything down."

Mr. Rumbold gave an exasperated sigh. "Miss Ainsworth, you don't put down what you say."

"Yes, Mr. Rumbold, shall I put that down?"

"No, no, no. Let us start again."

"Knock, knock," intoned Miss Ainsworth, "come in…."

Mr. Rumbold held up his hand to cut her off. "Please, Miss Ainsworth, be quiet. Now, Mr. Grainger, did you refuse to sign this book?"

"We all refused," said Mr. Grainger.

"I'm afraid that's not true," said the voice of Captain Peacock from behind him. "I only asked Mr. Grainger." Mr. Grainger turned, startled to see Captain Peacock sitting in a chair in the corner of the room.

"Sorry, Stephen," he said, "I didn't see you there. Please forgive me."

"That's quite all right, Mr. Grainger. As I said, I have had to report you."

"The rest of the department were all behind me," said Mr. Grainger defensively.

"I see," said Mr. Rumbold, "led by you. I think it's clear, Peacock, that we must make an example here."

"I'm afraid so," said Captain Peacock.

"One rotten apple," continued Mr. Rumbold, "can spoil the whole barrel." Captain Peacock stood up.

"I think I should like to say in Mr. Grainger's defence that he has never been a rotten apple."

Mr. Grainger turned. "Thank you, Captain Peacock, I am most grateful for that."

"Until," continued Captain Peacock, "today."

Mr. Grainger's smile of gratitude disappeared as there was a sharp knock on the door.

"Come in," said Mr. Rumbold.

"I'm in," said Mr. Mash, peering round the side of the door with a cup of tea.

"I wish," said Mr. Rumbold, "that you would wait until I have said 'come in.' I'm having an important meeting."

"Shall I go out again?" inquired Mr. Mash.

"No, no," said Mr. Rumbold, "put it down."

"Shall I put that down?" said Miss Ainsworth.

"No," said Mr. Rumbold, "I don't want that put down."

Mr. Mash, who had been about to put the tea down, picked it up again. "What shall I do with it then?" he inquired.

"Put it down," said Mr. Rumbold crossly.

"I thought," said Miss Ainsworth, "that you said don't put it down."

"I don't want you to put down 'put it down.' "

During this exchange Mr. Mash waved the tea up and down like a yo-yo, and when he became exasperated he slammed it down on the desk.

"I'm gonna put it down," he announced, "and as far as I'm concerned, you can stick it up."

"Miss Ainsworth," said Captain Peacock, "don't put that down."

Mr. Mash slammed the door loudly as he exited.

Mr. Rumbold produced a small bottle from his drawer, took out a pill and placed one on the end of his tongue and swallowed it with a gulp of tea.

"Now where were we?" he said in a low, controlled voice.

Miss Ainsworth glanced at her pad. "Never been a rotten apple in the barrel until today.' "

Mr. Grainger winced.

"Ah yes," nodded Mr. Rumbold. "Well, for the four minutes' unauthorized absence I am deducting 25p from your pay packet plus another 25p for refusing to sign the book."

"Could I," said Mr. Grainger, hopefully, "sign it now and save 25p?" Mr. Rumbold opened the book, and stabbed at it with his finger to indicate his point.

"I'm afraid not. Captain Peacock's remarks now occupy the place where you were supposed to sign. That is all; the matter is closed." To make the matter even more closed, he shut the book.

"Thank you," said Mr. Grainger, who walked leaden-footed towards the door, then turned. "But what about the others?"

"That's all," said Captain Peacock, "the matter is closed."

"Well," said Mr. Grainger, "I suppose that's a relief." Closing the door quietly behind him, he departed.

"I hope," said Captain Peacock, "you don't think I was sneaking, sir, but you know my feelings on discipline."

"That is all," said Mr. Rumbold, "the matter is closed."

"Yes, sir," said Captain Peacock.

An extraordinary sight met Captain Peacock's eyes when he returned to the department: Mrs. Slocombe and Miss Brahms were out of their territory and standing by the men's counter talking to Mr. Grainger. To Captain Peacock's surprise Mr. Mash was also there, nodding in agreement to what was being said.

"I think," said Mrs. Slocombe, "it's disgusting you having to pay 50p. I don't think you should stand for it."

"I think," said Miss Brahms, "you should have stood up for yourself and told them where to get off."

"Yes," added Mr. Lucas. "We were right behind you, Mr. Grainger."

Mr. Grainger sipped a glass of water that Mr. Humphries handed him. "I would prefer to forget it, it was a most unpleasant experience. I haven't been carpeted, since I was a junior."

"I think," said Mr. Humphries, "that we should all chip in and pay Mr. Grainger's fine. It's only 10p a head."

Mrs. Slocombe started counting on her fingers.

"Well," she said. "He was fined 25p for being late and 25p for refusing to sign the book. And we were only supporting him for not signing, so," she said, "we should only pay half."

"'Ang on, 'ang on, 'ang on, " said Mr. Mash. "There's a principle involved here," and elbowing his way forward he spoke in a loud authoritative voice. "Our brother here is being victimized. I refer of course to Brother Grainger here, "'cos he stood up to his rightful rights. It's up to us, brothers, to stand up for him. That's what brothers are for."

"Mr. Mash," said Mrs. Slocombe, "it has nothing to do with you, so please get back to the basement." Mr. Mash, to her surprise, stood his ground.

"It has everything to do with me, Brother Slocombe," he announced. "I am the shop steward and in that capacity, I am convening an emergency meeting in accordance with section 25 of the rule book."

Mr. Grainger looked surprised. "Can we do that?" he asked.

"I have done, brother," said Mr. Mash.

"But," said Miss Brahms, "what about the customers? There's somebody standing by my counter now."

"They," announced Mr. Mash, "will just have to wait. It all comes to a halt when the brothers say so. And I've just said so."

"Oh," said Mrs. Slocombe, "it sounds like the Mafia or the cosy nostril."

"Are you free, Mr. Grainger?" called Captain Peacock.

"Er…coming, Captain Peacock," said Mr. Grainger.

"Do not move, brother," said Mr. Mash putting a restraining hand on his arm.

"But," said Mr. Grainger, "Captain Peacock called. I…."

Mr. Mash shook his head. "He cannot touch us once I have convened an emergency meeting. We are sacrosanct."

"Oh, is that true?" said Mr. Humphries.

"That is true, Brother Humphries," said Mr. Mash.

Mr. Humphries smiled happily.

"Brother Humphries. Oh, it does bring you together when you have a Union."

Captain Peacock's voice rose and took on an impatient note. "I called you, Mr. Grainger."

"I have been convened," said Mr. Grainger defiantly.

Captain Peacock strode over. "I beg your pardon?"

"We are being sacrosanct at Mr. Mash's convenience." announced Miss Brahms.

Captain Peacock pointed towards the exit. "Get off the floor, Mr. Mash. Your place is in the cellar."

Mr. Mash pulled up Mr. Grainger's chair and stood on it.

"Unless," he announced in a loud voice, "you want everybody out from here to Harrods, I wouldn't use that tone of voice, Peacock. Now brothers, we are here to consider the case of Mr. Grainger."

Captain Peacock turned and glowered.

"So you're behind this, Grainger?"

"No, no," said Mr. Grainger hurriedly, "we're all behind it, aren't we?"

"Well, let's see how it goes first," said Mr. Lucas.

"As I see it," said Mr. Mash, "we have two things to decide. What we want and how we are going to get it. That's how the Union works, brothers."

"Well," said Miss Brahms, uncertainly. "I'm not sure what we want."

"In that case," said Mr. Mash, "it's lucky you've got me here. Firstly, we want to remove the stigmata attached to Brother Grainger here."

"Oh," said Mrs. Slocombe, "doesn't it sound just like *The Exorcist?*"

"Secondly," shouted Mr. Mash, "on the time element, we want to be free and unrestricted in the cloakroom."

Mr. Humphries shot up his hand. "I'll second that."

Mr. Mash stepped from the chair on to the counter and held out his arms. "Thirdly, a reappraisal of the whole archaic coffee-break system. Bringin' it in line with current Industrial Practice."

"What does that mean?" asked Miss Brahms.

Mr. Mash gazed down at her. "It means, Brother Brahms, that unless the management meets our demands, we'll take action. And if that don't work, we'll escalate."

"Hear! hear!" shouted Mr. Lucas.

"It's like Hyde Park Corner," said Mr. Humphries.

Again Captain Peacock pointed to the exit. "Mr. Mash, you've wasted enough time. Everybody back to work."

Mr. Mash wagged a warning finger at Captain Peacock. "You are out or order, Brother Peacock, and I don't want to have to reprimand you again."

Captain Peacock's eyebrows shot up with surprise. He started to speak but Mr. Mash interrupted him. "Now as I see it, brothers, the main point is that we must hold out for travelling time, to and from tea breaks. Tea should start not when you leave here," he clapped his clenched fist into his open palm to emphasize his point, "not when you get into the life, not when you queue at the counter, not even when you pay for it. Tea should start when you sit down and dip your biscuit in the cup."

"Blimey," said Miss Brahms, "don't he speak well."

"I'm now," shouted Mr. Mash, "about to put the motion on the table."

"But," said Mrs. Slocombe, "some of the phrases are strange."

"And I also move," continued Mr. Mash, "that this meeting authorizes me to put our demands before the management and to form a strike committee with *carte blanche* to take industrial action. 'Ands up those for the motion." There was a unanimous show of hands, except those of Captain Peacock which remained rigidly at his side.

"All agains?" inquired Mr. Mash.

Captain Peacock's right arm shot up in the air.

Mr. Mash shook his head. "You can't vote. You ain't got no standing."

"I happen," said Captain Peacock grimly, "to be a member of the Union."

"In that case," asked Mr. Mash, "where is you Union Card?"

Captain Peacock put his hand inside his breast pocket, his face fell.

"I'm afraid it's at home."

"Then," said Mr. Mash triumphantly, "that makes you out of order."

"Just a minute," said Captain Peacock, "have they got their cards?"

Mr. Mash gave a short laugh. "That is beside the point, brother."

"I move," continued Captain Peacock doggedly, "that we all show our cards."

Again Mr. Mash moved his admonishing finger. "You can't move anything unless you can show your card, and you ain't got no card to show, which means of course that the motion is carried unanimously." Cupping his hands he blew a raspberry in the direction of Captain Peacock.

Five minutes later a grim-faced Mr. Rumbold was standing facing Mr. Mash across his desk.

"I can tell you now, Mr. Mash," he announced firmly, "that there's absolutely no chance of us at Grace Brothers acceding to your demands."

Mr. Mash stared back at him belligerently. "Is that your final word, Brother Rumbold?"

"Absolutely. The management stands firm by its agreement off 1928."

Mr. Mash leant forward, placing both hands on the desk. "Are you saying, brother, that henceforth there is no point in our having meaningful discussions and the helpful exchange of views?"

"None whatsoever," confirmed Mr. Rumbold.

"In that case," said Mr. Mash, "you can get stuffed."

Hurriedly, Mr. Rumbold turned to Miss Ainsworth. "Don't put that down."

With a purposeful stride, Mr. Mash marched back into the department.

"Right, that's it," he announced in a loud voice. "Although the management kept me waiting nearly three hours to see them. Finally we had a confrontation, and from now on it's go slow from this moment in time."

"But," complained Mr. Grainger, "we're due to go home in three minutes."

"Never mind that," said Mr. Mash. "You will go slow right up to the bell."

"It won't be easy," said Mr. Humphries, "without any customers."

Mr. Mash climbed back on his chair. "In my official capacity as Shop Steward, I am ordering you to go slow." Stepping down he marched briskly across the department to Mrs. Slocombe as she started to put covers on the counter dummies.

"Hold that, Mrs. Slocombe, it's a go slow from now on."

"Don't be silly," said Mrs. Slocombe. "If we don't put these covers on I'll miss my bus."

"In that case," said Mr. Mash, "you'll have to leave 'em."

Ignoring him Mrs. Slocombe continued with her task. "I can't sell smutty undies."

"Of course you can't," said Mr. Mash. "And so the management through their intractable attitude will lose money."

"And I shall lose my commission," said Mrs. Slocombe.

"I'm afraid, brothers, we shall all have to make sacrifices."

Mrs. Slocombe shook her head. "Not just before my summer holidays we don't."

The sound of the floor bell announced it was closing time. There was a sudden rush to collect overcoats and hats.

"Don't forget, brothers," shouted Mr. Mash, "as soon as you arrive in the morning it's go slow."

Mr. Grainger wearily put on his overcoat helped by Mr. Humphries, who placed his homburg on his head. Then he walked up to Captain Peacock and shook his head.

"I don't like these Union things," he announced. "It all seems to be getting out of hand."

Captain Peacock stared at him unsympathetically. "Well," he observed, "you started it, brother."

Watched by a baleful-eyed Captain Peacock, the go slow continued all through the next morning, although in Mr. Grainger's case it was not so noticeable.

Lunchtime found Mr. Mash sitting at the head of the department table in the canteen with his mouth full of steak and kidney pie.

"I'm really proud of you, brothers. The go slow this morning was one hundred percent effective. I think you've put the wind up the management."

Mrs. Slocombe gazed at him anxiously. "If you don't go slow with that, Mr. Mash, you'll have the wind up somewhere else."

Mr. Grainger toyed unenthusiastically with his plaice and chips. "I know we are all behind the Unions, Mr. Humphries, but I think ten minutes is a long time to spend on an inside leg. Especially, Mr. Humphries," he added, "as the customer only came in for a pair of gloves."

Mrs. Slocombe chipped in. "My end has been a disaster."

"It always was," said Mr. Lucas.

"I'll ignore that," said Mrs. Slocombe, "as we're supposed to be united in a common cause. Otherwise, Brother Lucas, I would clip you round the ear."

"I had this lady Russian athlete come in for a bra," said Miss Brahms. "I took so long fitting it, she left me her address in Vladivostok."

"Well, brothers," said Mr. Lucas, "I think we must face up to it. It hasn't been a great success. With the few customers we get, it's very hard for anybody to know we're going slow."

Mr. Mash banged his fist on the table and made the crockery jump. "In that case, brothers, we shall have to escalate."

"How?" inquired Mr. Humphries.

Mr. Mash wiped a large piece of bread round his plate and stuck it in his mouth.

"Well, brothers," he said, indistinctly, "one way to bring our grievances to the notice of the hierarchy is to bung up the loos with plaster of paris."

"Isn't that," said Mrs. Slocombe, "rather cutting off our noses to spite our faces?"

"If that fails," continued Mr. Mash, "we can go lightning."

"What's that?" asked Miss Brahms.

Mr. Mash waved his fork at her. "You just drop everything without warning."

Mr. Lucas nodded approvingly. "I'm going to enjoy you going lightning, Shirley."

Mrs. Slocombe shook her head. "I don't think I like the sound of any of this; we all seem to be getting so militant and extremist."

"I can smell Karl Marx," said Mr. Grainger.

"Which table is he sitting at?" asked Miss Brahms.

"I mean," said Mr. Grainger, "I can smell reds under the beds."

"There are no reds under my bed, Mr. Grainger," said Mrs. Slocombe.

"Nor mine," added Mr. Humphries, "and I look every night."

Mr. Lucas snapped his fingers. "Think I've got it. Let's hijack the lift and keep Rumbold inside until he accedes to our demands."

Mrs. Slocombe popped a sweetener in her coffee. "Miss Brahms and I are not prepared to be cooped up for days in a lift with half a dozen men, except," she added, "as a last resort."

"Well," said Mr. Mash, "there's only one thing to do, and that is to bung up the loos followed by a lightning sit-in."

"What?" said Miss Brahms. "In the loos?"

"No, no," said Mr. Mash, "on the floor, and if that don't work, it's a walkout and pickets."

Mr. Grainger carefully folded his paper napkin and put it in his pocket. "I have been here for thirty-five years, and I'm not going to walk out now."

"Blimey," said Mr. Mash, "we're only doing it for you, brother."

Mr. Grainger turned to him in surprise. "What?" he spluttered.

"Yes," added Mrs. Slocombe. "If you hadn't been so insufferably rude to Captain Peacock, we wouldn't be in this mess."

"Well, I think," said Mr. Humphries, "that we should all vote on it."

Mr. Mash stood up. "Brothers," he intoned, "there is no vote needed. You gave me *carte blanche* by a democratic majority. I'm now going down to the shop floor on behalf of Brother Grainger to confront the management." And with a purposeful stride he headed for the exit watched by Mr. Grainger.

"I can see it now," said Mr. Lucas. "A bronze statue of Mr. Grainger nude on a pedestal in Hyde Park taking an inside leg, with the inscription 'To a hero of the Revolution.'"

"I don't think we have time for coffee," said Mr. Grainger, rising hurriedly and following Mr. Mash.

On the department floor Mr. Rumbold paced up and down frowning.

"It's not good enough," he snapped, then glancing at the department clock, "Three minutes past two and no sign of anybody."

Captain Peacock removed the black book from under his arm, and the propelling pencil from his outside breast pocket and pressed the button ready for action with a grim look on his face.

"I'm afraid, sir." he remarked, "that all the old values are disappearing. Is this what we fought for at Dunkirk?"

Mr. Rumbold stopped in his stride. "Were you at Dunkirk, Peacock?"

Captain Peacock shook his head. "No, sir. I just wondered if this is what the people who were at Dunkirk were fighting for."

Mr. Rumbold looked puzzled. "We don't have anybody here who fought at Dunkirk, do we?"

"Never mind, sir," said Captain Peacock. "Ah, here are the culprits now."

Members of the two departments followed Mr. Mash out of the lift. Halfway down the steps Mr. Mash stopped and holding out his arms caused the others to halt. In a loud voice he announced: "As democratically elected spokesman I have to tell you that unless you meet our demands, we are all out."

Mr. Rumbold walked to the bottom of the steps.

"The management," announced Mr. Rumbold, "represented by myself will not negotiate under intimidation."

Mr. Mash walked down two steps until he was nose to nose with Mr. Rumbold. "I'm not intimidating you, mate. If I was intimidating you, you would have a bunch of fives right up your hooter."

Mr. Rumbold glanced over his shoulder. "Do not let me lose my temper, Captain Peacock."

Captain Peacock shook his head. "No, do please carry on, sir."

Mr. Rumbold turned a bright shade of pink. "I'm like a wild animal when I am roused," he announced.

Mr. Mash's voice rose. "Did you hear that, brothers? That was a definite threat."

A ping indicated the arrival of the second lift and from it staggered Young Mr. Grace leaning on his stick, his wizened face wreathed in smiles.

"Good afternoon, everybody," he called in a weak quavering voice.

Automatically everybody switched their smiles on.

"Good afternoon, Mr. Grace," they chorused.

"I'm so glad you are here," wavered Mr. Grace, "I've got a copy of that memo of yours, Rumbold, about tea breaks." Mr. Lucas stepped forward and, taking Mr. Grace's elbow, helped him slowly down the marble steps.

Mr. Rumbold cleared his throat.

"Well, further to that, Mr. Grace, sir, the workers are now demanding that their tea break shouldn't commence until they have their coffee in their hands."

"And what's more," shouted Mr. Mash, "we'll get it, we're all behind Mr. Grainger in this."

"It's not just me," spluttered Mr. Grainger nervously backing away. "It's all of us."

"But mainly Mr. Grainger," added Mr. Lucas.

"Up brothers," shouted Mr. Mash, then turning back to Mr. Grace he announced, "we are not all travelling up and down in your rotten old lift, to get to your rotten old canteen in our own time."

Young Mr. Grace seemed quite unperturbed by the outburst.

"Quite right, Mr....er...um...er...."

"Mash from the cellar," announced Mr. Mash.

"Ah yes, quite right, Mr. Mash. The lifts aren't up to it, besides my tea break only starts when my tea is handed to me. And what's good enough for me is good enough for you."

Mr. Mash turned round and raised his arms triumphantly.

"That's it, brothers, we've won," and giving a 'V' sign to Captain Peacock and Mr. Rumbold, he announced, "That's the power of the Unions, brothers."

Mr. Grainger gave a sigh of relief. "You know," he observed, "I'm very glad I held out as long as I did."

Mr. Humphries patted him on the shoulder. "Well done, Mr. Grainger."

"We were always behind you," said Mrs. Slocombe.

"In future," said Mr. Grace, "your tea will be handed to you," and glancing over his shoulder he called, "Goddard."

The equally aged chauffeur in his green peaked uniform cap and coat pushed out a trolley with two urns perched on top. One marked coffee and the other tea. Mr. Grace pointed at it with his walking stick.

"There we are, now you won't have to leave the department at all. Carry on, everybody, you've all done very well." And assisted by Mr. Lucas he climbed back up the steps into the lift.

There was a moment's silence while everybody looked at the trolley, then Mrs. Slocombe shook her head sadly. "I used to enjoy my walk to the canteen."

"I even used to enjoy the lift journey," remarked Mr. Grainger moodily.

"And," said Mr. Humphries with a note of disappointment in his voice, "I won't see my friend behind the sandwich counter. The tall fair one that always gives me a double helping of everything."

Mr. Mash tried to keep the enthusiasm in his voice but without much success. "Never mind, brothers," he cried, "we've won a great victory."

"And," added Mr. Lucas bitterly, "lost our tea breaks."

Mr. Mash stared at their ungrateful faces and tried to think, unsuccessfully, of something to say.

"Mr. Mash," Captain Peacock called out. Mr. Mash turned and as he did so Captain Peacock cupped his hands and blew him a loud raspberry.

CHAPTER

# The Hand of Fate

"I sometimes wonder," Mr. Rumbold murmured, "if sitting
in this office I'm missing something."

# The Hand of Fate

MRS. SLOCOMBE GAZED DISAPPROVINGLY AT THE ANCIENT PORTABLE mirror on her counter.

"It's no good, Miss Brahms," she said, "I'll have to get these cracks filled in."

Miss Brahms, who had just arrived, was in the act of taking her coat off. She gazed at the mirror and nodded. "Either that, Mrs. Slocombe, or we could ask for a new one. It must have been here for donkeys' years."

"I'm referring, Miss Brahms, to the cracks in my face. Although we are superior to men in many ways, it's unfortunate that we don't seem to wear as well."

"Nonsense," said Miss Brahms encouragingly. "I mean, Captain Peacock must be your age and he looks much older."

Mrs. Slocombe shook her head. "With men," she remarked, "it's laughter lines, but with women it's old age."

"Well," said Miss Brahms, "I think you're only as old as you feel. You could easily pass for…," she paused. "Early forties," she said after some consideration.

"Thank you, Miss Brahms," said Mrs. Slocombe coldly, "that will be all." Then holding up her arms she exclaimed, "What on earth is that?"

Miss Brahms winced at the metallic clanking that was getting nearer every moment. Suddenly it stopped.

"'Ere," hissed the unmistakable uncouth tones of Mr. Mash. Turning, Mrs. Slocombe observed Mr. Mash decorated like a Christmas tree with buckets on each arm and a bunch clutched across his middle. Mrs. Slocombe turned her back on him.

"Don't answer to ''ere,' Mr. Mash."

"In that case," said Mr. Mash, "Oi," and blew a loud raspberry.

"I think," said Miss Brahms, "you were better off with ''ere!'"

With a long-suffering sigh, Mrs. Slocombe turned. "Mr. Mash, what is it?"

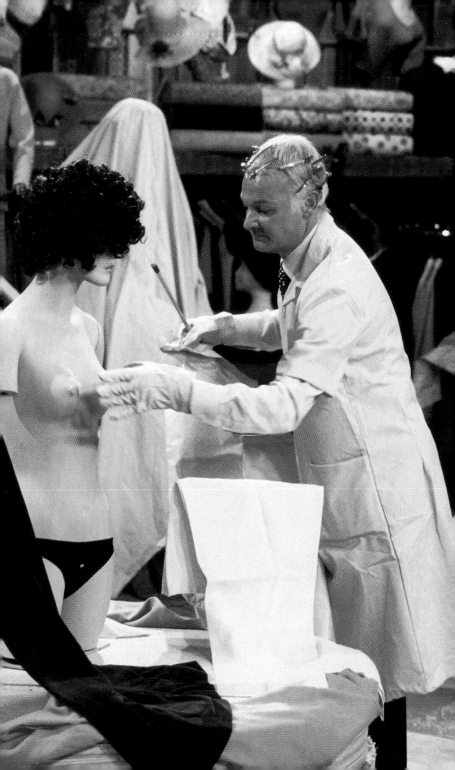

"Did you," said Mr. Mash, stepping forward with a lot of clanking, "put an order in for twenty-seven galvanized buckets?" Mrs. Slocombe gave a disdainful sniff. "Mr. Mash, what would I be doing in my department with twenty-seven galvanized buckets? This is ladies' wear."

"Well," said Mr. Mash, "you could be milking a Jersey."

The noisy clanking had attracted the attention of Captain Peacock, who strode hurriedly over.

"Mr. Mash," he called, "what on earth are you doing with those buckets?"

Mr. Mash turned to face him. "Morning, Captain Peacock. Sorry I can't salute you, sir."

Captain Peacock raised his eyebrows. "Have you taken leave of your send, Mr. Mash?"

Mr. Mash shook his head. "No sir, I'm just trying to ascertain who required these galvanized buckets?"

Captain Peacock glanced at Mrs. Slocombe sympathetically.

"I'm sorry about this," he said. "Mr. Mash, it's obviously nobody on this floor. Now be about your business."

Mr. Mash stood his ground with an aggressive clank. "Well," he grumbled, "hardware denies all knowledge of them."

"In that case," said Captain Peacock, "go and try musical instruments."

Mr. Mash grinned. "'Ere, that's not a bad idea, Captain," he said, and banging the buckets together he broke into strains of "Any old iron, any old iron" as he marched off.

"That'll do," shouted Captain Peacock at the departing figure, who completely ignored him as he headed for the main staircase. "Not that way!" shouted Captain Peacock. "Use the goods lift." Mr. Mash stopped to turn and gave an aggressive clank.

"Ain't working, Captain Peacock. I can use the public lift if you prefer it. Of course it will be a bit of a shock to our toffee-nosed customers to see a poor worker in his overalls carrying out his everyday lowly duties."

"That'll do," said Captain Peacock hurriedly. "Use the main staircase and be quick about it."

Turning and making as much noise as possible, Mr. Mash clanked out of sight.

Miss Brahms picked up a crocheted beret, and held it up towards Mrs. Slocombe.

"What price do I put on these 'ere berets?"

"Where did you get that from?" asked Mrs. Slocombe.

Miss Brahms pointed to a cardboard box under the counter. "I found it under here when I was clearing out last night." Mrs. Slocombe picked up the beret and gazed at it and gave it a sharp whack producing a cloud of dust. She nodded. "I thought so; we've had these for years. They were a special offer for the jubilee."

Miss Brahms picked up another beret and gazed at the label. "It says here, as worn by Princess Margaret Rose."

Mrs. Slocombe smiled reminiscently. "Oh yes. They were very popular at the time. I remember now."

"If they were so popular," remarked Miss Brahms, "how is it we've got so many left?"

"Ah," said Mrs. Slocombe. "Well, you see, they were only popular with Princess Margaret Rose."

Miss Brahms looked at her beret very doubtfully. "What shall I put on it then?"

Mrs. Slocombe pointed. "It's got a ticket on it; what does it say?"

"Two and eleven pence three farthing," Miss Brahms announced, peering at the small yellow ticket.

Mrs. Slocombe shook her head. "We can't put that on."

Miss Brahms frowned. "Now how much is that in new pence?"

"Well," said Mrs. Slocombe, "there's been devaluation, inflation, decimalization, purchase tax and V.A.T." She thought for a moment. Giving up the mathematics she said, "Put 'unrepeatable at 40p.'"

Miss Brahms pointed to the label again. "What about the Margaret Rose bit?"

"You can take that out, Miss Brahms, and we'll put a little notice up: 'As worn by Princess Anne at Badminton.'"

"You couldn't wear these playing badminton," scoffed Miss Brahms.

"Oh give over," said Mrs. Slocombe. "Just write the card out." Miss Brahms picked up a piece of cardboard and took a marking pen out of the drawer as the lift doors opened and a tall, horsy-looking lady in a tweed jacket and skirt and stout walking shoes appeared and gazed round anxiously. Captain Peacock's eagle eyes spotted her immediately and with an ingratiating smile walked up the steps to stall any possibility of her re-entering the lift before she entered the department.

"Good morning, madam. Are you being served?"

"Er, no," explained the lady. "I'm really in two minds as to whether to look at hats or not."

"If I may say so," said Captain Peacock, "Madam has a very good face for a hat."

"Er, thank you," said the lady uncertainly.

"And," said Captain Peacock taking her by the elbow and leading her down the steps and towards Mrs. Slocombe's counter, "you will find a great selection of hats in Mrs. Slocombe's department. Mrs. Slocombe, are you free?"

"Free," shouted Mrs. Slocombe and extending her hand, "over here, madam, this way if you please." Her fate sealed, the lady walked over to the counter.

"And what is it to be?" said Mrs. Slocombe smiling expectantly.

"A hat," said Captain Peacock. At that moment Miss Brahms finished writing her card and propped it up on the counter next to a row of crocheted hats.

"Perhaps," said Mrs. Slocombe, "you'd like to try on one of these Princess Anne hats that have just come in."

"Yes, we've been expecting those," said Captain Peacock.

"I'll deal with this, thank you," said Mrs. Slocombe, picking up a hat and handing it to the lady. "The mirror's here, madam."

The customer picked up the hat and pulled it down over her forehead and gazed at the effect in the mirror uncertainly. Mrs. Slocombe gave a gasp of admiration and clapped her hands together.

"Oh, just look at that, Miss Brahms, isn't it becoming?"

"Yes," said Miss Brahms as she was writing another card out. "They're all wearing them for badminton."

"How much are they?" inquired the customer.

"Here," said Miss Brahms, handing her the card. The customer gazed at the large 40 on it. "Is that four pounds?" she asked.

Mrs. Slocombe gazed at the customer keenly to detect any trace of surprise in her query.

"That's right," she said. "It was four pounds fifty, but they've just been reduced."

The customer nodded quite approvingly. "Quite reasonable considering today's prices," she observed.

"We think so, don't we, Miss Brahms?"

Miss Brahms nodded. "Shall I get my sales book, Mrs. Slocombe?"

"It's not really necessary, as I've just made the sale."

Miss Brahms's eyes narrowed, and she picked up the price card on the counter.

"I think I should point out," she said, "that I didn't put the dot after the…"

"That'll do," said Mrs. Slocombe hurriedly. "Get your sales book, Miss Brahms."

"Thank you, Mrs. Slocombe."

Although it was still only 9:15 in the morning, Mr. Lucas was hard at work wrapping a parcel watched by the elderly Mr. Grainger, who snapped his fingers encouragingly to hurry him along.

"Here we are," said Mr. Lucas, handing Mr. Grainger a parcel that looked as if it had been in the lost property office for a few weeks.

"It's not wrapped well," muttered Mr. Grainger, and then with a smile he turned to his customer, a very elderly gentleman with rheumy eyes and too large an overcoat. Mr. Grainger leant over confidentially as he handed the parcel to him. "The combinations are, sir," he said, "preshrunk, but it is advisable to wash only in lukewarm water."

"Or better still.," added Mr. Lucas, "no water at all. My grandfather always sends his combinations to the dry cleaners."

Mr. Grainger ignored him and addressing the customer, "I rinse mine through in the bath, then let the wind dry them."

Mr. Lucas shook his head. "It must be pure magic round your house, Mr. Grainger."

With a nod of thanks the elderly customer took the parcel and made his way slowly towards the steps.

"Thank you for your custom, sir," called Captain Peacock.

The elderly gentleman mounted the steps, the lift doors opened and a young, smartly dressed Oriental gentleman appeared and walked brusquely downstairs. Captain Peacock barred his way. "Can I help you, sir?" The little gentleman stopped in his tracks and bowing smartly from the waist said, "Ah so."

Captain Peacock bowed in return. "Ah so," he announced. "Unless I am mistaken, sir is Japanese."

The Oriental gentleman nodded, and bowed again from the waist. "Ah so," he repeated.

Captain Peacock bowed again and then gave a slight cough.

"Er, you wanty buy?" he inquired.

The Oriental gentleman nodded enthusiastically and bowed again smartly from the waist. Captain Peacock returned the bow and then clapped his hands imperiously. "Chop chop, Mr. Lucas."

Mr. Lucas glanced up in surprise. Captain Peacock beckoned imperiously. "Forward, Mr. Lucas."

The Oriental gentleman delved in the inside pocket of his smartly cut suit and produced a card and handed it to Captain Peacock with a bow. Captain Peacock stared at it.

"Cledit Card," announced the customer. Captain Peacock smiled.

"Ah so. Yes," and pointing to the bottom of the card: "You Mr. Kato," and then he pointed to himself, "I Peacock." The Oriental gentleman gripped his hand and shook it warmly. "How do you do, Mr. I Peacock." Before Captain Peacock could correct him, Mr. Lucas appeared at his elbow. accompanied by Mr. Humphries.

Ah," said Captain Peacock, "this is honourable Mr. Humphries."

The Oriental gentleman gazed at Mr. Humphries. "Mr. Humphries so," he announced and bowed smartly from the waist. Mr. Humphries gave an equally smart bow back.

"And this," said Captain Peacock indicating with his hand, "is honourable Mr. Lucas."

Mr. Lucas removed the tape measure from around his neck in a businesslike gesture. "What does the customer require?"

Captain Peacock turned back to the Oriental gentleman.

"I'll try and find out," he murmured.

"Oh, of course," said Mr. Lucas. "You were out East, weren't you? I forgot."

Clearing his throat, Captain Peacock spoke. "Whatee wantee?"

The Oriental gentleman smiled enigmatically. "Coat for lain."

Captain Peacock's eyebrows shot up in surprise. "I beg your pardon?"

"Coat for lain," repeated the customer.

Captain Peacock turned to him. "I think the customer wishes a raincoat, Mr. Lucas."

"Ah so," said the Oriental gentleman and bowed. Captain Peacock, Mr. Lucas and Mr. Humphries all replied "Ah so" and bent smartly from the waist. Everytime they bowed the customer bowed back and it started to get rather tiring. Fortunately, they were interrupted by the phone ringing. Mr. Humphries took advantage of it immediately.

"Scuzee," he announced, "phonee lingy. Me go get." And dashing round the counter he picked up the phone and announced, 'Men's leady-mades.'"

In Mr. Rumbold's office Miss Ainsworth, his secretary, took the phone away from her ear for the moment with a start of surprise, then put it back.

"It's Mr. Rumbold," she announced, "for Captain Peacock."

"Really," said Mr. Humphries, "that doesn't sound like Mr. Rumbold."

Miss Ainsworth shook her head. "No," she said, "It's Mr. Rumbold's secretary. Mr. Rumbold would like to see Captain Peacock in his office."

"In that case," said Mr. Humphries, "I shall acquaint Captain Peacock with Mr. Rumbold's wishes."

"There is no doubt," said Miss Ainsworth, "that you are terribly obliging."

Mr. Humphries shook his head. "Only up to a point," he said, and putting the phone down on the counter, he called, "Captain Peacock, Mr. Rumbold's office, chop chop."

In Mr. Rumbold's office, Mr. Rumbold's bald head was glistening and his eyes had a look of deep concentration as he continued his dictation to Miss Ainsworth.

"Now," he said, "no...damn, I've forgotten...er...what was the last thing I said?"

Miss Ainsworth glanced at her pad. "Would I please get them off." Mr. Rumbold hurriedly took off his glasses and polished them with his spotted handkerchief.

"Er...did I... I'm...are you sure I said that?"

Miss Ainsworth nodded. "Yes. The letters. You wanted me to get them off to catch the post."

"Oh, yes," said Mr. Rumbold with a sigh of relief and popped his glasses back. "No, I meant what was the last thing I said in the memo to Young Mr. Grace?"

Miss Ainsworth gazed at her shorthand. "I'm both flattered and honoured that you should be considering me for the vacant paste on the Board of Doctors..." Mr. Rumbold shook his head and gave a sigh of exasperation. "No, no, no, the vacant post on the Board of Directors."

Miss Ainsworth smiled apologetically. "I'm so sorry, Mr. Rumbold, it's my shorthand...'and of course I will accept readily if accepted. Signed yours crawly.' "

"Truly," snapped Mr. Rumbold.

"I'm sorry," said Miss Ainsworth apologetically.

Mr. Rumbold sat back in his chair with a sigh. "That will be all, Miss

Ainsworth. Do try and be a bit more accurate in future."

Miss Ainsworth lowered her eyes. "Yes, Mr. Rumbold."

"And," added Mr. Rumbold, "I want those things to go off tonight. I don't want any correspondence delayed like it was yesterday."

"Of course not," breathed Miss Ainsworth. As she stood up, there was a knock at the door and Captain Peacock popped his head round. Before he could speak, Miss Ainsworth said to Mr. Rumbold, "It won't be like last night, Mr. Rumbold. I promise I'll have it off before I go."

Captain Peacock raised his eyebrows.

"Good, Miss Ainsworth, well done," said Mr. Rumbold, and to Captain Peacock, "You have to be very firm with these girls, you know."

"Well you certainly seem to be getting results, sir."

Mr. Rumbold placed the tips of his fingers together and leaned back in his chair and gazed at the ceiling, while Captain Peacock sat down uncomfortably on a gold wickerwork chair.

"Now," he said, "no doubt you've heard that Mr. Theobald is retiring from the Board of Directors, due to continued ill health."

Captain Peacock nodded. "Yes, two bottles a day I believe, sir."

Mr. Rumbold sucked the air noisily between his teeth, and shook his head. "Well that's neither here nor there. Anyway, they've been asking for a short list of suitable people with the necessary requirements, which are of course: one, drive; two, experience; three, integrity; four, er…etc. And I thought it only right that you should be the first to know, and that's why I have sent for you."

Captain Peacock smiled. "Well. sir, it hasn't come as a complete surprise to me, and I need hardly say that I am both flattered and honoured and should I be selected for the post I would most readily accept."

The smile that had started on Mr. Rumbold's face had disappeared. "Captain Peacock," he said, "I feel I should explain that I am the one who is being considered, and if I do get the job I was intending recommending that you take over in here."

"I see," murmured Captain Peacock, hurriedly replacing the cigarette he had just taken from his case.

Mr. Rumbold stared at him. "You don't seem too pleased about it, Peacock."

Captain Peacock gave a thin smile. "I'm not sure, Mr. Rumbold, that a clerical job is really up my street. I do so enjoy the friendly personal contact with people." At that moment Miss Ainsworth gave a hurried knock, re-entered the office, walked over to the desk and bent over to retrieve her pen. Her miniskirt rode up, leaving a view for Captain Peacock to boggle at for a moment. Averting his eyes he continued: "But on the other hand, sir, perhaps I wouldn't entirely lose that personal contact."

As Mr. Lucas held the Japanese customer's parcel, Mr. Humphries handed over the credit card and the bill.

"There you are, sir," he announced, "£17.50."

As the Japanese gentleman extended his hand to receive it, Mr. Humphries stared at his upturned palm and gave a gasp of astonishment. "Oh, my word!" he exclaimed.

The customer gazed at the palm of his hand and then back to Mr. Humphries. "Please?" he inquired.

Mr. Humphries took the gentleman's wrist between thumb and forefinger, pulled the hand nearer to him and staring at the palm said, "There's a cross on your fate line."

The customer nodded. "Yes?" he said inquiringly.

"Yes, cross mean accident."

The customer stared at him not understanding. "Accident?"

"Yes," said Mr. Humphries. "Cross mean crash."

The customer shook his head again. "No, no, me no need clash," then with a smile, "Me got cledit card."

Mr. Humphries handed it to him. "Go home," he advised.

"Saya Nora," said the customer.

"Quanta la gusta," replied Mr. Humphries as the customer headed for the main staircase.

Mr. Lucas stared at Mr. Humphries with a puzzled look on his face. "What was all that about a cross on his fate line?"

"Well," said Mr. Humphries, "there are certain times when I can just see things."

Mr. Lucas gazed at him in disbelief. "You mean like a fortune teller?"

"Yes," nodded Mr. Humphries, "and I'm not often wrong." At that moment a series of violent crashes receding into the distance attracted their attention. As they glanced towards the main stairway, Mr. Mash came into view waving one bucket in his hand.

"Blimey," he announced, "some Japanese kama khazi pilot just tripped over my buckets when I was on my way upstairs and fell down." A further series of crashes sounded into the distance.

"Shall I go and give him a hand?" called Mr. Lucas.

Mr. Grainger shook his head. "He'll be in Haberdashery by now; let them deal with it."

Captain Peacock sprinted up the steps. "I'd better go and check." And as he disappeared Mr. Mash ran after him. Mr. Humphries tutted. "I warned him."

"Warned him about what?" said Mrs. Slocombe who'd come over to investigate the commotion. Mr. Lucas, who was by now a believer, said, "He saw it in his hands."

"Saw what in his hands?" inquired Miss Brahms.

"I saw an accident in his hands," explained Mr. Humphries, "and I told him it would happen."

"Oh you never," said Mrs. Slocombe shaking her head.

"He did," said Mr. Lucas, "and I heard him. I can vouch for that."

"Do you mean that you can read hands, Mr. Humphries?" Mrs. Slocombe was impressed.

"Yes, it's in the family, you know. My father noticed something funny about me when I was six."

Mrs. Slocombe stuck her hand out and held it under his nose. "Go on," she announced, "read mine."

"No, no, I'm afraid I can't. I have to be in the mood."

"Well," observed Miss Brahms, "you was in the mood when you were holding that Chinaman's hand."

"He was Japanese," corrected Mr. Lucas.

"Same thing," said Miss Brahms.

"I'm afraid," said Mr. Humphries, "I shall just have to wait until the vibrations are right. I could try over lunch," he added.

A clanking of buckets preceded the appearance of Mr. Mash at the top of the stairs.

"Oi," he called, "that Nip what fell down the stairs has got his head wedged in one of my buckets."

"Oh," said Mrs. Slocombe, looking concerned, "and so far from home."

"All I hope is," said Mr. Mash, "that he's got an account 'cos him and the bucket's gone to hospital and he wouldn't pay cash."

"I saw the hospital quite clearly," said Mr. Humphries, "but I didn't like to tell him."

The members of both departments were still gazing at Mr. Humphries with great respect as they sat at the lunch table up in the canteen, when Mr. Lucas arrived with the tray of coffees and placed them on the table.

"Here's the coffee, but I'm afraid there's only one spoon."

"Never mind," said Mr. Humphries, "I'll use my finger."

Miss Brahms giggled. "Mind you don't melt your nail polish."

Mr. Grainger produced a pencil from his pocket. "I prefer to use this. The taste of wood takes your mind off the coffee."

Miss Brahms held out both her hands and placed them under Mr. Humphries's nose. "Go on," she said, "do it now."

Mr. Humphries sipped his coffee and pulled a face. "Don't rush me. I'm trying to wash away the taste of the shepherd's pie."

Miss Brahms lowered her hands, looking disappointed. Mrs. Slocombe gave Mr. Humphries a nudge. "Go on, how did it start, Mr. Humphries?"

"I think," said Mr. Humphries, "it was yesterday's hot pot."

"No, not the pie, how did it start, this gift of yours, you know, when you first found out you had it?"

"Well," said Mr. Humphries, "you see, I kept having these funny turns. I remember when I was about fifteen and suddenly I had the sensation of floating out of my body and looking down at myself lying there in bed in my pyjamas."

"Ooh," said Mrs. Slocombe, "tell us what you were doing." Mr. Humphries looked surprised. "Doing? I wasn't doing anything, I was just lying there."

Miss Brahms shuddered. "Ooh. How creepy."

Mr. Humphries gazed round his enraptured audience. "Since then," he explained, "I have learnt to do it at will. You see, I can pop out of my body whenever I feel like it."

"I wish I could," said Mrs. Slocombe enviously.

Mr. Lucas nodded. "If I had a body like yours, I wouldn't come back," and held up his hands as Mrs. Slocombe started to rise. "I'm sorry, Mrs. Slocombe, it was only a joke."

Mrs. Slocombe sat down heavily and spoke through gritted teeth: "When I first joined this store, juniors were not allowed to sit with seniors." And then she tamed back to Mr. Humphries. "Go on then."

"Well you see," Mr. Humphries explained, "lots of people leave their bodies at night, but most of them don't remember it." Miss Brahms leaned forward eagerly, and pushing her coffee cup aside announced: "I have dreams like that."

"No," said Mrs. Slocombe incredulously.

Miss Brahms nodded. "Yes, I dream I fly around with no clothes on and all my friends look up at me." She dropped her eyes. "I wake up blushing all over."

Mr. Lucas leant across the table and put his hand on her shoulder sympathetically. "You don't want to be embarrassed by that, Shirley."

"Well," murmured Miss Brahms, "it's so humiliating."

"In that case." said Mr. Lucas, "just try flying on your back."

"Trust you to suggest that," said Miss Brahms, shrugging Mr. Lucas's hand away.

Mr. Lucas looked quite hurt. "It was a serious suggestion, and I'll tell you this. If ever I'm out of my body flying around and I happen to fly over you, I won't look."

"I have never dreamed I'm flying about," announced Mr. Grainger, "but I must admit that I quite often dream that I am wandering round the house looking for something."

"Do you find it?" inquired Mr. Lucas.

Mr. Grainger nodded. "Yes, fortunately. It happened again last night and on my way back I tripped over the cat."

"What? In your dream?" asked Mrs. Slocombe.

"No," said Mr. Grainger, "I actually did trip over the cat."

"Well," said Mrs. Slocombe, "animals are very psychic, you know. If there's a hint of danger, my pussy's hair stands on end just like a pollywog."

Mr. Lucas spluttered over his coffee.

"A built-in burglar alarm," he gasped.

Mrs. Slocombe gave him a withering look and then held her hand out under Mr. Humphries's nose. "Come on," she urged, "it will be time to go back soon. See if there's anything going on." Taking Mrs. Slocombe's hand in his Mr. Humphries examined it closely, turning it from side to side.

"Mmm," he murmured. "Um, ahh yes. Hmm, hmm, I'm not surprised at that."

"What? Tell us what you can see."

"Well for a start," said Mr. Humphries pointing at the base of Mrs. Slocombe's thumb, "you have a very pronounced Mount of Venus." Mrs. Slocombe's head turned sharply and stared sternly at Mr. Lucas, "One saucy remark from you, Mr. Lucas, and I'm going straight to Captain Peacock."

Mr. Lucas opened his eyes innocently. "I never said a word, Mrs. Slocombe."

"What does it mean?" asked Miss Brahms.

"It means," said Mr. Humphries, "that Mrs. Slocombe is a very passionate woman."

Mrs. Slocombe nodded. "True," she murmured, "very true."

"Is that because she's got such a pronounced one?" inquired Mr. Lucas.

"Shut up," said Mrs. Slocombe.

"Please," said Mr. Humphries, "I'm trying to concentrate here. Now let's have another butchers. Ah yes, your heart rules your head. See this line here." He traced his finger delicately across Mrs. Slocombe's palm. His finger stopped. "Ooh, and look, you've had very many affairs." The rest of the table craned forward and stared at Mr. Humphries as he stabbed his finger a number of times.

"One…two…three…ooh my word," he exclaimed, "that was a big one." Mrs. Slocombe hurriedly closed her hand.

"I don't think we want to go into the past too deeply. What I am more concerned with is the future." Cautiously she opened it up again and held it out for further inspection.

"Now if you look at this line here," said Mr. Humphries, who liked to be the centre of attention, "this is your life line. See, it goes all the way down your hand here. Oh yes," he nodded approvingly, "you'll live to well past middle age."

"That's just the present," said Mr. Lucas. "She wants to know about the future."

"Do be quiet," said Miss Brahms, "you're spoiling it." And she turned back to Mr. Humphries as he suddenly gave a gasp of surprise.

"Oooh, look at that!" he exclaimed.

"What?" said Mrs. Slocombe, staring at her palm anxiously. Mr. Humphries nodded. "Yes, it's quite clear to me now."

"What is?" said Mrs. Slocombe hoarsely. "It's nothing bad, is it?"

"Don't tell her she's about to kick the bucket," said Mr. Lucas. "It'll ruin the rest of the day for her."

"Nothing bad at all," said Mr. Humphries. "As a matter of fact, I can see a man at your feet." Mrs. Slocombe gave a gasp of pleasure.

"What's he like?" she inquired.

Mr. Humphries stared again at the palm and nodded. "Yes, he's a tall man. Very distinguished." He closed his eyes for a moment. "Yes, I can see him clearly."

"Oh," said Mrs. Slocombe, "can you really? Can you see who it is?"

"I wish I could," said Mr. Humphries. "I can see him clearly, but he's got his back to me and he won't turn round."

"In that case," suggested Mr. Lucas, "why don't you get out of your body and go round and have a look?"

"He'll turn round if we wait," said Miss Brahms.

"He probably doesn't know we're having lunch," said Mr. Lucas, "and that our time is nearly up."

"All I can tell you," said Mr. Humphries, "is that he has fallen at your feet."

"Oh," said Mrs. Slocombe. "Well, would you believe it?"

"You see," said Miss Brahms, "I told you it was never too late." At which moment Captain Peacock came over.

"I didn't know Mr. Humphries was a palmist," he said.

"Not only that," said Mr. Lucas. "Our Mr. Humphries can pop out of his pyjamas whenever he feels like it."

Captain Peacock looked dubiously at Mr. Humphries. "Really?"

"Captain Peacock," said Mrs. Slocombe enthusiastically, "Mr. Humphries is quite remarkable, he has looked in my hand and seen things in my palm I thought only I knew about."

"Surely," said Mr. Lucas, "there must have been someone else there."

"Come on, Captain Peacock," said Mrs. Slocombe, "why don't you let Mr. Humphries have a look at your palm?"

"I don't believe in that sort of thing," he said drawing up a chair and sitting next to Mr. Humphries, "although I must say it is something I've always wanted to do."

"Go on, Captain Peacock," urged Mrs. Slocombe, and Captain Peacock looked embarrassed.

"Well," he said uncertainly.

"Oh come on, Captain Peacock," said Miss Brahms, "unless," she added, "you've got some horrible secret you want to hide."

"I have nothing to hide," said Captain Peacock loftily, then he glanced at his watch. "Oh very well, but I only have a moment—so don't take too long, Mr. Humphries." And opening his hand he placed it under Mr. Humphries's nose. Mr. Humphries took the hand and gazed into it.

"I'm very privileged," he said and then, squinting at Captain Peacock's palm, nodded. "Oh yes," he murmured, "a born leader. Look at that prominent forefinger."

A supercilious smile crossed Captain Peacock's face. He nodded in agreement.

"Yes," continued Mr. Humphries, "this is a very ambitious hand. I haven't held one of these for a long time." A faraway look came into his eyes for a moment, and then he checked himself and continued the scrutiny. "My word, I've never seen such a long life line." He traced Captain Peacock's life line with his forefinger. "Look at it. It splits in two lines here. It goes right down your hand and disappears in your sleeve."

"What does that mean?" asked Captain Peacock, following the lines up his wrist and into the darkness of his cuff.

"Two lines disappearing up your sleeve," said Mr. Lucas, "can mean only one thing, Captain Peacock. You're going to die of old age in a railway tunnel!" Captain Peacock gave a withering look, then turned back as Mr. Humphries continued.

"Oh look," said Mr. Humphries. "Lots and lots of lines here. Head rules heart."

"He's got a big enough one," murmured Mr. Lucas.

"What have we here?" exclaimed Mr. Humphries. "There's a line here in your hand, Captain Peacock, that indicates a new opportunity." Captain Peacock raised his eyebrows inquiringly.

"Really?"

Mr. Humphries nodded. "And it's something to do with your job."

An excited look came into Captain Peacock's eyes.

"I see you as it were," said Mr. Humphries, "climbing a ladder and a door opens and suddenly you find yourself wearing a new hat."

Captain Peacock pursed his lips and sat back in his chair. "How remarkable," he observed.

Mr. Humphries gazed at him anxiously.

"Am I on the right lines?"

"Well," said Captain Peacock, "I wasn't going to mention this to anybody, but," he leaned forward as the rest of the table leaned towards him to hear what he wasn't going to mention to anybody, "only this morning I was informed that Mr. Theobald might be leaving due to ill health."

Mr. Grainger, who up till then had appeared to be half asleep, nodded. "Two bottles a day I hear," he murmured.

"And," continued Captain Peacock, "I was told that I should stand by to take over from Mr. Rumbold." Mr. Humphries looked surprised.

"Well," he said, "isn't that amazing? Well of course that's it."

"All fits in," said Miss Brahms, "that's climbing a ladder." Mr. Grainger nodded. "And taking over Mr. Rumbold's job is certainly a door opening."

"And of course," added Mr. Lucas, "he will have a new hat, because he will be allowed to wear a bowler."

Captain Peacock shook his head in amazement. "Most remarkable."

"May I have a look at your left hand now, Captain Peacock?" said Mr. Humphries.

"Certainly," said Captain Peacock with alacrity.

"There's something I want to have a look at," said Mr. Humphries, and taking the hand he turned it over and gazed at the back of it. A serious look crossed his face.

"I thought as much," he said.

An anxious look appeared on Captain Peacock's face.

"What is it, Mr. Humphries? What have you seen?"

Mr. Humphries pointed to Captain Peacock's watch.

"It's five past two," he observed. "We're late back from lunch."

All rose and hurried back to the department. A little while later, still flushed with success, Mr. Humphries was busy pricing a box of gloves, when Mr. Grainger sidled over to him.

"Are you free, Mr. Humphries?"

Mr. Humphries nodded. "Yes, I'm free, Mr. Grainger. I'm just pricing my gloves, but they can wait."

Mr. Grainger glanced round. "I'd like a word with you," he murmured.

And then seeing Mr. Lucas standing nearby straining his ears, Mr. Grainger added, "Would you mind stepping out of earshot, Mr. Lucas? This is for Mr. Humphries's ears alone."

"I can't hear you from here," replied Mr. Lucas from some distance.

"That's good," said Mr. Grainger. "Now, Mr. Humphries, for some weeks I have been watching the way you handle the customers."

Mr. Humphries gave an embarrassed cough. "I think I can explain that, Mr. Grainger. You see..."

Mr. Grainger held out his hand.

"What I am trying to say, Mr. Humphries, is this: I have been very impressed with your performance in trousers."

Mr. Humphries preened himself. "Thank you, Mr. Grainger."

"And," continued Mr. Grainger, "the point is that if Captain Peacock goes up in the world, somebody will have to take over as floor walker here."

Mr. Humphries gazed warmly at Mr. Grainger. "Oh, Mr. Grainger, you're going to recommend me."

Mr. Grainger stared at him with surprise. "Recommend you, Mr. Humphries? Certainly not, I'm going to recommend me."

"Oh," said Mr. Humphries disappointed. "Well, what are we talking about then?"

"Quite naturally," said Mr. Grainger, "I'm going to suggest to Captain Peacock that you take over my position. Do you think you could cope?"

Mr. Humphries nodded. "Oh yes I think so, Mr. Grainger, particularly with your hand to guide me."

"Do you think," muttered Mr. Grainger, "that Mr. Lucas is capable of taking over from you?" Mr. Grainger gazed doubtfully in the direction of Mr. Lucas, who was quite obviously straining his ears. Mr. Humphries turned and also stared at Mr. Lucas.

"Yes," he said, "I think so, with my hand to guide him."

"I think," said Mr. Grainger, "we'd better consult him."

"Yes I think we should," said Mr. Humphries.

"Are you free?" queried Mr. Grainger.

Mr. Lucas gazed round to see if there were any customers. Finally he spoke.

"Yes, yes, you appear to have caught me at a free moment." And taking two paces, he walked over and stood by Mr. Humphries.

"Shall I acquaint him with the facts, Mr. Grainger?" said Mr. Humphries. Mr. Grainger nodded.

"Now, Mr. Lucas. If Mr. Rumbold takes over from Mr. Theobald it's just possible that Captain Peacock will take over from Mr. Rumbold, in which case Mr. Grainger might take over from Captain Peacock and I might take over the responsibility of Mr. Grainger's position, which means there could be a vacancy for my position. Do you think you could handle it?"

Mr. Lucas paused to consider the question and then smiled. "Wouldn't it be simpler if I took over from Mr. Theobald myself?"

"No," snapped Mr. Grainger. "This is a serious responsibility we are discussing, Mr. Lucas. I would be obliged if you would stop being so filivolous." Mr. Grainger's teeth suddenly had great difficulty with the word "frivolous." Mr. Lucas raised his eyebrows inquiringly as Mr. Grainger tried again.

"Don't be frivolous," interrupted Mr. Humphries.

"Thank you, Mr. Humphries," said Mr. Grainger. "As I was saying, Mr. Lucas, this is a serious responsibility."

Mr. Lucas nodded in agreement. "Oh I can see that, Mr. Grainger. After all, it means that instead of me standing in the middle of the counter here," he pointed at the counter to indicate his point, "Mr. Humphries will have to stand at the end of the counter there." He turned and pointed to the other end of the counter. "I'll be standing in the middle here. It's certainly a big responsibility for me to stand at the end of the counter there," he pointed to a distance two feet away, "instead of at the end there." He turned and pointed to the other end of the counter. "I'll be standing in the middle here. It's certainly a big responsibility for me." He shook his head and adopted a very worried expression and a furrowed brow. "I don't know if I am ready for it. Mind you," he added, "it's not as big a responsibility for me standing there, as it is for Mr. Humphries who has to move up two feet and stand there. I don't envy you, Mr. Humphries. I'd be a nervous wreck if I had to move two feet and stand somewhere else on this counter."

Mr. Grainger stared at him stonily. "Have you finished, Mr. Lucas?"

"Yes," said Mr. Lucas. "Now let's put it another way. Do I get any more money?"

"You do indeed," said Mr. Grainger.

"In that case," said Mr. Lucas, "I'll do it."

"Good," said Mr. Grainger. "Now that I know your feelings in the matter, I shall confer with Captain Peacock." He glanced over in the direction of the centre of the floor to observe Mrs. Slocombe approaching Captain Peacock.

"Damn," he exclaimed, "that wretched woman's got there first."

Mrs. Slocombe's warm smile indicated that she intended to be extremely pleasant to Captain Peacock.

"Captain Peacock," she murmured. "Are you free?" Captain Peacock gazed round to make sure there weren't any customers about.

"At the moment I am free, Mrs. Slocombe. What can I do for you?"

Mrs. Slocombe positively purred, as she gazed at him.

"Well, it's like this, Stephen," she murmured. "If you do take over from Mr. Rumbold, and if I may say so, I think it's not before time, it would leave your position on the floor vacant here, would it not?"

Captain Peacock nodded. "That is of course true, Mrs. Slocombe."

Mrs. Slocombe continued in her buttering-up voice. "And I'm sure you will take over, Captain Peacock, because with your military background and big forefinger you were just born to lead."

"Well," said Captain Peacock, "I suppose advancement was inevitable."

Mrs. Slocombe put her hand on his arm and nodded enthusiastically. "It was indeed, especially with your posh voice, and you knowing all those long words." Lowering her voice slightly, she continued, "Will it be up to you to recommend someone to take your place?"

Captain Peacock smiled. "Of course if anybody knows of the strength and weaknesses of the people on the floor, 1 do. So no doubt it will be up to me."

"That's what I thought," said Mrs. Slocombe. "I think it's time we had a change of sex on the floor."

Captain Peacock gazed at her in surprise. "Do I understand, Mrs. Slocombe, that you are recommending Mr. Humphries?"

Mrs. Slocombe stepped back and stared up at him. "Good heavens no, Captain Peacock. I'm recommending me."

Captain Peacock gave a short, sarcastic laugh. "You, Mrs. Slocombe? A woman! A woman floorwalker." He laughed again at the possibility of the idea.

Mrs. Slocombe's sweet, buttery tone disappeared completely.

"Captain Peacock, women are equal to men these days, you know."

"Not that equal," said Captain Peacock shaking his head. "Floorwalking has always been a man's job."

"I don't see why," said Mrs. Slocombe. "Anyone can stand there looking stupid with his nose in the air."

Captain Peacock's smile disappeared as he gazed angrily back at Mrs. Slocombe.

"If that was all that was required I would recommend you without hesitation."

"You male chauvinistic pig," spluttered Mrs. Slocombe.

Captain Peacock's eyes narrowed. "I didn't hear that, Mrs. Slocombe."

Raising her voice Mrs. Slocombe screamed, "You male chauvinistic pig!"

With a tremendous effort Captain Peacock managed to control himself.

"I shall pretend, Mrs. Slocombe, that you haven't said that."

As Mrs. Slocombe turned her back on him, she called out, "I didn't want the rotten job anyway."

Mr. Grainger, who was busy measuring a customer's inside leg, gazed between them and observed Mrs. Slocombe walking away from Captain Peacock. He assured himself that his truss was firmly in place and stood up carefully, calling to Mr. Humphries.

"Yes, Mr. Grainger?"

"Would you mind," said Mr. Grainger, "taking over this customer? I've already taken the inside leg, and he is looking for something in Scottish tweed with broad shoulders."

"Aren't we all," said Mr. Humphries.

Adjusting an ingratiating smile on his face, Mr. Grainger approached Captain Peacock. "Are you free, Captain Peacock?" Still seething over his encounter with Mrs. Slocombe, Captain Peacock savagely adjusted the tie on a dummy.

"Just a moment, Mr. Grainger, can't you see I'm busy?"

Mr. Grainger waited patiently while Captain Peacock tugged at the tie to his satisfaction and then with a deep breath turned to Mr. Grainger. "I'm free now. What is it?"

Mr. Grainger adjusted his ingratiating smile. "I'm delighted," he murmured, "with the possibility of your promotion, Stephen."

Captain Peacock smiled and replied, "Thank you, Ernest."

"And if I may say so," continued Mr. Grainger, "it is well deserved and not before time."

"But," added Captain Peacock, "inevitable."

"Indeed inevitable," murmured Mr. Grainger.

There was a slight pause, then Mr. Grainger continued, "We've known each other a long time, Stephen."

Captain Peacock nodded in agreement. "You are one of my closest acquaintances, Ernest," he observed.

Mr. Grainger swelled up with pride. "Oh really, how very, very kind of you to say so, Stephen. Now I take it you will be recommending me."

Captain Peacock looked puzzled.

"Recommending you, Ernest? In what capacity?"

"For your job, of course," beamed Mr. Grainger.

"I rather doubt it, Ernest."

"Doubt it?" said Mr. Grainger. "Doubt it? Why?"

"Well," said Captain Peacock, "I think it needs a younger man to cope with it."

Mr. Grainger's smile disappeared, and his jowls shook with indignation. "Cope, cope," he spluttered. "Cope with what? All you do is stand there with your nose in the air, saying, 'Are you free, Mr. Grainger?'"

Captain Peacock's friendly look disappeared. "I have to check all the bills and make sure they are correctly made out," he snapped.

Mr. Grainger shook his jowls. "Any damn fool can do that."

"And," said Captain Peacock, "is that the qualification you are offering?"

Mr. Grainger stared at him for a moment, then jutting his head forward he announced: "Captain Peacock, as soon as I have had tea, I shall bring it up in front of Mr. Rumbold." And having issued this dire threat, Mr. Grainger turned firmly on his heels and marched back to the counter.

At exactly 5:31 the members of both departments assembled in front of Mr. Rumbold's desk. Mr. Rumbold glanced anxiously at his watch.

"Now let's make these complaints brief," he said hurriedly. "It is after all just after 5:30, and we have guests coming for dinner."

"Perhaps," said Mrs. Slocombe, stepping forward, "I could put it in a nutshell. Captain Peacock doesn't fancy a lady floorwalker."

"I see," said Mr. Rumbold. "Well, we have one in Haberdashery and one in Cosmetics. Now which one don't you fancy, Captain Peacock?"

Captain Peacock stepped forward. "I do not fancy one in men's wear, sir."

Mr. Rumbold's eyebrows shot up with surprise. "Good Lord, have we got one dressed up as a man?" he asked anxiously.

"I was," said Captain Peacock, "specifically referring to Mrs. Slocombe."

Mr. Rumbold nodded. "Ah, at last we're getting somewhere. So that's the complaint. Mrs. Slocombe has been dressing up as a man and it doesn't attract you." He stared at Mrs. Slocombe obviously trying to imagine the suggestion created in his mind. "Er…don't dress as a man anymore, Mrs. Slocombe."

"Oh don't be daft," said Mrs. Slocombe in an exasperated tone. "I don't dress as a man. It's just that I don't want to be under Mr. Grainger here on the floor."

Mr. Grainger gave a snort of disgust. "There's no danger of that, Mrs. Slocombe. Captain Peacock seems to think I'm past it."

Mr. Rumbold took his glasses off and polished them with his spotted handkerchief. "I sometimes wonder," he murmured, "if sitting in this office I'm missing something."

Mr. Humphries stepped forward and smiled ingratiatingly. "Well, Mr. Rumbold, if there is a vacancy I don't see why I shouldn't fill it. After all I have had fifteen years' experience." Mr. Rumbold frowned. "What vacancy are we talking about?"

"Well," interrupted Mr. Lucas, before Captain Peacock could speak, "when Captain Peacock takes over your job, we'll need a new floorwalker."

"Right," said Miss Brahms, "to stand there with their nose in the air, talking in a posh voice."

"Which," commented Mr. Lucas, "rules you out."

"And you," retorted Miss Brahms.

Mr. Rumbold placed his glasses back on his nose and stared severely at Captain Peacock. "My possible promotion was supposed to be a secret. I only got the memo about it yesterday. It's a very grave breach of secrecy."

"Captain Peacock didn't tell us anything," said Mr. Lucas, "but Mr. Humphries here saw it in his hand at lunch."

Mr. Rumbold stared even more sternly at Captain Peacock.

"What were you doing with my memo in your hand at lunch?"

"I did not have your memo," said Captain Peacock patiently, "I…," but Mr. Humphries interrupted him.

"No, sir, he didn't have the memo. I read the lines in his hand."

"That's right," said Mrs. Slocombe. "He's a palmist who can see into the future."

"And added Mr. Lucas, "He saw Captain Peacock climbing a ladder, opening a door and wearing a new hat."

"Which means," said Mrs. Slocombe, "that you're getting Mr. Theobald's job, and he's getting yours and that's why I'm applying for his."

"And so am I," said Mr. Grainger quickly.

Mr. Rumbold held up his hand for silence. "But it is by no means certain that I am going to get Mr. Theobald's job," he announced.

"In that case," said Miss Brahms, "why don't you let Gypsy Rose Humphries have a look at your hand, then he'll be able to tell you."

"I don't know," said Mr. Rumbold. "This really is most irregular."

"Well, do you want me to have a look or not," said Mr. Humphries, "because it's nearly twenty to six. I left my slippers in the oven at regulo 2, which switches itself on automatically. And if I don't get home soon they'll be overdone."

"Oh very well," said Mr. Rumbold holding out his left hand.

"Not that one," said Mr. Humphries, "that's the one we're born with."

Mr. Rumbold gazed at his hand in surprise. "I was rather under the impression that I was born with both of them," he remarked.

Mr. Humphries took hold of Mr. Rumbold's right hand. "I mean," he said, "in the world of palmistry, the left one you start with and the right one shows what you've made of it and how it's all changed." He stared at Mr. Rumbold's right hand with a concentrated look on his face. After a few moments Mr. Rumbold shifted anxiously in his chair.

"Well?" he inquired.

"Here," said Mr. Humphries, "didn't you have an unhappy childhood?"

Mr. Lucas gazed at Mr. Rumbold's bald head. "I expect his mother kept brushing his hair with sandpaper."

Mr. Rumbold gave Mr. Lucas a withering look. "Let's just stick to the future, shall we?" he said returning his anxious gaze to his hand. Mr. Humphries stabbed at an unseen line with his forefinger.

"Look at that," said Mr. Humphries. "I can see a cross. Yes, that definitely means there's a crossroad in your career," and peering even more closely he announced, "There. I can see a 'T,' there's a definite 'T.' Everyone craned forward to see the "T" that Mr. Humphries was pointing out. Taking Mr. Rumbold's hand, he passed it round for their inspection, pulling Mr. Rumbold across the desk.

"It's definitely a 'T,'" said Miss Brahms.

"What does it mean?" said Mr. Rumbold.

"It means," said Mr. Humphries, "that there is going to be a turning point in your life."

"The turning point," said Mrs. Slocombe excitedly, "must be Mr. Theobald. He's a 'T.'"

"Good heavens," said Mr. Rumbold, "this is most remarkable."

"When is it going to happen?"

"I can see something else here," said Mr. Humphries, turning the hand and peering at it closely. "Yes, I can see leaves. Brown leaves."

"In that case," said Miss Brahms, "it must be the autumn. That's when they go brown."

"Good heavens," said Mr. Lucas. "What a coincidence! It's autumn now." At that moment the phone on Mr. Rumbold's desk gave a shrill ring. Picking it up with his left hand, Mr. Rumbold held it to his ear, and half rose to his feet as Young Mr. Grace's voice crackled on the other end.

"Yes, sir…," replied Mr. Rumbold. "Yes indeed, sir….Thank you, sir… Good-bye, sir." He stared at the phone for a moment. "Most remarkable."

"What was it?" said Mr. Humphries.

"Er, could I have my hand back?" said Mr. Rumbold.

"Oh, I'm sorry," said Mr. Humphries, relinquishing his grip reluctantly.

"That," continued Mr. Rumbold, "was Young Mr. Grace who wants to have a word with me on his way out through the department."

"He's coming to break the news to you," said Mr. Humphries confidently.

"Oh dear," said Mrs. Slocombe, "we haven't even tidied up yet. Come on, Miss Brahms." And leading the way she rushed back into the department to cover up the dummies and close the display cabinet. Mr. Rumbold followed them out, waving his arms like a windmill.

"Hurry up, hurry up," he shouted. "You should have seen to this, Captain Peacock."

"I'm sorry, sir," said Captain Peacock apologetically. Then turning towards Mrs. Slocombe he pointed to some boxes on her counter. "Would you put those away immediately please, Mrs. Slocombe?"

Mrs. Slocombe turned to Miss Brahms. "Miss Brahms, would you put these boxes away immediately? They've got to go on the shelf in millinery. And you know I'm no good up on the ladder." Miss Brahms picked them up, tucking the top one under her chin, and entered the small room behind the counter. She put the boxes on the floor and crossed the room to get the ladder as Mrs. Slocombe came in.

"Miss Brahms, would you please hurry? We're all trying to go home."

"I am hurrying," said Miss Brahms.

Captain Peacock entered the room. "Come along, Miss Brahms. We haven't got all night."

"Do you mind closing the door?" said Miss Brahms. "I'm trying to put these boxes up there." She pointed to a cupboard over the door. Captain Peacock closed it, and helped her place the ladder against the door.

"Get up there," said Mrs. Slocombe, "and I'll hand you the boxes." Miss Brahms shook her head.

"I'm not going up that ladder with Captain Peacock standing down there, looking up."

"For goodness' sake," said Captain Peacock, "give me those hat boxes, I'll do it myself," and taking them he started up the ladder.

In the department Mr. Grace came out of the lift, and leaning heavily on his stick staggered to the edge of the steps.

"Mr. Rumbold!" he called in a wavering voice. Mr. Rumbold was waving his arms encouraging Mr. Grainger and the others to greater efforts.

"Yes, Mr. Grace, sir. As you see the members of my department are putting in a little overtime." Mr. Grace nodded and walked slowly down the steps.

"A strange thing happened this afternoon," he announced.

Mr. Rumbold rushed forward and took him by the elbow to help him. "Really sit, what was that?"

Mr. Grace paused for breath. "My tea bag broke," he announced.

Mr. Rumbold adjusted a sorrowful expression on his face.

"I'm sorry to hear about that, Mr. Grace. I shall tell the catering manager about it."

Mr. Grace shook his head. "No, I'm glad it broke. Lily the tea-girl read my tea leaves."

"I hope," said Mr. Rumbold as he helped Mr. Grace down the last few steps, "that it was good news."

Mr. Grace stopped again. "More of a warning really. It said beware of a bald-headed man with big ears, and so you're not getting the job."

Mr. Rumbold let go of Mr. Grace's elbow and took a step back with surprise.

"Carry on, everybody," said Mr. Grace. "You've all done very well." With an effort he turned and started back up the steps.

Mr. Lucas nudged Mr. Humphries. "Fine fortune teller you turned out to be."

"Well," said Mr. Humphries ruffled, "I wasn't far off. I said I saw the brown leaves and that tea would be a turning point."

"But," said Mr. Lucas, "Mr. Rumbold didn't get the job."

"Well exactly," replied Mr. Humphries, "the turning point was that he would turn back."

"And," added Mr. Lucas, "what about Mrs. Slocombe? With a man at her feet. Peacock going up the ladder and a door opening and all that rubbish about finding him wearing a new hat."

"Well," said Mr. Humphries, "I can't be right all the time. Let's go and tell him about Mr. Rumbold." Walking quickly and followed by Mr. Lucas he crossed the department and pushed open the millinery-room door. There was a wild cry from inside, followed by a crash. Mr. Humphries and Mr. Lucas popped their heads round the door and saw Mrs. Slocombe and Miss Brahms staring aghast at Captain Peacock who had fallen off the ladder. Next to him was an open box and on his head was a large Queen Mary hat, from under which Captain Peacock stared balefully at Mr. Humphries.

"I think," remarked Mr. Humphries, "that this would be a good time for me to leave my body."

CHAPTER

# The Clock

"May I continue," said Captain Peacock irritably.

"Oh please do," said Mrs. Slocombe. "We're all agog."

# The Clock

IT WAS A PARTICULARLY HOT JULY MORNING ON THE FIRST FLOOR AT Grace Brothers and no doubt equally hot on all the other floors. Nevertheless, Captain Peacock still wore his pale grey waistcoat under the immaculate black jacket as he stood and peered at his reflection in one of the long mirrors near the men's counter. He'd spent quite a few lunchtimes standing in the staff entrance doorway to Grace Brothers' roof garden—staff not actually being allowed on the roof garden or restaurant—but there was no law forbidding any member of the staff standing on the top step when the door was open. The resulting suntan showed up well against Captain Peacock's white stiff collar reminding him of the one he had had when in the desert army. He raised one eyebrow and stroked his moustache. It had often occurred to him that he did not look too unlike David Niven and had he had any memoirs worth recounting, he would certainly have written them up.

He suddenly became aware of another pair of eyes gazing over his shoulder and, straightening up, came face to face with a very fat military-looking gentleman with a pug nose, a small bristling moustache and under his chin a blue and red striped tie. Instinctively Captain Peacock stood to attention.

"Can I help you, sir?"

"Yes," barked the customer. "Show me some sports jackets."

"I don't actually show anything personally, sir," admitted Captain Peacock, "but I'll summon our senior assistant to attend to your wishes." With a snap of his fingers and a quick movement of his head he called, "Are you free, Mr. Grainger?"

"Yes, I'm free, Captain Peacock." Mr. Grainger came ambling from behind the counter, his fingers automatically bringing the tape measure down from round his neck.

Captain Peacock gazed at the customer's striped tie. "Unless I'm mistaken, sir, that is a Guard's tie you're wearing, isn't it?"

The gentleman shook his head. "No it's not," he barked. "It's the Stork margarine table tennis club tie."

Captain Peacock stood at ease. "Oh is it?" he said casually. "Table tennis, yes," and then peering more closely at it he nodded. "Yes, the band is a little narrower."

"Yes, Captain Peacock," puffed Mr. Grainger at his elbow. With a casual wave of his hand Captain Peacock indicated the customer.

"Something in the sports jacket line for this customer, Mr. Grainger, with plenty of room underneath the arms for overhead smashes." The customer stared at him aggressively for a moment, then followed Mr. Grainger to the counter.

Mr. Humphries looked up from the box of ties he was sorting through. Mr. Grainger indicated his customer.

"I would say this gentleman is a forty-four, wouldn't you, Mr. Humphries?"

Mr. Humphries put down a tie and, casting a critical eye over the customer, nodded. "Certainly, Mr. Grainger, a forty-four without a doubt. Wouldn't you think so, Mr. Lucas?" He turned as he spoke. Mr. Lucas, who had been dozing on the counter, woke up with a start. "What was that, Mr. Humphries?"

"I said that this gentleman certainly looks a forty-four."

"Oh yes," said Mr. Lucas, "a definite forty-four. In fact, if he isn't a forty-four, we're in trouble because we haven't got anything bigger."

Mr. Grainger shook his head. "I wouldn't recommend a check, sir; they do tend to make one appear more portly, not that sir is portly," he added hurriedly, "but that's the effect that checks tend to have." He turned for confirmation to Mr. Humphries. "Don't you agree?"

Mr. Humphries raised his hand and spoke behind it into Mr. Grainger's ear. "I'm afraid we've only got checks in a forty-four." Mr. Grainger nodded and turned back to the customer.

"On the other hand, sir, you do have the height to carry a check."

"A forty-four check please, Mr. Lucas," shouted Mr. Humphries.

Mr. Lucas headed for the appropriate rail. "Forty-four check coming up."

"It is particularly clement weather we are experiencing at the moment," remarked Mr. Grainger.

The customer nodded. "It is indeed."

There was an awkward pause and Mr. Grainger fiddled with his tape. "Please hurry up, Mr. Lucas. We are waiting."

"Coming sir," called Mr. Lucas, and extracting a large check jacket from the rail, he rushed over with it. Mr. Grainger took it from him.

"This range is made in pushcon, isn't it, Mr. Humphries?" Mr. Humphries felt the sleeve of the checked jacket.

"Right first time, Mr. Grainger," he affirmed, "If I remember rightly, it's 35% wool and 35% pushcon."

The pug-nosed customer frowned. "Just a moment. That only makes 70%."

"You're quite right of course," said Mr. Humphries, "but there's a lot of air between the fibres to allow the fabric to breathe. Isn't that right, Mr. Lucas?"

Mr. Lucas nodded. "Absolutely, Mr. Humphries. If you're quiet, you can hear it."

"Thank you, Mr. Lucas," said Mr. Humphries heavily.

Mr. Lucas indicated the rail. "We've got a whole rail full there, just panting for breath." Mr. Grainger hurriedly interrupted him. "Er…the long mirror please, Mr. Lucas."

Mr. Lucas ran over to the long mirror and wheeled it over, and while he set it up, Mr. Grainger helped the customer off with his jacket, and handed it to Mr. Humphries, who put it on the counter. Mr. Grainger then took the new large checked jacket and helped the customer into it. Buttoning up the front he stood back and admired it as the customer looked at his reflection.

"Well, what do you think, Mr. Humphries?" inquired Mr. Grainger.

Mr. Humphries gripped the loose jacket at the back and held it firmly, looking at the customer's reflection.

"I must say it's very snug in the front, sir."

"Very snug indeed," agreed Mr. Grainger.

Mr. Humphries addressed the customer. "If sir could turn round we'll have a look at the back."

"I'll bet," said Mr. Lucas, "that's going to be very snug too."

As the customer turned, Mr. Humphries grasped the front of the jacket and pulled the back in.

"With this back," said Mr. Grainger, "it could have been made for him."

"Of course those broad shoulders make all the difference," agreed Mr. Humphries. This time the customer gave a small smile while desperately trying to peer over his shoulder. Eventually he gave a nod of approval.

"Yes, that seems fine. Tell me, is it hard wearing?"

"Very hard wearing," Mr. Grainger assured him.

"I think you should know, sir," said Mr. Humphries, "that pushcon was discovered when they were developing Concord."

"So," added Mr. Lucas, "if you were thinking of travelling through the sound barrier, you couldn't have chosen better."

"How much is it?" asked the customer.

Mr. Humphries gazed at the ticket on the sleeve.

"Thirty pounds, sit, including V.A.T."

The customer's small eyes almost disappeared. "That's rather a lot, isn't it?"

Mr. Lucas shook his head. "Not when you consider it cost sixty million to develop, sir. It's very reasonable."

The customer still shook his head. "Well, I still think it seems an awful lot of money." He suddenly turned round to look at the front again. With a hurried grab Mr. Humphries just managed to gather up a handful of material at the back.

"Actually, sir," said Mr. Grainger, "it has been reduced from forty-two pounds."

The customer suddenly looked interested. "Oh has it indeed?"

"That's right," said Mr. Humphries, "you're saving ten pounds, sir."

"I'll tell you what I'll do," said the customer, "I'll think about it."

"Very well," said Mr. Grainger. He folded his arms and stood staring at the customer. The customer glanced at Mr. Humphries, who glanced at his watch and then folded his arms and stared back. Thirty seconds elapsed without a word being exchanged. Finally the customer gave in.

"Er, I'll take it."

"Sale, Mr. Humphries," called Mr. Grainger.

"Scribble out the bill, Mr. Lucas," called Mr. Humphries. Mr. Lucas scribbled out the bill and said admiringly to Mr. Grainger, "Well done, Mr. Grainger."

As the customer departed with his purchase, Mr. Grainger gazed after him with a satisfied look in his eye.

"Tell me," asked Mr. Lucas. "What if his wife tells him it's too big?"

"In that case," said Mr. Grainger, "he will bring it back and we shall charge him for the alterations."

"They can't win, can they," said Mr. Lucas.

"Not if I can help it," said Mr. Grainger.


At Mrs. Slocombe's counter there was a middle-aged lady trying on a bridal veil. She gazed at the effect in the mirror that Miss Brahms held up for her. She shook her head.

"No," she said, taking it off. "I think it's just a little too young for me."

"I know exactly what you want," said Mrs. Slocombe. "Miss Brahms, get the bridal veil with the blue orange blossoms."

Miss Brahms put the mirror down on the counter. "Yes, Mrs. Slocombe."

"I hope you don't mind me asking, madam," said Mrs. Slocombe, "but where are you going for the honeymoon?"

"Well," confided the lady, "we're torn between Eastbourne and Brighton."

"I had mine at Shrewburyness," said Mrs. Slocombe. "The weather was terrible and there was absolutely nothing to do…in the daytime that is," she added, with an arch smile.

"What about the veil, Miss Brahms," called Mrs. Slocombe. "Why don't you try Brighton, madam?" she suggested. "It's much livelier than Eastbourne. If the weather is bad there, you can always play bingo."

"Here we are," said Miss Brahms, producing an orange blossom–encrusted bridal veil.

"Here we are," Mrs. Slocombe repeated. "Try this on." The customer bent her head forward and Mrs. Slocombe adjusted the veil. She stood back and gazed at the effect. The veil was so thick that the customer's face was completely hidden.

"There," said Mrs. Slocombe. "How's that?"

"I can't see anything," said the muffled voice of the bride-to-be.

"I tell you," said Mrs. Slocombe, "that from our side, it looks lovely. Doesn't it, Miss Brahms?"

"A treat," agreed Miss Brahms.

"I can't see anything at all."

"Never mind," said Mrs. Slocombe, "you'll have someone holding your arm."

The voice took on an anxious note. "But he won't recognize me."

"He'll know you by your voice, won't he?" said Mrs. Slocombe, a little impatiently.

"Yes," said Miss Brahms, "and think of the surprise he will get when he lifts the veil up."

"That'll do, thank you," said Mrs. Slocombe. "Now, madam, the blossom is detachable should you wish to use it for decorative purposes afterwards."

The customer removed the veil and looked at it with little enthusiasm.

"Well, I suppose I had better take it if you think it's all right," she said with a sigh.

"Pack it up, Miss Brahms," said Mrs. Slocombe hurriedly.

"I haven't said anything," said Miss Brahms defensively.

"I mean," said Mrs. Slocombe, "pack the veil up, girl."

"Sorry," said Miss Brahms.

"Well," said Mrs. Slocombe, "will it be cash or account?"

"As a matter of fact," confided the lady, "my fiancé has just opened an account here."

"Oh really?" said Mrs. Slocombe with renewed interest. "In that case, Miss Brahms, get out that Grace Kelly bridal assemble with the detachable train."

A short while later the bride-to-be headed for the lift carrying an enormous parcel and leaving behind a smiling Mrs. Slocombe.

"When her fiancé gets that bill," said Miss Brahms, "it won't be Brighton or Eastbourne, it'll be Beachy Head."

"Pssst," hissed the unmistakable voice of Mr. Mash. Mrs. Slocombe's smile disappeared and a stern expression crossed her features.

"Oi." Slowly Mrs. Slocombe turned around and gazed along the counter to observe Mr. Mash peering round the fixtures at the end.

"Is that the way you normally attract a lady's attention, Mr. Mash?"

"No, Mrs. Slocombe, I usually go up behind them and give them a quick goose." A pained expression crossed Mrs. Slocombe's face. Glancing around to make sure he wasn't observed by Captain Peacock, Mr. Mash edged his way round the fitting room.

"Ere," he hissed, "are you going to old Grainger's farewell dinner tonight?"

Mrs. Slocombe shook her head. "It is not his farewell dinner, Mr. Mash. Just because he has reached his sixty-fifth birthday, it does not mean he is retiring."

"Well it does if they give him a cuckoo clock," said Mr. Mash. "That's what they did to old Mr. Fredericks in Hardware. I remember it clearly. He had been with us 'ere forty-six years. They had the dinner and as soon as they got to the coffee they give him his clock and one chorus of 'For He's a Jolly Good Fellow' and shoved him in the lift."

"That may be," said Mrs. Slocombe, "but I do find there is a different class of person in Hardware. Now will you get off the floor, please."

"I will," said Mr. Mash, "as soon as I have completed my tasks. I'm here in my official capacity as porter. 'Ang on a sec..." and disappearing, he re-appeared with his noisy trolley from which he took a large box and put it on the counter.

"What have you got in there?" said Mrs. Slocombe suspiciously. Mr. Mash pulled the lid off the cardboard box and produced several pairs of carpet slippers.

"Six pairs of pussy boots."

"Six pairs of what?" said Mrs. Slocombe, her eyebrows shooting up with surprise. She took the glasses that hung on her ample bosom and put them on the end of her nose.

"Pussy boots," said Mr. Mash. "Fur slippers. We got a little sales gimmick too," and reaching into the basket on his trolley he produced a stuffed cat on a stand.

Mrs. Slocombe looked at it in horror. "Whatever is that?"

"This," said Mr. Mash, "is an electric pussy. Battery operated." Placing the cat on the counter, he pressed the switch. The tail started to revolve, there was a loud mechanical purr followed by a faint miaow, and then a Walt Disney–type recorded voice announced: "These are Pussy Boots, these are Pussy Boots."

Mrs. Slocombe shook her head in dismay. "How could anyone do that to a cat?"

"Thank your stars," said Mr. Mash, "that you aren't selling elephant hide luggage."

"I've a good mind," said Mrs. Slocombe, "to write to the R.S.P.C.A."

Mr. Mash switched the cat off. "It's a bit late," he said. "It's dead."

"What's going on over here?" said Captain Peacock coming over.

"Oh, I'm glad you have come over," said Mrs. Slocombe. "Just look what they've sent me."

"Here, Captain Peacock," said Mr. Mash, "do you want to see it work?"

Captain Peacock nodded condescendingly. Mr. Mash switched on the apparatus again and once again the cat went through its paces. The tail revolving, head turning from side to side, the mouth opening while it passed its message. Captain Peacock smiled.

"Well, you must admit it's a novelty, Mrs. Slocombe." The smile started to disappear as the tail began to revolve at an ever-increasing speed.

The pitch of the voice went higher and higher till suddenly with a loud "boing" something snapped inside. The head left the body and hung grotesquely on the end of a long spring.

"I think," said Captain Peacock solemnly, "that you'd better take it to the vet, Mr. Mash."

"Very whimsical," commented Mr. Mash. He picked up the remains of the cat, threw it back in the basket and wheeled it off. Mrs. Slocombe gave a sigh of relief.

"By the way," said Captain Peacock, "Mr. Grainger's just gone for his coffee break, so it will be a good opportunity to discuss his birthday dinner."

"Oh yes," said Mrs. Slocombe, "what a good idea. Come on, Miss Brahms, gather round."

Captain Peacock glanced across the floor.

"Mr. Humphries," he called, "are you free?"

Mr. Humphries's blond head nodded in the distance. "I'm free, Captain Peacock."

"Are you free, Mr. Lucas?" called Captain Peacock.

Captain Peacock waited until they had gathered round. He glanced towards the lift to make sure that Mr. Grainger hadn't come back early.

"Now," said Captain Peacock, "I've had a word with the canteen manager and it seems that the most economical way of staging this function is to give the dinner down here."

"Oh poor Mr. Grainger," said Mrs. Slocombe. "Can't we have a proper do in the restaurant upstairs?"

"If we do," said Captain Peacock, "it will cost us another pound per head."

"In that case," said Mr. Humphries, "let's have it down here. It's more personal after all."

Removing his spectacle case form his inside pocket Captain Peacock opened it and placing the executive pair of horn rims on the end of his nose, he removed from another inside pocket a small folded piece of paper which he opened and studied earnestly.

"Now," he said, "I have made a note of the menu which is as follows: First vegetable soup or hors d'oeuvre."

"The staff canteen's idea of hors d'oeuvre," commented Mr. Lucas, "is a sardine and a piece of tired lettuce."

"You're forgetting," said Captain Peacock, "that it also comes with a dollop of Russian salad."

Mr. Lucas clapped his hands to his forehead. "Oh yes, I'm sorry, Captain Peacock, I'd forgotten the Russian salad."

Mr. Humphries clutched his middle in mock agony. "I have never forgotten the Russian salad," he commented. "I had roller skates for a week afterwards."

"And," continued Captain Peacock, "there is a main course which I shall bring up later."

"Won't we all," said Mrs. Slocombe moodily.

"May I continue," said Captain Peacock irritably.

"Oh please do," said Mrs. Slocombe. "We're all agog."

"There will," said Captain Peacock reading from the list, "be cabinet pudding with custard or simulated cream. Followed by coffee *ad lib* and one After Eight mint."

"Is there one each," said Mr. Lucas, "or just the one?"

"How much does all that come to?" asked Miss Brahms.

Captain Peacock gazed at her over the top of his glasses. "The price, Miss Brahms, depends on what we choose for the main course. Roast pheasant would be £2 a head. *Poulet rôti* 1.50…"

"'Ang on," said Miss Brahms. "What was the last one?"

"That," said Captain Peacock, "was French for roast chicken. As I was saying that would be £1.50. Steak Pie £1.25 or macaroni cheese £1.00."

Mr. Lucas put his hand up. "I vote for macaroni cheese."

Mrs. Slocombe shook her head and clicked her tongue disapprovingly. "Mr. Lucas, you can't give the poor soul a farewell dinner with macaroni cheese."

"Unless you want him to go out with a bang," added Mr. Humphries.

"No," said Mr. Lucas, "I think he'd prefer it. I mean, if he gets those teeth of his into a pheasant, we'll be here all night."

"If we have the canteen's steak pie we'll be here all night so what's the difference?" said Mr. Humphries.

"I'll go for the macaroni cheese," said Miss Brahms. "It's not too bad if you close your eyes."

"Come on," said Mrs. Slocombe, "let's be reasonable. I think as it's his farewell dinner we should at least give him the chicken."

"Any other votes for chicken?" asked Captain Peacock, as he removed his pencil from his top outside pocket.

Mr. Humphries nodded. "I'll vote for chicken. It goes so well with cabinet pudding and simulated cream."

"As a matter of fact," said Captain Peacock, "I favor the chicken myself. So the vote is three chicken to two macaroni."

"That was a close finish," said Mr. Humphries, "and it appears that the steak pie has lost its deposit."

Captain Peacock made a careful note on his piece of paper and murmured, "so that will be £1.50 per head."

Mr. Lucas glanced lecherously at Miss Brahms. "I'll tell you what, Shirley, we'll share the wishbone."

"I know what you're going to wish," whispered Mr. Humphries waspishly.

"I heard that," said Miss Brahms, "and even if he wins he won't get it."

"If I may continue," said Captain Peacock, pencil poised.

"Please do," said Mrs. Slocombe.

"That price of course," said Captain Peacock, "includes Mr. Grainger and his good lady wife. Now is anybody else here bringing guests?"

"I was thinking of asking the Aga Khan," said Mr. Humphries, "but I'm not sure that he can eat meat."

"I'm definitely not bringing anybody," said Miss Brahms.

"I quite agree," said Mrs. Slocombe. "I think it will be very nice to keep it all intimate."

"I'm all for a bit of intimacy," said Mr. Lucas, "although I had thought of inviting the Galloping Gourmet."

"If he saw that menu," commented Mr. Humphries, "he'd gallop the other way."

"If," said Captain Peacock heavily, "the witty thrust and riposte could cease for a moment and I could be allowed to continue..."

"Continue," said Mr. Lucas. "I'm sorry for the interruptions but the thought of spending £1.50 has made me a bit lightheaded."

"Thank you," said Captain Peacock. "Now as far as dress is concerned. I think it should be black tie."

"And something else, I trust," said Mr. Humphries.

"Black tie?" said Miss Brahms. "Anyone would think it was a funeral. I think it's morbid giving farewell dinners."

Captain Peacock shook his head. "Now then, Miss Brahms. We don't know it's a farewell dinner. That's up to our manager, Mr. Rumbold."

"That's right," said Mr. Humphries, "it's only a farewell dinner when they give you the cuckoo clock. You drag yourself home for the last time, stick it on the mantelpiece and watch the rest of your life to tick away."

"Well," said Mr. Lucas, "the way old Mr. Grainger was staggering around this morning they should save the money and give him an egg timer."

"That will do, Mr. Lucas," said Captain Peacock. "Now I think we have covered everything. So you can all go back to your places."

At that moment Mr. Grainger appeared at the top of the steps on his way back from his coffee break.

"Have I missed anything?" he called.

Captain Peacock turned. "Aah no, er...no, Mr. Grainger, we're just setting the menu for your dinner."

Mr. Grainger made his way gingerly down the steps. "I do hope," he remarked, "that we're not having steak pie. I travel home on a non-corridor train."

"As a matter of fact" said Captain Peacock, "we are having the chicken by an overall vote."

Mr. Grainger smiled with pleasure. "Oh, I'm delighted to hear that, Stephen." His smile disappeared slightly and he paused by the Captain.

"Mr. Fredericks had the chicken," he confided, "and unfortunately he got the clock as well and he wasn't quite sixty-four."

Captain Peacock introduced an encouraging note in his voice. "Come now, Ernest, I'm sure that Grace Brothers will require your services for many years to come." The smile returned to Mr. Grainger's face.

"Is that official?" he asked hopefully.

"I'm afraid not, Ernest. Not in my hands. It's all up to Mr. Rumbold."

The telephone at the back of the men's counter started to ring and Mr. Humphries picked it up.

"Men's ready-mades." he announced in a deep voice. Then nodded. "Yes, I'll tell him. Are you free, Mr. Grainger?" he called.

"At the moment," said Mr. Grainger, after taking a brief look round.

"In that case," said Mr. Humphries, "you're wanted in Mr. Rumbold's office."

A troubled look crossed Mr. Grainger's face and he glanced anxiously at Captain Peacock.

"Oh dear," he mumbled, "I wonder what it's about?" Captain Peacock put a comforting arm on Mr. Grainger's shoulder. "Probably nothing to do with your retirement at all, Ernest."

Mr. Grainger's shoulders sagged slightly. "Well," he murmured, "whatever will be will be. Of course I've had many happy years here, Stephen."

Captain Peacock nodded sympathetically. "I must remind you, Ernest, that if Grace Brothers are going to announce your retirement, Young Mr. Grace would attend your dinner personally."

A glimmer of hope shone in Mr. Grainger's eye. "Isn't he coming?"

Captain Peacock looked around, bent forward and spoke confidentially. "Off the record, Ernest, I have not been so informed."

The years seemed to slip away from Mr. Grainger and his face beamed with delight. "Oh good," he said, and turning he disappeared with a springy step in the direction of Mr. Rumbold's office.

Mr. Rumbold sat at his desk gazing thoughtfully at the inscription on the cuckoo clock which he held in his hands and which read "For service above and beyond the call of duty, Grace Brothers thanks you." A knock on the door interrupted his scrutiny. Jumping up hurriedly from behind his desk, he placed the clock in a filing cabinet and then returning to his desk called, "Enter."

Mr. Grainger's beaming face popped round the door. "I understand you wish to see me, sir."

"Ah yes," said Mr. Rumbold. "Come in, shut the door, Grainger. Er…it's about Young Mr. Grace."

Mr. Grainger carefully closed the door and turned round with an inquiring look on his face.

"Er…yes, sir," he said cautiously.

Mr. Rumbold shook his head. "He won't be attending your dinner tonight, I'm afraid."

"Good," beamed Mr. Grainger.

"Unfortunately," said Mr. Rumbold, "he has a very bad cold."

Like a change in the weather the beaming smile disappeared from Mr. Grainger's face and a cloud took its place. "You mean, sir, that if it wasn't for his cold, he would have been there."

Mr. Rumbold settled himself back in his chair and gazed at Mr. Grainger with what he fondly imagined was a kindly expression.

"Well, when anyone has been here as long as you have, Ernest." He waved his hand vaguely in the air to indicate the importance of Mr. Grainger's sojourn at Grace Brothers. Then leaning forward slightly he inquired, "How long is it now?"

"Well," said Mr. Grainger, "I joined Grace Brothers, let me see, in 1937. That was the day Mr. Baldwin resigned."

"Resigned from Grace Brothers?"

"No, no, no. He handed over to Mr. Chamberlain."

"Ah yes," said Mr. Rumbold knowledgeably. "That would be Chamberlain of China and Glass."

"No sir," said Mr. Grainger irritably. "The Prime Minister."

"Good heavens!" said Mr. Rumbold looking startled. "He wasn't at Grace Brothers, was he?"

"No sir," said Mr. Grainger patiently. "Mr. Chamberlain who went to Munich."

Mr. Rumbold shook his head trying to collect his thoughts. "I didn't know we had a branch there," he muttered. "I must look into that."

Mr. Grainger leant on the desk. "We haven't, sir, he went to see Hitler."

"What?" gasped Mr. Rumbold, sitting bolt upright in his chair. "Mr. Chamberlain of China and Glass? How extraordinary."

"Perhaps we should start again," said Mr. Grainger. "In answer to your question I have been here thirty-seven years."

"It's a long time," said Mr. Rumbold nodding approvingly.

"Yes," said Mr. Grainger. "It is."

There was an awkward pause as Mr. Rumbold searched his mind for something encouraging to say. During the awkward pause Mr. Grainger cocked his head to one side. It seemed to him that he could distinctly hear the ticking of a clock somewhere. Mr. Rumbold suddenly became aware of the ticking as well and coughed noisily to try and hide it.

"Er...I'm looking forward to the dinner, Mr. Grainger."

Mr. Grainger dismissed the ticking to his fevered imagination.

"Yes, sir, so am I. I understand from Captain Peacock that we are having the chicken. A welcome choice if I may say so."

"Yes indeed," said Mr. Rumbold. "I'm so glad it wasn't the steak pie. Mr. Fredericks had the steak pie."

"No," corrected Mr. Grainger, "he had the chicken, and," he added, "the cuckoo clock." He gazed intently at Mr. Rumbold for some reaction. Apart from dropping his pencil, taking off his glasses and wiping them nervously, coughing, noisily clearing his throat and shifting uncomfortably in his seat, there was none.

"Yes the clock," he mumbled, "yes, yes...well that'll be all, Mr. Grainger. Thank you for coming in."

"Thank you, Mr. Rumbold," murmured Mr. Grainger. He paused again and cocked his head to one side. "Is it my imagination, sir, or can I hear something ticking?"

"Ticking," shouted Mr. Rumbold and then controlling the level of his voice. "Ticking?" he said. "No, no, I don't think so, it's probably the central heating pipes expanding."

"The central heating isn't on," said Mr. Grainger. "The weather is too hot."

"In that case," said Mr. Rumbold, "that's probably why they are expanding. Well that'll be all, Mr. Grainger," and getting up and extending an arm, he propelled Mr. Grainger towards the door.

As the door closed behind him Mr. Grainger paused and gave a deep sigh of relief. All seemed to be well, then he froze. For quite distinctly through the closed office door, he heard the sound of a cuckoo. Inside the office Mr. Rumbold desperately wrestled with the filing cabinet and as the cuckoo came out for the third time grasped it in his hands and silenced it. Outside the door Mr. Grainger's shoulders slumped and, like a man condemned to death, he trod the weary path back to the department. Mr. Humphries was the first to notice the appearance of Mr. Grainger at the end of the counter.

"Oh my word," said Mr. Humphries throwing his hands up in dismay. "Mr. Grainger, you look as if you've seen, a ghost."

Mr. Grainger sat down heavily on his chair. "Mr. Humphries, I have just heard the cuckoo in Mr. Rumbold's office."

"My word," said Mr. Lucas, "and it's only the third of March. You'd better write to The Times about that."

"It was a cuckoo clock," said Mr. Grainger, "and you know what that means."

"Oh dear," said Mr. Humphries. "Quickly, Mr. Lucas, a glass of water for Mr. Grainger."

"Perhaps," said Mr. Lucas as he paused before he dashed away to carry out his mission, "you'd like to try on a pair of carpet slippers, Mr. Grainger? Just to get used to them." Mr. Grainger slumped visibly in his chair.

"Shut up," said Mr. Humphries, "and put a spot of brandy in it."

Eight o'clock that evening, the entire first floor of Grace Brothers had been transformed for Mr. Grainger's farewell dinner by the effervescent Mr. Mash and his cronies from the basement. Twine stretched across the department and from it a number of streamers hung down from the novelty department. A piano from the music department with a sale ticket still on it stood by Mrs. Slocombe's counter and in the centre of the floor three long tables were joined together and covered with a customer's returned table cloth which had been damaged in transit. The knives and forks were laid out neatly and in the centre of the table there was a bowl of plastic fruit and at either end a small posy of dried flowers. Waiting expectantly at the foot of the marble steps was Mr. Rumbold immaculately clad in his dinner jacket upon which was pinned a large pink carnation with a lot of green fern sticking out round it, and next to him stood Mr. Mash similarly attired but his immaculate appearance rather spoiled by his working boots protruding from under his rather short evening trousers. In his hands he held a large tray of drinks. Mr. Rumbold glanced anxiously at his watch.

"I hope someone turns up soon," said Mr. Mash. "The bubbles in this champagne is all drying up."

"Remember, only one glass each, Mr. Mash," reminded Mr. Rumbold sternly.

"Right! We don't want 'em losing control, do we?"

At that moment one of the lifts went ping, the doors opened and Mr. Humphries in a frilly shirt with an enormous purple bow tie, black velvet evening jacket and sparkling patent leather shoes made his entrance. With him was Mr. Lucas still dressed in his day suit but sporting a spotted bow tie. Mr. Mash stepped forward and in a grandiose M.C. voice announced.

"Mr. James Lucas, accompanied by Mr. Wilberforce Clayborn Humphries."

"Hello, Wilberforce," called Mr. Lucas, and holding out an arm, "Shall we?"

"Why not?" said Mr. Humphries, putting his arm through Mr. Lucas's as he accompanied him down the steps. Mr. Humphries held out a hand languorously towards Mr. Rumbold. "How do you do, your Grace? I do hope we're not late. We just popped into the Oklahoma Pancake House for a cup of cocoa and a Danish pastry. The excitement was almost too much."

"It certainly was," said Mr. Lucas. "There was a lovely bit of Danish crumpet in there. But when we said we were going to our anniversary dinner, she took one look at Mr. Humphries and went right off me."

An interested look came into Mr. Humphries's eyes as he saw the champagne glasses on the tray.

"My word," he exclaimed. "Grace Brothers have really pushed the boat out. Could it be Dom Pérignon?" he inquired.

"No," said Mr. Mash. "It's Japanese tinned, extra dry."

Mr. Lucas took a glass and sniffed it. "I see," he commented, "the bubbles don't tickle your nose, they just give you karate chops."

A ping announced the arrival of the lift again and from it stepped Mrs. Slocombe and Miss Brahms. Mrs. Slocombe was wearing her best emerald green evening dress with a large spray of orange plastic orchids pinned to the cleavage of her bosom. Miss Brahms wore a white miniskirt and white high-heeled sandals. Mr. Lucas gazed at her legs appreciatively and gave a low whistle of admiration.

"Knock it off," said Miss Brahms.

Mr. Mash took a deep breath and again in his loud M.C. voice announced: "Shirley Brahms and the Duchess of Slocombe." Then, holding out the tray as the ladies came down the steps, "Drinks, ladies?"

"Why not?" said Mrs. Slocombe taking her glass and pressing it unsteadily to her lips.

"I don't think," said Miss Brahms, "that Mrs. Slocombe should have anymore."

Mrs. Slocombe turned and with difficulty focused her eyes on Miss Brahms. "Are you inferring that four vodka martinis are more than my capacity?" Then throwing back her head, she took a step forward, tripped over the edge of the carpet and was caught by an anxious-looking Mr. Rumbold.

"It's these shoes," complained Mrs. Slocombe. "I've just had them re-soled and I'm not used to the extra rubber."

Mr. Humphries stepped forward. "Well you know what they say about vodka, Mrs. Slocombe. One's all right. Two's the most. Three's under the table and four's under the host." Mrs. Slocombe gave a wild shriek of laughter, and put her arm round Mr. Humphries's shoulder.

"Oh Mr. Humphries, what will you say next?" Mr. Humphries gazed at her anxiously.

"Only that Mr. Rumbold's the host."

The lift appeared again, the doors opening just as Captain Peacock was in the act of taking off his raincoat to reveal a bow tie and dinner jacket. Mr. Mash stepped forward again to the bottom of the steps with the drinks and with a stentorian bellow announced: "Captain Stephen Peacock, R.A.S.C., C. of E., Hero of the battle Catterick Naafi, holder of the Hot Cross Bun and arch enemy of the fuzzie wuzzies in the packing department..."

"That will do, Mr. Mash," called Captain Peacock holding up his hand authoritatively and then, marching down the steps, he handed his hat and coat to Mr. Lucas and took a drink from the tray.

"Make it last," said Mr. Mash, "we've got no more reserves."

Ignoring him Captain Peacock addressed himself to Mr. Rumbold. "The group are coming up in the other lift, sir."

"Oh good," said Miss Brahms. "Who have we got, the New Seekers?"

When the lift arrived three very elderly ladies emerged. One held a music case containing a cello, another a violin. As the trio came out from the lift Mr. Lucas shook his head sadly. "I don't think it's the New Seekers. Looks more like the Old Knockers to me."

The lady without an instrument led the other two down the steps and approached Mr. Rumbold. "Good evening," she announced in a deep musical voice. "I am Madame Trixi and this is the Trixie Trio." She turned and waved her hand with a flourish at her two elderly companions. Captain Peacock and Mr. Rumbold exchanged anxious glances. Mr. Rumbold cleared his throat.

"Madame Trixi, may I say welcome to Grace Brothers."

"Thank you," said Madame Trixi and then glancing at the tray held by Mr. Mash gave a tinkling laugh. "Oh my word, look, champagne." Mr. Mash half turned his back on her moving the tray out of her reach.

"The beer for the band is under the piano," he announced. Madame Trixi's friendly smile disappeared.

"I see," she said. "In that case, where do you want the orchestra?"

"Er…I think over by the pianoforte," said Mr. Rumbold pointing.

"Very well," said Madame Trixi and leading her companions over to the piano she sat on the stool, opened the lid and played a cascade of ill-assorted notes.

With an inane grin on her face, Mrs. Slocombe watched the ladies opening their music cases and producing their instruments.

"My word, Captain Peacock," she hiccoughed, "it looks as though we are going to be able to trip the tight lanfastic."

Captain Peacock raised his eyes in surprise. "I beg your pardon, Mrs. Slocombe. I didn't quite hear that."

"She wants you to rip her tight elastic," said Mr. Humphries.

Captain Peacock took Mrs. Slocombe by the elbow and led her towards the table. "Perhaps you'd better sit down, Mrs. Slocombe. We'll be starting in less than an hour." Then he paused and turned to Mr. Rumbold. "By the way, sir. Since it will affect my speech, is Mr. Grainger going to get the farewell clock or not?"

Mr. Rumbold nodded. "Yes, I'm afraid so, and due to Young Mr. Grace's indisposition I'm going to have to be the one to present it."

"It's a pity," said Captain Peacock as he helped Mrs. Slocombe into a chair, "that he's going. He's a very useful member of the department and we shall all miss him very much indeed."

"Trousers will not be the same without him," said Mr. Humphries.

"Never mind," said Mr. Rumbold. "It happens to us all eventually. We shall just have to carry on. Mr. Humphries of course will have to move up one and we shall have to get another Mr. Lucas as he will be moving up one as well."

"What a terrible thought," commented Captain Peacock.

"That's it," said Mr. Humphries to the others. "He's going!"

"Who is?" said Miss Brahms downing her Japanese champagne with a gulp.

"Mr. Grainger," said Mr. Humphries. "He's getting the clock."

"Poor old sod," said Mr. Lucas. "Fancy being thrown on the scrap heap like that. He could probably have gone on for weeks."

"It'll break his heart," said Miss Brahms, taking another drink from the tray.

"I feel very sorry for him," said Mr. Humphries. "I'm very fond of Mr. Grainger."

"Hey," called Madame Trixi.

Mr. Rumbold turned. "Are you addressing me?"

"Yes," she replied. "Is there anything in particular you wish us to play?"

"Oh yes," said Mr. Rumbold, "When Mr. Grainger comes down the steps, I would like you to play something appropriate."

"How about 'Goodbyee'?" suggested Mr. Lucas.

"Oh, I do think that's a bit sudden," said Mr. Humphries. "I mean, don't you think, how about er…something romantic," and he started singing: "A tinkling piano in the bedding department, those foolish words told me what your heart meant, these foolish springs remind me of you."

"Something cheerful," said Miss Brahms. "A Beatles' number or the Rolling Stones."

"As I'm in charge," said Mr. Rumbold, "may I suggest, 'A Fine Old English Gentleman.' "

"That's a splendid choice," agreed Captain Peacock. "Did you get that, Madame Trixi?"

After a hurried consultation with her colleagues, Madame Trixi nodded and smiled. "Yes," she said. "You just wave your hand when you want it."

"Not many girls are that accommodating," commented Mr. Lucas.

"The lift's coming up," cried Miss Brahms.

Mrs. Slocombe staggered unsteadily from her chair, and headed towards the stairs. "Hip hip hooray!" she cried.

"Not yet," said Mr. Rumbold sternly. "Be quiet, Mrs. Slocombe."

Captain Peacock held his arm up, and shouted, "Stand by, orchestra."

"We're standing by," said Madame Trixi, hands poised over the keys.

The doors opened and out stepped two aged cleaning women with mops and buckets. Mr. Mash stepped forward and in his stentorian bellow announced Miss Elsie Makepeace and Miss Doris Poland. Captain Peacock turned with surprise and his arm dropped. Immediately the band started playing, in spite of Captain Peacock's frantic signals to make them stop. The women started back in surprise.

"Oh my gawd," said Elsie. "It must be *This is your Life.*"

Mr. Rumbold marched up the steps. "What on earth are you two doing here? It's a private dinner."

"It's half past seven, sir, we've come to do the floor."

"Well, you can't do it now," said Mr. Rumbold. "Please go away." And ushering the cleaning women back into the lift, he pressed the button.

Just before the doors closed one of them shouted, "I'll see Mr. Hetherington about this." And on that dire threat the doors closed and the lift disappeared. Mr. Rumbold, looking hot and bothered, wiped his forehead with his spotted handkerchief and called to Captain Peacock.

"Didn't you speak to Hetherington about this, Peacock?"

Captain Peacock shook his head. "It's not in my province, sir."

At that moment the telephone behind Mrs. Slocombe's counter rang. Running as quickly as she could on her white high-heeled sandals, Miss Brahms crossed the department and answered it.

"Lingerie and blouses," she announced breathlessly. Then paused for a moment. "Right." Hanging up the phone she turned. "Mr. and Mrs. Grainger are on their way up in the lift," she announced.

"Places, everybody," shouted Captain Peacock. No sooner had everybody got to the bottom of the steps when the lift doors opened to reveal Mr. and Mrs. Grainger attired in their best evening wear. Mrs. Grainger, a grey-haired elderly lady, leaned heavily on Mr. Grainger's arm, and gazed nervously at the reception committee. Mr. Grainger patted her hand comfortingly and stepped towards the top of the steps. Mr. Mash stood forward and shouted "Mr. and Mrs. Ernest Grainger arriving for his possible farewell party, or not as the case may be."

Captain Peacock waved his arm feverishly and galvanized the Trixi Trio into action. As the strains of "A Fine Old English Gentleman" echoed through the department at Grace Brothers, a burst of applause broke for Mr. and Mrs. Grainger as they walked slowly down the steps. Mr. Grainger beamed with delight and wiped the corner of his eye with his sleeve. It was obviously one of the more emotional moments of his life.

Mr. Rumbold stepped forward and cleared his throat. "Mr. and Mrs. Grainger, on behalf of Grace Brothers, welcome to your anniversary dinner."

"Thank you," said Mr. Grainger, then glancing up at the bunting hanging from the line exclaimed. "You shouldn't have done all this for me."

"Oh look," said Mrs. Grainger, "they've even got an orchestra."

Mr. Grainger gazed at the Trixi Trio and wiped his eye again. "Mr. Fredericks never had an orchestra," he said with a lump in his throat.

"You'll be doing the Gay Gordons before the evening is out," said Mr. Humphries.

"That should round off the evening nicely," said Mr. Lucas.

As all the drinks had left the tray, Mr. Mash held it out in his left hand and with his right one banged his fist against it. "My Lords, Ladies and Gentlemen," he announced, "please take your partners for the tinned vegetable soup." Quickly sensing the atmosphere, the Trixi Trio struck up with "We'll Gather Lilacs in the Spring Again" and the guests made their way to the table where Mr. Grainger helped Mrs. Grainger to her seat.

The time on the department clock indicated that the hour of ten had been reached. The Trixi Trio was playing "Hit the Road, Jack," and Mr. and Mrs. Grainger were dancing with the zest of a much younger couple, Mr. Grainger humming off-key in his wife's ear. Madame Trixi gazed over her shoulder approvingly at the scene as her aged fingers tripped up and down the keyboard.

Miss Brahms tried to remove Mr. Lucas's hand from her posterior as he danced closely to her.

"What are you doing?" she grumbled. "This is supposed to be a waltz."

"Sorry," said Mr. Lucas. "It's that Japanese champagne. It's turned me into a wild animal."

"I've had enough," said Miss Brahms and leaving him in the middle of the floor she marched back to the table and joined Mr. Humphries and Mr. Rumbold.

"He's like an octopus," she announced gazing at Mr. Lucas who continued dancing on his own in front of one of the female dummies.

"I think," said Mr. Rumbold, "that Captain Peacock is having a bit of trouble with Mrs. Slocombe."

"I'm not surprised," said Mr. Humphries. "She's on her second bottle." Captain Peacock clung grimly on to Mrs. Slocombe, supporting her as he turned. Mrs. Slocombe gazed up at him with a vacant smile on her face.

"I must say," she muttered, "you're very light on my feet."

"I'm sorry," said Captain Peacock grimly, "but if you will keep putting them in the way."

With a sudden movement Mrs. Slocombe spun round again clutching on to Captain Peacock, tripped over his foot, and it was only with a desperate effort that he managed to stop her from falling.

"Oops," said Mrs. Slocombe gaily. "Nearly went then."

Captain Peacock shook his head. "It's strange how potent cheap music can be," he murmured.

Mr. Rumbold turned to Mr. Humphries and with attempted humour announced, "Well, you and I appear to be the only ones not dancing."

"Oh all right," said Mr. Humphries, standing up and taking Mr. Rumbold's hand. "If you promise not to lead." Mr. Rumbold hurriedly removed his hand and glanced at his watch.

"Er...I think it's time we got on with the speeches." He waved across the table to attract Mr. Mash's attention. "Mr. Mash."

"Yes, sir."

"Would you give my compliments to the Trio and ask them to take an interval?"

"Right you are," said Mr. Mash scooping up a large helping of cabinet pudding from Mrs. Slocombe's plate and stuffing it in his mouth. Then clapping his hands noisily he addressed the Trio.

"Oi. Belt up."

As the music stopped, Mr. Grainger staggered over to the table and, helping Mrs. Grainger to her seat, sat down next to her.

"I feel quite puffed," he announced. "It's just as well I'm going to put my feet up."

Mr. Rumbold stood up and pushed his chair back. "Would everybody please be seated."

Mr. Lucas nudged Miss Brahms. "Well, this is it. Time for the judge to pronounce his sentence."

"I was enjoying that dance," said Mrs. Slocombe as Captain Peacock helped her to her chair. Looking up at Captain Peacock, her jaw hanging slightly, she confided, "I shall always remember dancing with you, Stephen. It is not an experience that I will forget in a hurry."

"Thank you," said Captain Peacock, sitting down.

Mr. Rumbold cleared his throat to attract attention. "I would ask," he said, "that those present should make sure that their glasses are charged."

Mrs. Slocombe immediately picked up her empty glass and stared at it unsteadily. "Mine seems to be empty," she announced. Mr. Mash picked up a bottle and refilled her glass.

"What have you got, Mrs. Slocombe?" he asked with a chuckle. "Hollow legs?"

Mr. Rumbold felt in his inside pocket and took out a copious sheath of notes, and tapping on the table with his knuckles, called for silence. Everyone turned and looked at him expectantly.

"I shall now call upon Captain Peacock to propose the toast." Placing his copious notes back into his pocket, he sat down again. Captain Peacock also produced a large wad of notes from his inside pocket, studied them for a moment, then looked at Mr. and Mrs. Grainger.

"Ladies and gentlemen," he started in a deep sepulchral voice. "Mr. and Mrs. Grainger…" Mrs. Slocombe raised her glass. "Hear, hear, I'll drink to that," and with a quick movement she downed the champagne in one.

Captain Peacock looked at her disapprovingly. "Mrs. Slocombe, we haven't got to that bit yet."

"In that case," said Mrs. Slocombe holding out her empty glass, "I'd better have another."

Mr. Mash raised his eyebrows and filled it. "You must have got a hollow body," he muttered.

Captain Peacock glanced down at his notes again and then up at the ceiling. "How can one sum up a career like Mr. Grainger's?"

"Quickly, I hope," whispered Mr. Lucas.

Captain Peacock glanced back at his notes and continued: "He started literally on the ground floor at Haberdashery and after two short years was given his own counter in Stationery." He glanced approvingly at Mr. Grainger, who lowered his eyes modestly. "Already," intoned Captain Peacock, "the writing was on the wall. It spelled success." He laughed at his own joke, and then a look of surprise crossed his face as nobody else joined in. He cleared his throat and continued: "His amazing drive and enthusiasm soon came to the notice of the Board of Management."

"True," murmured Mr. Rumbold.

"And," continued Captain Peacock, "he was transferred to Bathroom Furniture. Where he remained for five triumphant years before moving on."

"Flushed with success," interjected Mr. Lucas. Captain Peacock pretended not to hear the remark.

"Before moving on to Gentlemen's Shoes," he continued. "Already one might say his foot was on the ladder." He paused for further laughter and a look of relief crossed his face as Mr. Grainger threw his head back and gave a chuckle. "Thank you, Ernest," he murmured. Then glancing back at his notes he searched for his place.

"Ah, here we are. Er…because from there, fortunately for us and Grace Brothers, he finally found his niche in Gentlemen's Trousers."

"What's a niche?" asked Mrs. Slocombe leaning forward, her head lolling from side to side as she tried to focus on Captain Peacock's face. Captain Peacock ignored her.

"I would now like you to raise your glasses as I close on these words from Pope." As everybody raised their glasses, Captain Peacock peered closely at his notes. "Oh happy man," he quoted, "whose wish and care a few paternal acres bound content to breathe his native air in his own ground."

"Is that it?" asked Miss Brahms.

"Yes," said Captain Peacock.

Mrs. Slocombe burst into wild applause and the others followed suit. Mr. Lucas shook his head sadly. "It's a pity he lives in a flat in Eltham."

"Perhaps," said Mr. Humphries, "we could give him a window box."

"I must now ask you," said Captain Peacock, "to all be upstanding," and raising his glass he announced, "Mr. Grainger, coupled with Mrs. Grainger." In unison the voices replied, "Mr. Grainger, coupled with Mrs. Grainger." The only voice not in unison was Mrs. Slocombe's as she was struggling to her feet at the time. She eventually raised her glass and announced loudly, "Mr. Grainger, coupled with Mrs. Grainger."

"Thank you, Mrs. Slocombe," said Captain Peacock. "Perhaps you would just care to take your seat again."

"Certainly," said Mrs. Slocombe and fell down heavily, narrowly missing the seat and disappearing on to the floor. She was helped up by Mr. Mash.

"Who moved that?" asked Mrs. Slocombe aggressively. "I'll give them a bat round the ear 'ole."

"If you've quite finished, Mrs. Slocombe," said Mr. Rumbold, "perhaps we could ask Mr. Grainger for a speech."

"Yes," said Miss Brahms. "Speech! Speech!"

Mr. Grainger looked rather abashed.

"Go on," said Mr. Lucas. "It may be your last chance."

As the cries for speech, speech continued Mr. Grainger slowly rose.

"I had not," he said, "expected to make a speech," and reaching in his pocket, he brought out a small notebook, opened it and peered into it intently.

"Ladies and gentlemen," be continued, "may I call you dear friends. My heart is very full…"

"My glass is very empty," shouted Mrs. Slocombe.

"You have," said Mr. Grainger, "done me a great honour tonight by giving me this banquet. The chicken and these wonderful presents." Mr. Grainger picked up a box and extracted a brush with a shoehorn on the end. "Especially," he commented, "this combined shoehorn and back scratcher. And as I look back over the years, it all seems to have passed very quickly…" He paused, emotion getting the better of him for a moment. Then straightening his shoulders he continued, "but I have the most happy memories of you all, and all I can say is," and a husky note came into his voice, "thank you." Noisily blowing his nose, he sat down to a wild burst of applause.

As the applause died down, Mrs. Slocombe collapsed across the table sobbing wildly, "Oh it's so sad," she moaned, "so sad." Busily, Mr. Mash moved glasses, crockery and cutlery out of the way as she rolled about.

"For goodness' sake," said Captain Peacock, "get that woman to sit up and be quiet."

Mr. Mash pulled Mrs. Slocombe upright in her chair.

"I'm afraid I must blow my nose," she announced, holding her hand out hopefully. Captain Peacock pulled his immaculate handkerchief out of his top breast pocket and handed it to her. Mrs. Slocombe took it and blew her nose noisily and handed it back.

"Please keep it," said Captain Peacock.

Mr. Rumbold rose from his seat and Mr. Mash banged noisily with a spoon on the table.

"Pray silence for Mr. Rumbold."

"Thank you, Mr. Mash," said Mr. Rumbold. "That will be all." Mr. Mash sat down.

"Ladies and gentlemen," said Mr. Rumbold, "Mr. and Mrs. Grainger. You know it has been the custom of Young Mr. Grace to announce whether or not he wishes employees who have reached the age of sixty-five to take advantage of the pension scheme or remain in the saddle."

The look of contentment disappeared from Mr. Grainger's face and he sat gazing pensively at his cabinet pudding.

"But as you know," continued Mr. Rumbold, "Mr. Grace is indisposed, due to a severe cold. So it falls to my lot to perform the ceremony."

At that moment a ping announced the arrival of the lift. Everyone turned to see Young Mr. Grace supported by Goddard, his chauffeur, entering the department leaning heavily on a stick.

"It's Young Mr. Grace," said Captain Peacock.

Everybody stood up as Mr. Grace gingerly walked down the steps. Mrs. Grainger stared in surprise.

"Is that Young Mr. Grace?" she inquired.

Mr. Grainger nodded. "Yes, Old Mr. Grace doesn't get about much anymore."

"Good evening, Mr. Grace," intoned Mr. Rumbold.

"I hope I'm not too late," called Mr. Grace.

"You're never too late, sir," said Captain Peacock standing up and offering his chair.

"There's plenty of cabinet pudding left," announced Mr. Lucas.

Captain Peacock held up his hand and whispered hurriedly to Mr. Rumbold, "He's obviously come to hand over the clock."

"Just in time," hissed Mr. Rumbold, and to Mr. Grace, "May I carry on, sir? I was just in the middle of making a speech."

"Oh, please do," said Mr. Grace, tucking into Captain Peacock's cabinet pudding.

"Er…where was I?" said Mr. Rumbold glancing at his notes. "Oh yes, I was saying how very much we appreciated the long years of devoted service and great consideration you have shown to all the people who have worked with you."

"Hear, hear," echoed the staff.

"That's very kind. Thank you very much," said Mr. Grace.

Mr. Rumbold gave him a surprised look, then reaching under the table produced the clock. "And we feel that after these long years, you truly earned a rest and it only remains for this to be presented." Leaning across the table he handed the clock to Mr. Grace, who nodded his thanks as he took it.

"I must say," said Mr. Grace, "that this comes as a complete surprise to me. And how very nice of you all." Mr. Grainger who had raised his hands to receive the clock from Mr. Grace sat back confused.

"Yes," continued Mr. Grace. "I've given lots of these clocks away but have never actually got one." Clutching the clock and helped by his chauffeur, he rose from his seat.

"Well," he wavered, "my doctor said I shouldn't be out, so I am going back to bed," and then, turning to Mr. Grainger, "Another five years, Ernest, and you'll be getting one of these. Well good-bye, everybody. You've all done very well." With a wave of his stick, he staggered off towards the lifts.

There was a moment of stunned silence. Captain Peacock turned to Mr. Grainger with a smile. "It seems that you're staying on after all, Ernest."

Mr. Grainger nodded, a broad smile crossing his face. "Yes, indeed, Stephen. Well, I'm very glad, of course. At the same time I was looking forward to a little more leisure." He turned to Mr. Rumbold. "Is it possible for me to have Monday off, sir?"

"Certainly not," snapped Mr. Rumbold.

"In that case," said Mr. Lucas, "if he's not leaving he won't need the presents." Reaching over he retrieved the combined back scratcher and shoehorn.

At that moment Mr. Mash appeared at the table with a large birthday cake with rows of flickering candles on it and Madam Trixi struck up with "For He's a Jolly Good Fellow." Mr. Grainger stood up, then inhaling deeply, expelled a breath that blew out all the candles, except twenty-five.

"Grace Brothers wouldn't have been the same without you," said Captain Peacock.

"I won't mind not moving up," said Mr. Humphries.

"I'm glad you won't have to look for another Mr. Lucas," admitted Mr. Lucas.

"It's all too much," wailed Mrs. Slocombe and she flung herself face downward on the table and started sobbing uncontrollably.

"I shall remember this evening," said Mr. Grainger nodding nostalgically and with a final supreme effort he blew out the remaining candles.

## ABOUT THE AUTHORS

JEREMY LLOYD CREATED AND THEN CO-WROTE (WITH DAVID CROFT) ALL ten seasons of *Are You Being Served?* and its sequel series, *Grace and Favour*. The pair also collaborated on the immensely popular comedy *'Allo 'Allo*, set in a café during the French Resistance. Like the earlier series, it's now seen widely on PBS' stations; and the shows have fans in over 60 countries. His other television writing credits include *Rowan and Martin's Laugh In, Come Back Mrs. Noah* (starring Molly Sugden), and the game show series *Who Dunnit.*

His long acting career has included numerous television series and more than twenty films, and he spent four years in two long-running musicals in London's West End. The animal poems from his children's book *Captain Beaky and His Band* have been dramatized for the stage. His latest stage play, *The Late Late Lady McVain,* has been well reviewed in Canada and he hopes to bring it to the States. He lists his hobby as resting.

ANTHONY BROWN (FOREWORD WRITER) IS THE CO-AUTHOR OF THE celebration book *Are You Being Served? The Inside Story,* and the Reviews Editor of Britain's best-selling science-fiction magazine *SFX.* A former editor of the British magazine *Dreamwatch,* he has discussed television on BBC Radio programmes, has written TV previews for a variety of national newspapers, and is currently working on his first radio drama. He lives next door to the Abbey in Bath, Somerset, and remains single, but hopeful.

221

## SUPPORT YOUR LOCAL PUBLIC
## BROADCASTING STATION!

EVERY COMMUNITY ACROSS AMERICA IS REACHED BY ONE OF THE 346 member stations of the Public Broadcasting Service. These stations bring information, entertainment, and insight for the whole family.

Think about the programs you enjoy and remember most:

*Mystery!* . . . *Masterpiece Theatre* . . . *Nova* . . . *Nature* . . . *Sesame Street* . . . *Reading Rainbow* . . . *Baseball* . . . *The Civil War* . . . *The NewsHour with Jim Lehrer* . . . *Three Tenors* . . . *Great Performances* . . . *The American Experience* . . . *Washington Week in Review* . . . and so many more.

On your local PBS station, you'll also find fascinating adult education courses, provocative documentaries, great cooking and do-it-yourself programs, and thoughtful local analysis — as well as amusing comedies like *Are You Being Served?*

Despite the generous underwriting contributions of foundations and corporations, more than half of all public television budgets come from individual member support.

For less than the cost of a night at the movies, less than a couple of months of a daily paper, less than a month of your cable TV bill, you can help make possible all the quality programming you enjoy.

Become a member of your public broadcasting station and do your part.

**PBS**

Public Television. You make it happen!

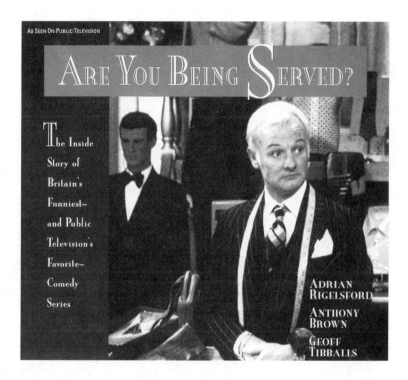